COLD SILVER

FOR SOULS

Cold Silver for Souls

Shadesilver: Book One

Tori Tecken

Books by Tori Tecken

SHADESILVER SERIES

COLD SILVER FOR SOULS

PHASED DUOLOGY
PHASED
TRUEBLOOD*

LEGENDS OF THE BRUHAI
THE BLOOD STONES
QUEEN'S WOLF*

*WORK IN PROGRESS

Dedicated with love to my friends Kayla and Andrew Wizard

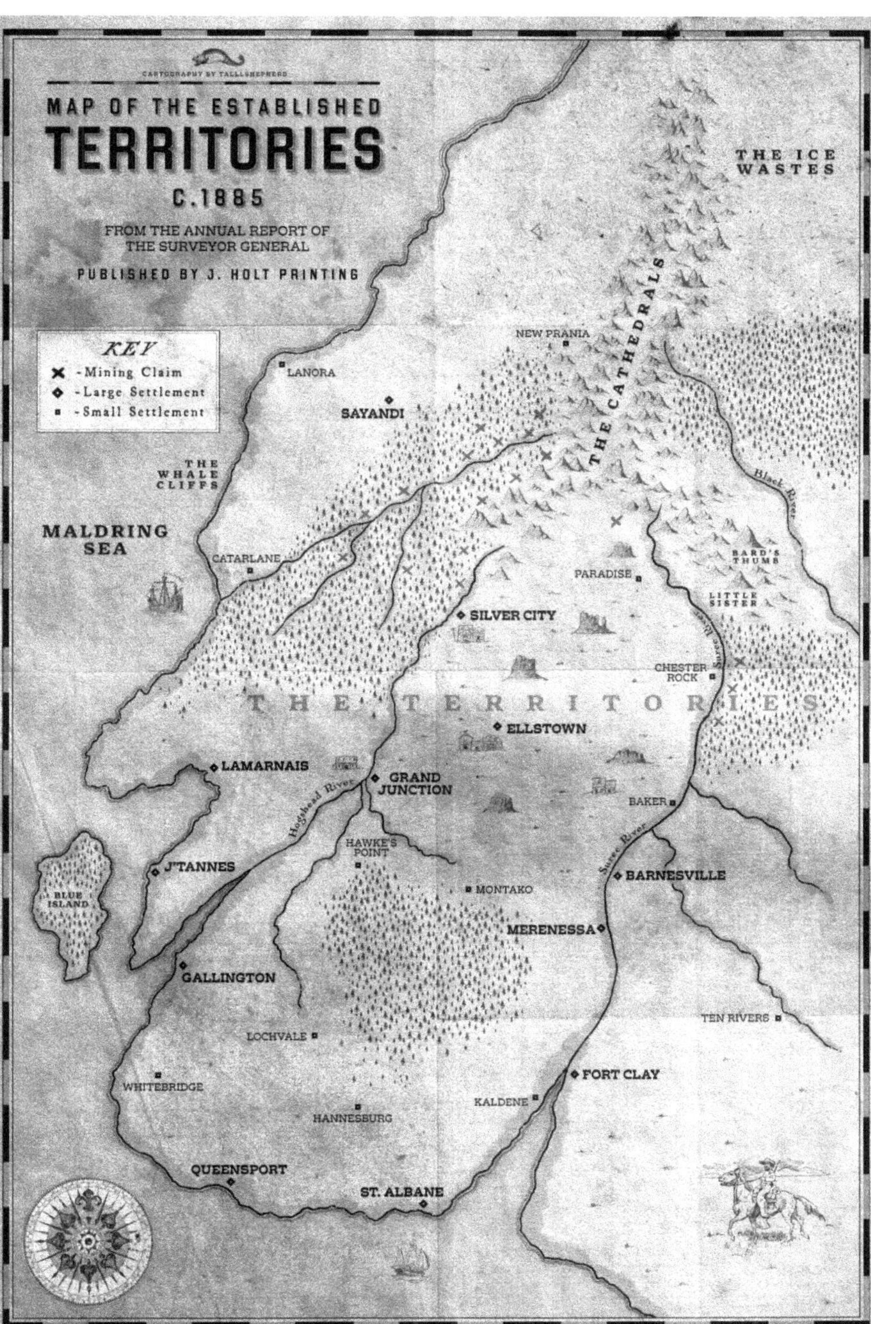

CARTOGRAPHY BY TALLSHEPHERD
MAP OF THE ESTABLISHED
TERRITORIES
C.1885
FROM THE ANNUAL REPORT OF
THE SURVEYOR GENERAL
PUBLISHED BY J. HOLT PRINTING
KEY
✗ - Mining Claim
◆ - Large Settlement
■ - Small Settlement
THE ICE WASTES
THE CATHEDRALS
NEW PRANIA
LANORA
SAYANDI
THE WHALE CLIFFS
MALDRING SEA
CATARLANE
Black River
BARD'S THUMB
PARADISE
LITTLE SISTER
SILVER CITY
CHESTER ROCK
THE TERRITORIES
ELLSTOWN
LAMARNAIS
Hogshead River
GRAND JUNCTION
HAWKE'S POINT
BAKER
J'TANNES
Surre River
BARNESVILLE
BLUE ISLAND
MONTAKO
MERENESSA
GALLINGTON
LOCHVALE
TEN RIVERS
WHITEBRIDGE
FORT CLAY
KALDENE
HANNESBURG
QUEENSPORT
ST. ALBANE

CHAPTER ONE

WALKING DEAD

Silver City sounds bigger than it is. To a northerner like me, it's the south. But to the folk that live here, you'd have to ride a fair way further to find a true southern city. It's a strange mix of southern finery and northern grit, a town masquerading as something fancier than it is. Streets aren't too dusty though. Down south the dust and smog are worse. Bigger cities, drier air, and the crusted filth of too many people living too close together.

Here, the main street of Silver City is busy, even at this hour of the morning. The groggy thickness of my eyelids makes me think of my rented bed back at Tabitha's place. A driver unhooks his mismatched team of draft horses from a supply wagon outside the general store. The wagon is packed with crates and sealed boxes. I'll have to remember to stop in and see if he's restocked the taffy. I'm almost out.

Mr. Thomas is flipping the sign in the front window of his barber shop to 'Open' and gives me a solemn nod. The sign outside the shop shows a pair of barber's razors alongside the dentist's picks. I've always wondered which one he was first, a barber or a dentist. I've let him cut my hair before, but I don't know as I'd trust him anywhere near my teeth.

A mother hurrying her young child along the boardwalk notices me and avoids my gaze when I tip my hat. Her face is flushed, and her corset makes her waist look like the thin stem of a wine glass. I've never worn one, but I can't imagine how she breathes. It's not really me she's avoiding as she pulls her little girl past me toward the far end of town where the schoolhouse bell is ringing. It's the massive, animated corpse behind me. He tends to make people a bit uncomfortable.

Rip pauses when I glance back at him, hulking and unsettling. Black, blank eyes stare into the space beyond my head, and his unnaturally gray skin shows through all the ragged holes in the remnants of his clothing. The little girl is staring, practically dragged along by her mother across the boardwalk. Necromancers are a rare breed, so I'm probably the first one she's seen. Probably the first walking dead man she's ever seen too.

I'm not an important enough person to see Hector McBride in the flesh. His head foreman handles all McBride's business with me and the other bounty hunters out of a little office in town. A bell chimes above my head when I push open the front door. There are no chairs to sit in, and a wide counter separates me from the honeycomb-shaped arrangement of boxes nailed to the far wall. Slips of paper nestle in many of them. Contracts, payment stubs, collection notices, and weigh outs for silver.

A small, stout man appears from the back room, squinting at me as he rounds the corner. July Kinney, head foreman of McBride Silver Industries. His beard is combed, but his face still manages to look dirty even though it's been washed. His eyes are too small for his face, and he's not a big man, so they get lost in the beard, sideburns, and his extra wide nose.

"Hunter. You're late."

The clock in the corner clicks to 8 o'clock sharp. He follows my gaze and his squinty scowl deepens. When somebody tells me to be at a place at a certain time, I'll be there. It's not my fault if he secretly means something else. I fix him with a patient stare. Rip hulks silently behind me. I could've left him outside, but I find that having a giant dead man at my shoulder tends to make folks like Kinney a little less high and mighty.

"You said you had a job for me," I remind him.

He shuffles through a stack of papers behind the counter longer than he needs to. He's making me wait. My stomach growls, and a smirk appears beneath the bushy mustache on his upper lip. I should've taken Tabitha up on her offer of breakfast before I left. I take one step and lean forward on the counter. I'm uncomfortably close to him now, I can smell the tobacco and sweat and the faint hint of whiskey as he wheezes slightly with each breath.

He manages to find the paper he was searching for and shoves it at me. There's a hastily sketched picture of a man at the top, followed by a name and last known location. A short list of people he's been in contact with. What he's stolen.

"Two shadesilver nuggets?" That's a decent haul these days, especially for a down-on-his-luck miner. It's also a sign that McBride trusts me. At least trusts me enough not to make off with it myself.

"Aye. He's a fool and then some."

I glance over the rest of the information, noting that the mark has worked for McBride for nearly two years. Biding his time, I suppose. The sketch doesn't do this man any favors. Bushy eyebrows. Mean squint to his eyes, not unlike the man standing in front of me. I wonder if his jaw really is that crooked. The thing about wanted men is that they always seem to have mean eyes in the drawings.

"Name's Cutter. Was in one of the boss' scout teams that went up north a while back. Last person who saw him thinks he might have headed that way. Left four days ago," says Kinney. "Boss wants him dead, no need to bring back anything but the silver."

I carefully fold the paper and tuck it into my coat. "What's the pay?"

"One of the nuggets you bring back, you keep."

If the offer had come from anyone but McBride, I'd have been picking my jaw up off the waxed floorboards. Depending on the size of the shadesilver nuggets, I'd be able to pay a year's rent with Tabitha for that much. Hector McBride was an extravagant man, and from the months I'd already worked for him, I also knew that extravagance extended to his sense of justice. McBride Industries was not a company you stole from if you wanted to live to tell about it.

He'd pay me a whole shadesilver nugget to bring down this Cutter fellow, and then the man would be turned into an example. Sheriff Brady was in McBride's satin lined pocket, and so was the Silver City Justice of the Peace. Whatever else this Cutter fellow was, he was indeed a fool. Pops always said fools got what was coming to 'em. I guess for Cutter, that was me.

"You can tell Mr. McBride that I'll leave in the morning."

"If I were you, I'd leave sooner than that," retorted Kinney. "He's got a few days' lead on you."

My time would be wasted trying to explain to the foreman that heading quickly in the wrong direction doesn't get you to your mark any faster.

"Wax is looking a little lean on the floorboards, July," I say quietly. "I'd pay it some mind, if I were you."

Without waiting for the man's reply, I lead my silent shadow out of the office. The stink of the street hits me as soon as I step outside, and I pause to watch a stagecoach roll by. The horses are still stepping briskly but I can see the lather and sweat under the harnesses. It's a two-day journey from the next stop to the southeast: Ellstown. I catch a glimpse of a brightly rouged feminine face peering out of the side window, perhaps some young debutante seeking an adventure in the wild north. I scuff the toe of my boot on the porch boards.

You shall not judge.

It's been a while since I sent Reverend Ambrose a letter. Maybe I'll scribble something down for him before I leave. But first I have business with one Mr. Ulysses Hadley. A name I'm familiar with, as I've seen its owner frequent the cheaper of the two saloons in town. He's been a miner since the early days of the Rush, but everything he had to show for it has filtered right through his pockets like a sieve. There are a thousand others just like him, so deep in with the current that brought them up here that they can't find it in them to go anywhere else.

There's a cheap boarding house out behind the saloon. It's a dingy mess of dark rooms and dirty men, and that's where I'll find Hadley. I flip a copper coin to the girl lugging a wash bucket down the hallway and she points me to a room close to the end of the row. I offer to take the bucket off her hands, and she seems relieved. I leave Rip in the hallway.

Hadley's door isn't shut, and the stench from inside turns my gut a little. He is there, lying in a filthy pile of blankets that might once have been considered a bed. He's snoring louder than anything and reeks of the booze he drank all night at the card tables.

I pull back the bucket of sudsy, murky water and let it fly. A second later Mr. Hadley is lunging up like a half-drowned rat, spluttering curses and roaring and swinging. I step back out of reach and wait for him to wipe the soap away from his eyes. He sees me lounging against the doorframe and that brings him back to his senses a little. He presses a fist to his temple. I don't envy him the ache in his head.

"Mr. Ulysses Hadley."

He grunts, still blinking water out of his eyes. "Yeah."

The paper appears out of my pocket, folded carefully to show only the sketch drawn on the top half. "You know of a man who works for McBride by the name of Cutter?"

He peers at the sketch for a minute and shakes his head. "I told him he'd gone soft in the head. 'McBride'll send one of his dogs after you, sure as a cockroach don't die,' is what I said to him." He returns his attention to me. "You the dog?"

"When was the last time you saw him?"

He frowns and runs a hand through what's left of his hair. "Gee, I couldn't tell ya. Days all sorta run together…"

I sweep my duster aside and settle a palm on the grip of my right revolver. "Think a little harder, Mr. Hadley."

That sobers him up quicker than the water. "Well, uh… must have been five nights ago? Down at the card tables."

I shift my palm ever so slightly. "What else did he tell you?"

"Nothing. I swear."

"Mr. Hadley, I'm here for Cutter. But it seems to me that you knew he intended to steal some silver, and you didn't think you needed to bring that to your foreman's attention. I imagine Mr. McBride would be interested in that kind of information." The revolver slides up a little way out of the holster and my thumb smooths the hammer of the gun back with a click.

His hands fly up, palms open. "No! I swear I didn't never think he'd do it! You know how it is, man gets a little whiskey in him and talks a big talk, doesn't mean anything by it!"

The hammer clicks back down, and the gun returns snugly into the leather. "I know how it is. And I'd like to get on my way. So why don't you tell me what else Cutter said to you?"

CHAPTER TWO

BAD DECISIONS

Tabitha's boardinghouse is a sight cleaner than the one I just left. She's a widow that came north with her husband years ago, and when he died in a mining accident, she decided to stay and run a business. She's the kind of woman who's got enough grit and fire in her soul to survive raising seven children of her own and a few others who weren't, plus keep a boardinghouse full of tenants in line, fed, and paid up. Not much rattles a woman like that. I respect it.

She's scrubbing one of her giant cookpots in the kitchen when I walk in with my saddlebags over one shoulder. She stands and wipes her hands dry on the apron tied over her gray work dress. Brown eyes look me up and down, and then she pulls a chair out from the little table in the middle of the room and sits.

"Stepping out again, are ya?" Tabitha asks.

"Got a job up north. I'd be grateful to you for keeping my room while I'm gone."

A handkerchief appears from her pocket and she dabs at the perspiration lining her forehead under wisps of graying hair. "How long?"

"Few weeks, probably."

She nods toward Rip, who lurks behind me like a dark shadow. "You'll be taking your corpse along with you."

"Yes ma'am."

"Well then I don't suppose you'll mind me renting out his stable stall while you're gone. You got money for me?"

I pull a small leather bag off my belt and place it carefully on the table by her hand. She'll find more than enough coin inside to pay my rent for another month, plus a few extra for her trouble. The money inside jingles as she takes the bag and points a calloused and slightly crooked forefinger in my direction.

"You got another month. I'll keep your room for you. But you don't come back, and it'll be cleaned out. Everything in it becomes my property."

I feel a grin tugging on the corner of my lips. "Sounds pretty tough for a lady who tells me I'm her best customer."

"Stuff and nonsense. Makes no difference to me so long as you pay. Get along with you, then," she says gruffly as she waves me away and tucks the leather bag into her apron pocket. "I'll set out a plate of breakfast for you before you leave."

She busies herself with the cookpot again, scrubbing away with a vengeance. Pops would have said she was scrubbing the dickens right out of that pot. She's a good woman, and I've been a good customer.

In my room on the second floor, I pull out a map. It's the good one that Pops paid the surveyor for when he came traveling north. Sharp, neat lines. There's a town or two missing that have sprouted since the map was made, but it's still the one I use. I fill in the gaps here and there with my own memory, and that works just fine.

Hadley said this fellow talked a big talk about knowing the

land around the Cathedrals, and that he'd been to some of the old mining haunts. I squint and follow a likely route from Silver City up into the Cathedral Mountain Range. A rip in the paper catches on the rough skin of my finger, peeling a little section of map away. I smooth it back down and can't help but wrinkle my nose at the town name inked at the center of the ripped bit.

Paradise.

I was hoping I'd be wrong about the route. But it turns out that fate or angels or the Almighty God Himself has decided I'll be heading straight back into that hellhole despite my best efforts to avoid it. Looks like I'll be delivering my next letter to Reverend Ambrose in person. At least somebody will be happy to see me.

I get the jittery feeling beneath the skin of my hands and arms that always comes with the thought of returning to Paradise. Reaching into my pocket, I find a taffy, twisting the little paper apart to reveal the soft candy hidden inside. I pop it in my mouth and suck in a good deep breath that strains my ribcage. Cleaning the extra taffy out of my teeth will give me something else to focus on. I should be able to pass through Paradise quickly. I do have some business with the reverend, but that won't keep me in town longer than a few hours at most.

It doesn't take me long to gather what I need and pack the saddlebags. I fold the map, smoothing my thumb over the town of Paradise one more time. Then my stomach growls and I start thinking about the food waiting for me downstairs at the table. Tabitha makes some of the best food in town, and I can already imagine the taste of some good, seasoned pork sausage.

As promised, a plate of late breakfast tucker sits steaming in my usual place at the table. A cup of fresh, frothy milk sits above the bowl. I set my saddlebags down, hang my hat on the chair, and dive in, stabbing a piece of ham and then some salt and peppered eggs onto my fork. She's even included a few extra slices of apple because she knows I like them. I'm late for breakfast, so I've managed to miss eating with the other boarders, which suits me just fine. There are always one or two new ones passing through town, and I don't feel the desire to be the topic of conversation around a breakfast table. It's not as bad as Paradise, but even here, I'm still the necromancer. The corpse raiser. The northerner. It's like they're never quite sure if I'm human or not.

I finish the eggs. Just a few bites of sausage left, and I've saved the apples for last. Boots tromp into the room behind me, and a chair scrapes back.

"Mornin', Hunter."

I nod to the lean woman who is now two chairs to my right. Her brown hair has more than a few gray streaks in it, and it's pulled back tightly into a braid at the back of her head. Jo Farstep, fellow bounty hunter and former soldier. There's nothing soft about Jo, she's all hard edges. She's always observing the world with a certain suspicion, as if she's never had a reason to trust another person in her life. She fought in the war like Pops, but she was a whole lot younger than he was when she volunteered. Now she walks with a slight limp on her left side for her trouble.

"Mornin'," I return the greeting and push back my plate. Jo eyes my saddlebags.

"Got a job?"

"Yeah. North a ways."

She nods. "I heard McBride had himself a couple nuggets stolen. That your man?"

It's no surprise that she knows. News gets around pretty quick in Silver City. I'm surprised that McBride didn't send her after the mark. She's been a bounty hunter longer than I have, and she's a veteran sharpshooter. I'll have to get up close and personal with Cutter to bring him down, but Jo could find a cliffside to perch on and put a bullet through his forehead before he even knew she was after him.

"That's him."

"You the one that roughed up Ulysses Hadley?"

I raise one eyebrow. Tabitha comes into the room with a plate of sausage and eggs for Jo, and Jo says 'thank you ma'am' as our host bustles back into her kitchen.

"He came into the Sheriff's office talking a big talk about you going around messin' with folk just minding their own," she says. "Says you sicced that corpse of yours on him and threatened him with a gun."

I sip the last of the milk from my glass and set it down. "You believe him?"

"Only when he says he's been drinking. That's the only truth ever comes out of his mouth."

"I might have reminded him I carry a gun," I admit. "But I don't need to use Rip to threaten a man like Hadley."

Jo eyes me for a moment, then takes a bite of sausage. "No, don't suppose you would."

I push back my chair and throw the saddlebags over my shoulder again, settling the wide-brim back on my head. "I'll see you around, Farstep."

"Good hunting."

Renting two stable stalls from Tabitha costs me more than I'd like to spend, but it's necessary. My roan mare wouldn't stand for sharing a stall with a corpse, she's flighty enough as it is.

Good legs, steady on any kind of ground we cover, but she's not much for brains. I bought her cheap, and I guess I got what I paid for. Pops wouldn't have paid half of the twenty-five bills I'd bought her for, but I always did like a challenge.

She sees me over the stall door and pricks up her ears with a little snort, wide black eyes fixed on me like she's never seen me before. I've never found a name that quite fits her. The only names I've ever called her aren't civilized enough to stick around.

Next to her, Rip is standing in the middle of a stall staring straight ahead like he always does. It's downright unsettling, even though I suppose it would be stranger to see a dead man blink. I pull my saddle off the stand and head into the mare's stall. I pull up the cinch around her middle until it's tight and lead her out into the stable corridor. The cinch gets pulled again, tighter, so I can make sure the saddle stays on after she puffs out her belly. She'd like nothing better than for me to slip right off her back, the infernal devil.

I hear a shuffled step behind me and pivot just in time to dodge a fist that would've smashed into the side of my face. A surprised grunt accompanies the large body that trips forward and falls nearly underneath the roan mare's dancing hooves. By the time Ulysses Hadley stands and turns with his fist drawn back again, my revolver is out of its holster and pressed against his forehead.

"You're not about to make a bad decision, are you Hadley?" I ask.

He licks his thick lips. A little fear, maybe a little anger, but he has a whole lot of respect for the muzzle of the gun pressed against his skull. Not much brain to spare. He looks at me with some hate in his eyes, but I could build a boardinghouse of my own if I had a copper pithing for every person who'd ever looked at me like that.

"Get out of here. You're not worth the drink you drown in."

His eyes glitter, but he slips away from the barrel of my Barrington revolver and shuffles out of the barn. By the time I ride back into Silver City, I expect he'll have cooled down a bit. If he hasn't, I'll have to watch my back.

CHAPTER THREE

THIS IS PARADISE

Paradise isn't even a small town, it's a jumble of shanty buildings all holding each other up with jury-rigged beams, some spit, and a pinch of luck. Pops always did say folk this far north had to be equal parts hardy, innovative, and crazy. The buildings look it.

The only real sturdy buildings in Paradise are Gerdy's Saloon and the little chapel at the edge of town. If a town goes to the Dark After, a person wants a priest and good stiff drink to be waiting for them when they climb out of the rubble.

I pass a broken sign about a quarter mile out of town that reads P-A-R-A-D. Half the sign broke off years ago and nobody's had a hankering to fix it. My roan mare spooks at it a little and does a jig sideways. I shift my weight and give a tug at the reins to remind her I'm still here. The fool horse is steady as a rock if someone fires a bullet right by her head, but she draws the line at creaky wooden signs.

Behind me, Rip lumbers along with deceptively light footfalls despite his bulk. I'm taking a risk, bringing him into the town in broad daylight like this, but I've been away from Paradise for too long and seen too much of the world to be afraid of these people anymore. As my strange little posse saunters through the narrow main street, I catch the eye of old Mr. Gibbs sitting there on his bowed porch, watching nothing happen on the street. I tip my hat. He hawks and spits in my direction.

It's good to be home.

There's only one hitching rail in front of Gerdy's, and a scrawny bay gelding is standing in front of it. His reins aren't even tied around the wood, but he stands there, one back leg cocked, lower lip drooping as he snoozes and flicks the occasional fly away from his belly with his tail. I stop the mare next to him and slide down, stretching out my legs a little before tying one rein around the rail. Rip's ashen gray skin is a bit dusty from the road, but I think the dust is the last thing anyone in this town will be worried about when it comes to the giant corpse. Gerdy's got a twitchy trigger finger waiting for us.

Instead of the usual thuds my boots make on floorboards, there's a shaky rattling sound with every one of my footsteps. I wonder if there are more than three nails in the whole place. Gerdy stands behind the bar, coarse gray hair tied back under her faded reddish bandana, a few more wrinkles on her face than the last time I saw her. A pair of regulars sit at one of the three rickety tables, playing cards. Gerdy sets her squinty eyes on me and her usual frown goes into a full scowl. When Rip walks through the doors behind me, she looks like she's swallowed a boulder and her eyes go all bugged out.

I sit down on a stool and sweep my duster behind me, letting her get a good look at the pistols hanging from my belt. "Afternoon, Gerdy. It's been a while."

She waves a forefinger in my direction. "Filthy, shade-cursed Soulless!" she manages to spit out between the gaps in her teeth. I glance over my shoulder at Rip, who stands motionless against the wall by the door.

"I'm just here for a drink, Gerdy. I've been on the road a while and I could use a glass of your best," I offer, amiable. But that's the thing about small towns that aren't really towns at the edge of civilization. Time doesn't move so fast in these parts. When folks make up their mind about something, that's the way things are for a good long while. It's been years since Gerdy saw me last. I was shorter, scrawnier, and didn't have a hulking Animated trundling after me then. But her opinion of me hasn't changed. In her mind, I'm still that little girl hiding behind Pops and trying to bring dead cats back to life.

There are a lot of names for what I am. Some of them are nicer than others. But Gerdy doesn't call me any of the nicer ones. She reaches for the old smoothbore Thomason musket I know she keeps behind the counter. It's ancient, probably a weapon her grandfather used, but well-kept, and I've seen her shoot it before. My proximity to her negates the low accuracy of the weapon. She levels the barrel toward my chest, finger shaking on the trigger.

"You shoulda stayed there with your southern folk," she hisses. "Your old man is gone, no reason for you to come back."

I hear one of the men at the table scrape his chair back over the floor. He's six feet away from me behind my right shoulder. He's not armed, he's just here for a glass of whiskey and a game of Spades. But still, I judge the distance, the speed at which I would have to draw to fire on them both. I imagine Gerdy falling backwards into the row of glass behind her, the man toppling to the thin floorboards while the last one raises his hands, telling me not to shoot.

I just want a drink. I swallow a little bit of spit down my dry throat, ignoring the wavering muzzle of the gun a foot away from my collarbone. "I'm here to set some things in order," I say calmly. "But I could do with a drink first." I slip my thumb and forefinger into a front pocket and place one silver coin up on the counter with a clink. Gerdy shakes her head.

"I don't want a lick of silver from you," she says, venom lacing her tone. "You just pour it yourself, and if that Almighty-cursed Shade of yours so much as moves, I'll blow your head off."

The glass bottle of whiskey sits next to two cups a foot or two away from me on the counter. I pour just enough to chase the dust out of the back of my throat and swirl a little bit on my tongue before swallowing. It's awful stuff, nothing like the refined whiskeys I've had in the south. But I set the glass back on the counter and nod.

"Thank you kindly, Gerdy. Y'all have a nice day now."

I leave the silver on the counter. The musket barrel follows me back outside, and then it follows Rip until we're both out the door and Gerdy's Saloon has been cleansed of our presence. I breathe in the crystallized cold mountain air and feel it burn inside my nose. The old clapboard chapel sits waiting for me at the edge of town, but I'm not quite ready to face it yet. Maybe I'll save a conversation with the reverend for tomorrow.

I untie the roan mare and she nips at my sleeve when I mount. Cantankerous piece of horseflesh. I'd taken pity on her when a trader was trying to sell her for dirt cheap to anyone who would take her off his hands. She'd have probably been butchered if I hadn't, mean and skittish thing that she was. I've always had an easier time than most with the Almighty's creatures, but this mare tests me.

The invisible tether connecting me to Rip pulls as we move, the magic that keeps him on his feet drawing its energy from the soul fragment he carries in his chest. My soul fragment.

Gerdy would call it "soulless trickery" or "corpse magic". Down in the south they have a fancier newfangled term for it that is just a nicer way to say the same thing. Necromancy. It's rare, I've only met a few other folks who had that kind of magic, and not one of them has held an Animated as long as I have.

Rip shuffles along behind the roan mare as we continue down the short main street of Paradise and out of the north side of town. The dirt road disappears into a pair of wagon ruts in the frosty grass as we head into the last wide-open space before the forested foot of the mountains. The smell of pine mixed with the fresh snow from the night before fills me with a familiar kind of joy. If the man in St. Albane selling Mr. Ackinvald's Wondrous Cure-All Miracle Elixir could bottle that smell, they might actually do someone some good.

The slope evens out as we continue down the trail and turn further toward the mountain. At first glance, the little clearing looks just the same as when I left it seven years ago. The roof of the little barn has caved in a bit, and one of the cabin windows is broken out, a bit of jagged glass clinging to the bottom of the frame. Weeds and grass have grown up around the place without any animals to crop it down and keep it neat. The garden is all swallowed up, and I can only tell it was there by the slight dip in the shape of a rectangle beneath the grasses.

After dismounting, my boots crunch through the stiff weeds as I make my way to the cabin door. We're not into true winter yet, so the cold is still mild for these parts. I turn the handle, and it sticks. It isn't until I put my shoulder to the wood and shove that it budges inward, leading me into the remnants of my life with Pops.

Our two rope beds still sit on either side of the far wall, each with a drooping curtain of cotton scraps sewn together. The one broken window has let in a bit of the elements, and I can see where the last few winters have left their damp rot in the floor beneath it. There is still a stack of dried wood next to the fireplace. A scant amount of food lies rotten in the cupboards. I'd left in a hurry.

Before I do anything in the cabin, I need to patch that barn roof so the roan mare has a dry bed for the night. I make my way back outside to find her nipping at a patch of grass under a tree. I'll find the extra planks in the side of the barn. The hay won't be any good anymore, but there are a few sacks of plain rolled oats that Pops had laid up on the shelves to stay dry.

Clambering to the top of the barn roof is as easy as pie. I used to sit up there during the warmest parts of the day to read my books or twist grass braids. Pops would always say that Mama would've told me to get right down, but she was dead and gone of the typhoid by the time I was five. It was a miracle I'd survived it. Some folk in Paradise claimed I should've died, and that's why I was touched with the corpse magic.

A mean little boy at the one-room schoolhouse had even followed me to the outhouse one day and told me through the crack in the door that my Mama had died because of me. I had come out of that little shack with my fist drawn back, threatening to throw the fruit of my labors at his face. I hadn't had any in my hand, of course, but the memory of his horrified screams as he tripped and fell face first into the mud on his mad rush to get away still gave me a chuckle.

I lay the planks in a neat row over the small hole in the barn roof and nail them in place. I don't intend to stay long, so a simple patch job does the trick. I shimmy down and bolster the inside of the roof with the rest of the planks, so the hole is firmly clamped between the two lines of boards. I shed my big jacket and hat, sweaty hair sticking to my forehead. Gathering up the mare's reins, I bring her into the stall and pull off her saddle, rubbing her down for a good long while until her head is lowered nearly to the dirt floor. She makes a whoofing sound and cocks one back foot, not interested in taking a chunk out of me for the moment. I leave her with a small pan of oats.

I don't let Rip into the cabin. I make him hunker down outside on the porch. He can't feel the cold anyhow. Inside, I rustle around the cupboards, throwing the ruined food out the broken window. There's still a good jar of halved tomatoes and another of beets. Pops and I left quite a bit of canning in the small pantry. On the top shelf are three corked bottles of wild raspberry mead.

After I cover the window with a couple of loose boards I find laying around and get a small fire going, I settle down in the rocking chair with a sigh. I pop open the jar of tomatoes and quietly savor the richness of them one at a time until the whole jar is gone. I could use a good slab of beef to go along with them, but they'll do. I make it a fair way into the jar of beets before my belly tells me that I've eaten quite enough.

I can't bring myself to open the mead. The honeyed taste will bring me far closer to Pops than I'm willing to get right at this moment. Pops always did love to sit back in his rocker with a cup of sweet mead.

With a ragged quilt spread over my legs, I kick my feet up on a short stump in front of the fire, one pistol drawn and lying in my lap. I'm being overly cautious with Rip sitting like a hellish guardian on the front porch, but one can't be too careful in these parts, so I keep my guns close. Tomorrow, I'll go and visit the reverend. Then I'll head into the mountains to kill a man.

CHAPTER FOUR

A KINDLY GATHERING

A cold mountain sunrise is a beautiful thing. I admire it from my front porch with a chipped mug of hot tea. The sky can't choose between purple, gray, orange, or pink, so it just paints with all of them. The air is crisp and colder than it was yesterday. Rip sits in a haphazard pile, staring out toward the wagon-rut road leading back toward Paradise. His blackened eyes are set a little too deep in the dead, gray-skinned skull. Shreds of his shirt hanging from his shoulders. He's an awful mess. At least he doesn't smell.

I sip my tea. The roan mare whinnies plaintively from the barn. She's ready to leave, but I'm content here for a moment more. The topmost branches of the pines sway slightly, and the leaves of the smaller white birch trees glitter. I could stay here. I could hunt, grow crops, and leave the chaos of the world behind. But it's a fleeting thought. There are too many memories haunting me here. And the ones that I choose to keep are as painfully fresh as the day itself. I yank on Rip's tether.

"Get up."

He awkwardly unfolds and lurches to his feet, enough humanity left in the movement to be unsettling. There were a few useful supplies in the house to add to my saddlebags, which I sling over my shoulder on the way back to the barn. It will save me some coins back in town when the general store owner tries to rob me blind.

The roan mare steps briskly out on the trail, and after one last glance around the old place, I face south and let it lie. Someday I'll be back.

My return to Paradise is early enough in the morning that most folk haven't begun bustling around the tiny shanty town yet. Gerdy is out on her saloon porch, sweeping dust back into the air with her scraggly broom. She flips the three-fingered warding sign against evil up in my direction, and I tip my hat. This time, I turn right, down the secondary street toward the chapel. As always, it is pristine, the worn clapboards freshly painted. Reverend Ambrose may not have an enthusiastic congregation in the citizens of Paradise, but he keeps the building with as much pride as a father.

I leave the mare and Rip outside and pull my wide-brim hat from my head, freeing my unruly red hair from its confines. I've always felt a little out of place here, and I step into the brightly lit sanctuary with a light tread, as if a heavy footstep will bring down the wrath of angels.

Reverend Ambrose runs a dusting cloth over the frontmost wooden pew. His hair is all gray now, and he squints down at his work through circular spectacles. When he looks up and gives me a wide smile that crinkles the corners of his eyes, some part of me becomes a little girl again.

"Hunter!" he exclaims, dropping the cloth. He holds out his arms, and I walk into them. It's the first time another human being has touched me in months. I quickly step back, worrying the brim of my hat between my fingers. The reverend gestures for me to sit. The wooden pew back digs into my spine, and I fight the urge to sit on the floor instead.

He sits next to me, far enough to give me my own space. "It's so good to see you again," he says. "You've been in the south a long time."

I nod. "There's plenty of work down there."

"I don't see your Animated with you."

There's a glimmer of hope in his eyes, and I hate to disappoint him. "I left him outside. Didn't want the good folks of Paradise to think I was polluting your sanctuary with the Dark After."

"I see."

He folds his hands on his lap. He understands the hard things I can't say. He always did, somehow. The stares and prejudice of the other folks in Paradise never seem to bother him. He just goes about his work with a steady calm. Where Pops was driven by his ambitions, Reverend Ambrose was content with whatever happened to come his way. They had both been my fathers, in their own way.

"Did you get my last letter?" I ask.

"I did, and I wasn't expecting to see you so soon." He reaches into his pocket and pulls out the folded piece of paper. "Planning on heading into the mountains?"

I nod. "Got a mark that stole goods from a businessman down in Silver City. Knows the land around the Cathedrals, so he probably thinks he can hide up there until it all blows over." I pause. "Did you… did you make them?"

"Let's talk in the forge. Less chance of being overheard."

We step out the side door and down the little path toward the humble house that the people of Paradise built for him back when the town was first founded. Adjacent to the house is a small forge. Warm, lazy fire glows in the kiln, beckoning to the artist in me. Reverend Ambrose spends most of his time fixing broken tools and shoeing horses, making gadgets for the folks in Paradise. But the cupboard in the back houses an impressive array of blades. He learned blacksmithing from his father before fighting in the Two Seas War as a naval captain. When he came home, he turned in his captain's cords for a pastoral collar and never looked back. I'd heard the story countless times as a little girl sitting in his forge to watch him work. He never spoke of the war, or what had driven him to the life he led now.

In my letter I asked him to return to that life for a moment, because he is the only one I can trust with my secrets. He removes a block at the lower half of the kiln, and retrieves a package hidden inside. Inside the cloth are two brand new knives, which he places carefully on the worktable. They're like nothing I've ever seen before. The hilts are wrapped with soft gray calf leather, the blades long and slender. If they had been made from the usual blade steel, they would shine and reflect my face as I stare down at them. But these do not. These blades are a deep slate gray, dull and lifeless. And as I reach out to touch them with my fingertips, there is a hum of magic in them. They reach into the power in my veins, wrap around it, and I feel strength rush through me.

Shadesilver.

This is what sparked my father's dream to strike it rich. To press further into the Cathedral Mountains and dig holes in the earth in hopes of finding the same dull metal lying on the table. It's what drove thousands of men and women from their comfortable homes in the south, away from their families, and into the unforgiving wilderness – the dull gray metal that amplifies magic.

"They'll do." I slide each knife into its tooled leather sheath, and the magic buzzes against my hands until the leather covers it completely. The necromancy in my blood quiets, and I feel the questing strain on Rip's tether. "They're a beautiful piece of work, Reverend."

He watches me in that oddly all-knowing way of his. It's not the first time I wonder if he can read my mind. His magic is tied to iron and steel, if he knew everything I was thinking it wouldn't surprise me in the least.

"Hunter, you know I'm not going to ask you where you got the shadesilver. And I'm not going to ask you what you're planning on doing with it. You've a rare gift, and I don't pretend to know why the Almighty gave it to you. I know there's a reason. But that Animated out there…" he reaches out and grips my shoulder. "Don't let that darkness swallow up everything in you that's good."

"It's what I am. You know that."

He shakes his head. "No. Who you are is something else entirely." He drops his hand away from my shoulder. "But I know you have a journey ahead of you to find her."

Before I reply, a gunshot rips through the air somewhere back by the chapel. The invisible tether holding me to Rip shudders, and I jerk forward a step. I'm out of the smithy and running back along the path seconds later, tearing around the corner of the chapel to see Rip standing in the same spot I left him. Gerdy stands a good twenty feet away, her smoothbore musket smoking and pointed in his direction. Behind her stands a pathetic crowd of nervous folk. One man even holds a pitchfork.

Rip stands silent, a hole torn through his jaw from the bullet, exposing teeth just as gray as his skin. I turn to face Gerdy.

I'm not a natural-born patient person. I learned that a measure of self-control can keep a body out of trouble. Back in the south, I avoided a good number of fights and mis-understandings just by keeping my cool. It took me some time, but I learned it. And now

I unlearn it, just a little.

"Gerdy Adams, you old bag!" I snap. My right hand sweeps my duster back, palming the smooth butt of the revolver at my hip. A gasp runs through the gathering, and I think it's directed at me until I realize none of them are looking in my direction. I turn, already knowing what it is they see.

Rip's ruined jaw looks like a patch of hazy smoke, swirling and reforming, setting the bones and teeth back in order. When the smoke fades away, it's as if Gerdy's bullet hadn't ever been there. The crowd's sudden silence turns dangerous as they realize Rip is impenetrable. But I'm not.

Gerdy's musket barrel moves a foot to the right, and now it's trained directly at my chest. Despite her obvious fear, her hands are steady. Credit where credit is due, as Pops would say. My finger loops around the revolver's trigger.

"You put that down now, Gerdy," I say, regretting my earlier insult. "Decent folk like you wouldn't want to be adding murder to your shiny clean slates, now would you?"

"Ain't murder if you're already dead!" pipes up one of Gerdy's regulars. Gerdy squints down the barrel of her gun at me.

My pistol slides free of the holster, ready to give the crowd proof that I'm still alive and breathing, and that I intend to stay that way. A warm hand presses against my arm, and the reverend steps around me. Gerdy's gun doesn't budge.

"Get yourself away from there, Reverend," she says. "I aim to drive this Soulless heathen out of our town one way or another. She can go back to the rest of her kind in the south, or she can drop dead in the dust."

"We're driving out the heathens now, are we?" replied Reverend Ambrose with an easy smile. "Paradise will be a mighty empty town. I'll pack my things."

A rustle of slighted opposition rolls through the gathering. I'm nothing like these folk. They know it. I know it. Only Reverend Ambrose doesn't know it. For an all-knowing man, sometimes he can't see the truth when it's as close as the end of his own nose.

"Seems to me what Hunter could use is some provisions and a quiet ride out of town," the reverend continues calmly. "I'll come along to the general store and see that no trouble is had. You folk go back to your business, now."

Gerdy holds her gun on me for another minute, but she finally lowers it, still squinting in my direction. "You go on then," she grinds out from between the gaps in her teeth. "You're not wanted here, so find your way somewhere else. Next time I see you or that abomination, I'll not feel so kindly."

I'd hate to see Gerdy when she's not feeling kindly.

Reverend Ambrose walks with me to the edge of town. A few fresh supplies are stowed away in my saddlebags and the pack on Rip's back. Hiram Bowles, the general store owner, took my silver coins as if they'd give him the plague just by contact with his fingers. Gerdy stood like a self-appointed sheriff on her saloon porch and watched me ride all the way down the street. She's probably still there, hoping I turn around so she can finally put a musket ball between my eyes.

The shadesilver knives are tucked safely in their sheaths, hanging from my belt with the pistols. It'll take some getting used to the pinpricks of discomfort they cause so close to my skin. Reverend Ambrose says I may never grow accustomed to it. Says it may be the price I pay for their magic. The tether to

Rip feels stronger, bolder. So I guess they're worth it.

We stop at the point where the road disappears into the wagon-rut trails. One leads straight off toward Pops' cabin. Another curves away to the left toward the middle of the Cathedrals. The mark has a good head start on me, but that's where patience comes in. I'll find him in the end. But I have another goodbye to see to first.

Reverend Ambrose is looking at Rip in that way of his, trying to put some pieces together. He's never outright asked me about what happened all those years ago, but now he does. "Who was he, Hunter?"

The big Animated stands there, silent. His ripped shirt might have been a color once, but it's nothing more than drab shreds now. It's enough to cover most of the gray skin beneath, and the killing wound I gave him that still looks as fresh as the day I sent the bullet through his heart. It's the only wound that stays now. His dark hair and beard are wild enough to make him look a bit feral. He's stocky, with thick arms, and he stands a good head and a half taller than the reverend. He stands out in a crowd, that's for darn sure.

But the worst part about him are those empty, blackened eyes, staring at nothing. Sometimes I think I catch him staring at me and it gives me the creeps. The reverend means well, but I also know what he would say if he knew what Rip was. Part of me fears that he already knows.

"I don't know as I'm ready to tell that tale yet, Reverend."

He nods. "I suspected as much. You be careful up in those mountains. Keep a scarf around your face. And keep your faith."

He presses something into my hand. I look down at a little cross on a chain, and the shadesilver hum against my skin is gentler than the knives. The simple silver bars are less fine than a jeweler's work, but the stamp of a blacksmith's careful restraint marks the smooth sides. I immediately imagine what my mother might've looked like wearing it.

"Thank you, Reverend." I pause, squeezing the small cross in my palm. "You take care of yourself, now. I'll see you around."

He pats my knee. "I'll hold you to that. I put some fresh lefse rolls in your pack, I know they're your favorite. Come on back to Paradise when you've found your man."

We both know it will be a spell of time before I try my luck walking through Paradise again. Gerdy meant every word of her murderous threat, and she'll shoot me on sight, like as not, the next time I come around. I wish things could be different, that I could stay in that forge with Reverend Ambrose and spend my time hammering out the iron in the town. But I'm a corpse raiser, and that's the way things are for people like me. It could be worse.

The roan mare breaks into a brisk trot, bouncing her hindquarters a little before settling into her pace. I don't look back, because the sight of the old man standing there watching me leave his town will break my heart and might make me feel like testing Gerdy's promise. Besides, I've got a man to catch in return for the money waiting back in Silver City. Mr. McBride is a man that expects his coin to be earned.

So I sit – or bounce – the mare's lurching trot as we make our way into the foothills of the Cathedrals. I saw those peaks every day of my life until I left Paradise, but they still take my breath away a little bit every time. Makes a person feel small looking up at those white-capped giants. Real small. So small it starts to get a little bit uncomfortable.

Rip lumbers along behind me. His run is just as disconcerting as his sitting down, all jerky movements and hitch-steps. He stares forward, dragged on by my consistent pull on the tether.

At the other end, there's the constant unnatural emptiness and the faint glimmer of my soul fragment. It's familiar, but it's the same wrongness that happens when you play two notes next to each other on a piano. Discorded, I think they call it.

The man that Rip was before sure isn't there now. And that's fine by me. The rest of him can rot away at the edges of the Dark After for all I care. I give the tether a yank just for spite.

CHAPTER FIVE

CROSSING OVER

As I make my way into the higher foothills, the cold gets meaner. The knitted scarf is wrapped twice around my neck, ends tucked into the front of my heavy coat. I left the roan mare down in a little fenced-in pen and shelter by an old hunting cabin. She's got enough to eat for a good long while, and I asked Reverend Ambrose to check in on her in a day or two. The climb into the Cathedrals is too steep for her, and the nooks and crannies we'll use for shelter along the way won't fit an animal her size. Rip carries most of my supplies now, lashed onto his back in an oversized rucksack.

Already I'm keeping a weather eye out for the dangers that the north brings. We're close enough to the border of the Wastes now that a stray Shade wouldn't be amiss, and I sure as the Dark After don't want to be caught with my britches down by one of those.

The animals up here are meaner too, the wild and the cold turns them into something monstrous. A pack of wolves or a mountain bear aren't as bad as the Shades, but they're not something I want to run into either. Rip makes me harder to kill, but I'm not about to take chances I don't need to. Pops once told me the story of Killian Wainwright, a keen old hunter who trekked into the Cathedrals to trap and shoot during the autumn and winter. He knew every tree and boulder like the back of his gnarled hands and was almost as wild as the animals he hunted.

Old Killian ran up the wrong side of a big old mountain bear, and when his brother went out to find him, all that was left was his rifle and a bloodied ribcage. You don't mess around with things up here. If it's not the cold that gets you, it's teeth and claws. And if it ain't either of those two things… then it's the Shades. When you've met a Shade face to face, getting eaten by a mountain bear doesn't sound all that bad.

Suddenly it seems like McBride has gotten the better end of our deal. But no one else is mad enough to put themselves at the mercy of the Cathedrals. That's why I get paid more than the others.

I take a big breath of cold mountain air in through my nose to clear the thoughts out of my head. When you've only had yourself for company as long as I have, you get to thinking too much.

The first and smallest mountain in the range is the Little Sister. After that it'll be the Bard's Thumb, and a journey down the other side to an abandoned shanty town near the headwaters of the Mule River. Seems to me if someone knew enough to hide up in the mountains, they'd know about a place like that.

I make it most of the way over the Little Sister by the end of the day, and there's still enough forest that I can tie our packs up in a tree with rope pulleys and climb up to an old hunting platform that still hangs on to the tree trunk by a few rusted nails. I settle in, wrapping myself tightly in the two blankets I've hauled along, tired to my bones from the long walk. This will be the last night I'll be able to sleep without a fire.

Rip stands guard at the bottom of the tree. I'm glad he doesn't smell like a dead thing, or he'd have every mean creature within miles stalking us by the middle of the night. He's not actually dead. I'm not much good at explaining things, but he's sort of stuck. When a person dies, they go along to whatever After claims them. But an Animated doesn't get to cross over, not really.

There's a piece of my soul in the empty space where his should be. It stopped him from dying all the way. I glance at the bright glitter of stars through the tree branches above me and wonder if Rip's soul is stuck in the Between, watching me and what's left of his body trundle around the Cathedrals. Maybe he isn't, but I give the sky a smirk anyway and pull my hat down over my eyes. If he is watching, stuck and silent, that would be a fine thing.

The first mining outpost on the other side of the Little Sister huddles next to a wide creek. It's one of the bigger outposts this far north. Broken sluice boxes and the remains of a few wooden buildings dot the edges of the creek. I kneel down at the rippling water and take a drink from the mountain's crystal clear blood. This is the Fifth Creek stakeout, and a decent amount of shadesilver was found here, but not enough for the lives lost in the first winter. Seven people froze to death, soft southerners who thought the legends of the north were a load of codswallop and decided to test their luck without the proper gear. It was their last lesson learned.

The largest draw for the Shadesilver Rush had started farther to the west, in the lowland runoffs of the Cathedrals. The climate is milder there, and after the first strike, men flocked to the streams and the rivers. First they came in dozens, then hundreds, each searching for the next bonanza that would make him a rich man. More than a few men went mad sifting pebbles, sand, and grit through their pans and sluice gutters, their eyes strained and squinting as they prayed to see the telltale dull glint of the magic silver.

Shadesilver was as rare as an honest man once upon a time. But a pair of brothers discovered some pebbles of the stuff in a creek streaming down from the western side of the mountain ranges, and then they found a rock of it the size of a grown man's fist. Very quickly, the properties of the shadesilver became apparent to someone with magic. Word got out, and the prospect of getting rich in a hurry was better than any lure Pops ever put on the end of a fishing line. Every man jack figured he could try his hand at mining and have better luck than the next.

More shadesilver was found in more places, and even Pops had given in to the promise of adventure. He'd led expeditions for a few brave souls into the Cathedrals to dig and sift in places that most folks weren't fool enough to go. I touch the hilts of my knives. The amount of shadesilver attached to my belt was worth a fortune.

The Rush was still going on, but nobody was finding fist-sized rocks of it anymore. They scrounged for pebbles and dust, mostly contracted miners working for bigger men like Hector McBride. Men who could afford to pay poorer folk to rustle up the shadesilver for them and pay bounty hunters like me to chase them down when they stole it. Men who could afford to keep their boots polished and propped up on a desk.

I straighten and look down at the flowing creek, wondering how much shadesilver dust is making its way south to the bigger land claims and into the pockets of those polished men. Across the creek, there's a sad little collection of stick crosses stuck in the graves of the less prosperous who chose this spot to make their fortune. The cold wind bites at my face under my hat, but I still remove it for a moment to pay my respects.

When people get swallowed back into the earth, their last little bit of defiance stands above their resting place within those little stick crosses. If there's something people fear more than death, it's being forgotten. Of being insignificant like the dirt somewhere underneath the snow. But I figure sticks tied into a cross aren't much of a remembering. If there aren't people living and breathing who remember you fondly, well then, I guess you might not be worth remembering much.

As I jam the wide-brim back on my head, the first few flakes of white snow flutter down around Rip and I. By noon tomorrow this whole valley will be white as a nun's bonnet, some places ankle deep, some places as high as knee deep if the wind picks up. And it likely will. The northern winds are vicious, and they'll remind you mighty quick if you forget.

I turn and just about run into Rip. There are a few snowflakes stuck into the scraggly remains of the beard clinging to his sharp gray jaw. I walk up to him, peer into those black blank eyes. He stares back, never blinking. I pull the tattered front of his shirt aside just enough to see the bullet hole torn through his chest. I don't know why I do it. It's not like I need to see the bullet trail to remind myself he's dead. Sometimes I think I wish he'd wake up a little and give me a reason to kill him again.

Truly, I don't know why the folks in Paradise are so shook up by Rip. It's not a natural thing for a person to walk around after they're dead, sure, but most of the time he's nothing more than a pack mule. My supplies and bedroll are all tied onto his back. Might as well make some use of those broad miner's shoulders.

I tug the tether after me as we start to head further up into the tundra. Looming above us is the peak of the Little Sister, and then the crooked top of the Bard's Thumb. It's time to chase down our man. I pull my heavy coat tighter 'round my neck.

CHAPTER SIX

SARDINES

Damn this cold. There are icicles on my lashes, and my breath steams beneath the woolen scarf. My toes feel like nothing inside my boots. I haven't been able to feel them for the past half hour. The storm picked up with a terrible fury last night. At least Rip's hulking shoulders block some of the wind as he clears a path through the knee-high drifts. There's something morbid about the fact that my Animated has better eyesight in this hellish whitescape than I do.

The magic between us feels strained as I struggle to keep my body temperature high enough to maintain the steady push forward. I don't want a repeat of this morning. My arms are still aching from the effort it had taken to help while the worthless brute pulled himself out of a snowdrift.

I could've left him there. An Animated doesn't feel the cold, the freezing winter biting you in the nethers. Sometimes I wonder how much he does feel, connected to me the way he is through that tiny splinter of soul. He might get a little of whatever I experience, tiny wisps of emotions through the magic linking us. If that's all he gets, held in the Between, then that's fine by me. He was damned long before I found him.

His eyes changed color when I brought him back, black veins running through his face from those dead pools of nothing. I shake my head, clearing the unpleasant memories like cobwebs out of corners. Freezing to death is sure not my favorite way to spend an afternoon. Gives me too much time to think.

Rip stops abruptly in front of me, and I groan behind my damp and sticky scarf. I can feel the thread between us growing brittle like a thin sheet of ice over water as I get colder. I'm tired of it. I suppose I have no one but myself to blame. Not many bounty hunters willing to work up near the Northern Wastes, and I can't blame them. But the ice is already in my blood, like Pops used to say. Somebody has to go after the insane marks who think fleeing to the snow will save their hide from a trip to the gallows.

I glare at Rip, who has taken one shuffling step through the snow. For a dead man, he sure needs a lot of my body heat to stay upright. I look around at the swirling white. I've probably overestimated my limits again.

I shake free some of the snow that's settled over my hood and scarf and try to see past my frozen eyelashes. We're on the Eastern face of the Bard's Thumb after cresting the Little Sister most of yesterday and this morning. As soon as the storm clears, the massive spires of the rest of the Cathedrals will be visible again, and they'll take my breath away. They always do, no matter how many times I see them. No matter how close they come to killing me off. Seeing them from a distance is a spectacle, but seeing them up close? Nothing else like it.

If we're about halfway up the Eastern slope, that means fifty or so yards ahead we should find a wooden post. Then a sharp left across a wide shelf of snow-covered rock to a crack in the mountainside that hides an old cave hideaway of mine. You get to know the nooks and crannies of a place when you trudge up the side of it dozens of times. We're still on the crude stone staircase up the Bard's Thumb. I keep knocking my boot tips against it as we climb.

My Pops would've given me a soldier's earful for getting caught up here in a snowstorm. He'd have known that I'd ignored the signs on purpose too, stubborn enough to want to use it as an opportunity to close some of the distance between us and the mark I was chasing. And then stupid enough to try it. He'd have said I had spring mud for brains. I glance up at Rip. At least I have brains.

A step hidden beneath the snow trips me a little. I swear under my breath, swinging one hand out wildly. Pain shoots through the backs of my fingers as they collide with something hard. A wooden post. I almost missed it. A weird little trickle of adrenaline runs down my spine as I realize how close I've come to just continuing up the Bard's Thumb. There isn't another shelter until we reach further down the opposite side. I'd never have made it. That was for darn sure.

My gloved fingers twitch toward the silver cross buried beneath my innermost layers of clothing. *Suppose I best not try my luck by cursing,* I mutter inwardly. Sharp left at the post. Not far now.

Fighting through the sleeves of two coats, I manage to pull my arms inside against my shirt to conserve more heat. Getting my deerhide gloves off is a struggle, and I gasp at the frigid touch of my fingers against much warmer skin.

I kick at the back of Rip's ankle, trying to urge him faster through the snow. But now that we are making our way onto the rock shelf, the snowdrifts are bigger. His broad shoulders hunch forward even more as he pushes his way through, making a small path for me to follow behind. The snow is light and fluffy over the packed ice beneath, making for treacherous steps. I've turned my ankle on that ice before and have no hankering to do it again.

I'm not sure how long we've walked until Rip pulls up short. I open my mouth to hurl some kind of insult at his back but then realize that he's stopped in front of a crack in the rock directly to our right.

Well hang me, he remembered. Maybe I'm not as cold as I thought.

Inside, the small opening widens out into a cozy cave. It's more than comfortable enough for two bodies, especially when one of them doesn't do a lot of moving around. Despite the cold, I can still feel the threads connecting me to Rip like puppeteer strings. The emptiness I feel at the other end no longer feels foreign the way it did when I first animated him. But nothing will ever make us anything near natural. Maybe the purist factions have the right of it. Maybe my soul wasn't ever really alive.

I push at Rip and he sits… or sort of crumples awkwardly against the far wall, his eyes staring at nothing. I pull my scarf away from my face first, feeling the raw, chapped skin of my cheeks. Goopy snot strings break away from my nose, half frozen and still stuck to me. I can handle the north, but I never said it was glamorous.

The small barrel of kindling and the stack of dry wood are untouched since my last visit. I build a log cabin at the bottom of the fire-pit and strike my flint twice before the tiny spark catches. I drop to my knees and blow gently, coaxing a larger flame from the dead moss and sticks. The larger pieces take some work, but the burgeoning warmth brings a bit of life back into my lungs and face.

Wrestling the many layers of clothing off my body takes me a good few minutes with my half-frozen limbs. When I'm down to my light jacket and trousers I can begin the painful process of thawing out my fingers and toes. The knife belt around my hips is a comforting weight, and that's just as well because there's no unbuckling it right now with my fingers this numb.

I settle down on top of my thick outer fur coat, cross-legged and making no effort to hold my hands directly near the crackling fire. The pain will be bad enough as it is.

The pins and needles are faint at first. Then it's like being stung by a hundred red ants all at once. I bite my lip, refusing to show any discomfort in front of Rip. It's the principle of the thing. I study the Animated sitting motionless across from me, trying to distract myself from the agony of my blood learning to recirculate through my hands.

There he is. Proof that some of us can avoid letting go of the past. I'll never say what he was before, not even to myself. I took that much away from him, and more. He looks like a ghost in more ways than one. He's so quiet he could sneak up on a body in broad daylight, but his shoulders and arms can still swing a forge hammer. Makes no sense that someone can be that strong when they're dead. Or at least mostly dead. It's almost unfair.

Unnatural.

I snort, unfolding my long legs and scuffing at the dirt with the toe of my boot. Folks always warned Pops that I was going to grow up strange like, and here I am, sitting across from a walking corpse and thawing out my blue toes. "She's touched," they'd mutter. Touched by what they never did say, but most folks don't understand corpse magic. How can they if they haven't lived with it tied up in their blood?

Pops always sorta hoped I'd be a businesswoman, someone respectable. He didn't want me to go the soldiering way like he did. He carried too many scars from the Silver War. But bounty hunting isn't the worst way to go, as I've found it. I like the silence of the chase, the way I can focus on nothing else until it's done and the silver hits my palm.

And the thing about the people hiring an Animator as a bounty hunter? They love a two-in-one deal. They might say my line of work is strange and unnatural, but nothing beats getting two hunters for the price of one. Bigger odds of their mark getting bagged. I could charge more, having an Animated, but I won't take silver for Rip. Silver isn't why I do what I do.

I glare at the corpse under the stringy damp curls of my hair and stretch my arms, feeling the crackle-snap of the discs in my spine as I lean back in an arch. When we get back down south I'll have a stop at Old Man Bernard's house and he can put my bones back in the places they're supposed to be. I fish around in my pack to find the little tin of sardines and Reverend Ambrose's lefse rolls in their paper wrap. They're better with butter but I'll take them plain. It's cold, but soon the thin, soft layer of potato bread melts between my teeth as I lean back against the cave wall. The small fire heats the space nicely, smoke escaping from the crack in the ceiling.

The lefse gone, I stare at the little package of sardines. They stare back. I plug my nose and swallow them down. Pops used to say there was nothing you couldn't eat with a little willpower.

Now that all the frozen bits of me are thawed out, and I've had something to fill my belly, I need sleep. My body feels like it weighs twice what it should. Even with Rip doing the brunt of the work, shoving your way through snow up a mountainside isn't the easiest thing you'll ever do. With a yawn, I finally unbuckle my belt, laying my long knives at the end of the blanket I've rolled out on the ground. There's some melting snow still clinging to the wool, but I've slept on worse. I lie on my back, arms folded over my stomach and head resting on top of the pack.

I count to slow my breathing. Hard to slow my brain down, ever. Pops used to say I could talk the hind leg off a mule, and eventually I quit saying so much on the outside and just started talking on the inside. Safer that way.

Even once I fall asleep, I will dream of chasing my quarry. The lingering taste of sardines leaves a slimy film on my tongue. I think about the way Pops pulled at his shaggy hair when he was thinking extra hard. I think about the hand-drawn picture of my mark hidden away in the pack and how it probably looks nothing like him. I think about how the fresh snow outside will glitter like diamonds when the storm blows over and the moon comes out for a spell. I think about the first time I met Rip. Before he was Rip. I squeeze my eyes shut and think about the sardines again.

Exhaustion catches up with me eventually, and I can't tell if I'm dreaming or awake when I see Rip's eyes staring at me.

CHAPTER SEVEN

A DEAD MAN IN THE MOUNTAINS

The storm is gone in the morning and the mountains are breathtaking, cresting into the sky like frozen ocean waves. And it's not just the air. There's something even more magical about the untouched white than the invisible tethers linking me to Rip. The drifts are deeper now, up to my knees in the low places, but it's light and fluffy like a featherbed. The packed ice underneath is less forgiving.

Rip pushes through the drifts, and it's slow going. Curls of hair stick to my forehead. The wide-brimmed hat is shading me from the sun but not from the blinding glimmer of the snow. My eyes ache, but I can't close them. It's time to think about the next day of my journey.

Over the other side of the Bard's Thumb is an abandoned mining settlement. Well, maybe settlement is a generous word. It's a ramshackle collection of shanty houses and a few abandoned silver-dust pans down by the stream. The original miners who crawled up here with their brains full of shiny nuggets and the idea of living like kings got a real shock when they discovered how rough the mountains can be. For most of 'em, they ended up with lighter pockets than they came with. Or dead.

If they wanted to strike the real shadesilver veins, they would've gone further into the Cathedrals. But nobody wants to venture that far into the ragged peaks. And nobody knows the fortunes that sit underground in the North. There are too many Shades there. If they catch wind of you, then you'd better clutch your silver cross. I've never seen one this far down the peaks, but there's a first time for everything, as Pops used to say.

The mark I'm looking for would have probably stopped in the settlement if he needed shelter on his way to wherever he was going. Most of them don't go much farther than that anyway. I guess they think that because the place is abandoned nobody will find them up there. But Rip and I always find them. The settlement isn't the only place to hole up in the peaks, but if he's hidden away in a crevice somewhere, I'll find him.

Cresting the Bard's Thumb takes us until midday, and then we start down the other side. The going is a bit easier now, but I'm breathing hard from the exertion. I can feel my heartbeat thrumming through the necromantic tether toward Rip. The beats disappear into emptiness. The only thing keeping him on his feet is the fact that I'm still breathing.

That's the thing with an Animated. I gave up a piece of my soul and years of my life to bring him back. Without me, he'd be rotten bone dust in a shallow grave like my Pops. There's no rest in peace for Rip. I'll drag him out on every hunting trip I ever take until I keel over. I glance down at his hands, swinging limply by his sides, and my jaw clenches.

Focus. He's not your mark today.

I force the image of the mark's face drawn in shaky charcoal lines on the paper back into my wandering brain. "Over thirty, got a mean look about him," the foreman had told me. That narrowed it down to just about every miner in the region except a handful who were fresh-faced and bright-eyed youngsters.

They didn't last long. Usually came up to try sifting through a couple pans before they went back to easier work back down the valley.

The foreman had told me the mark's name was Cutter. That was his last name, of course. Nobody knew anybody's given name in these parts. Even I was just 'Hunter'. No reason to call me anything else. Even Pops used to call me Girl.

Two shadesilver nuggets. That's what Cutter had decided his life was worth, making off with them right out from under the foreman's nose. The foreman wouldn't tell me how he'd done it. But he was paying me to bring those nuggets back. Whether I bring Cutter back whole or in multiple pieces is up to him. Personally, I prefer to bring them back whole and let whatever passes for law deal with them.

We're down the slope a good way now, and I can see the little ridge in the distance. The settlement is on the other side, hopefully along with Mr. Cutter. I did have to consider the fact that he could have moved on or holed up somewhere else. I stop midstride and rub at the shin splints starting in my legs. Hopefully I won't have to chase him further into the peaks. I want to get back down through Paradise before the week is out.

I stumble over a hard chunk of ice and catch myself just before I go sprawling into Rip's back. I bang up my knee though, and that hurts like a snitch.

When I stand, grimacing at the new weakness in my sore leg, the hairs on the back of my neck rise. I look up to meet a pair of eyes staring blankly down at me. Rip has turned around to face me without any pull on the tethers. I take a half step back involuntarily.

"Get to it, corpse," I growl. My voice doesn't tremble but my hands sure do. Rip obeys, back to his task of pushing through the snow, his eyes never blinking once.

Reverend Ambrose's warning from a long while back comes to mind. *Once you put that little piece of soul inside someone else, you can't get it back. And the tethers will pull you closer together the longer you leave them there. Make sure you know what you're giving away, Hunter.*

Seven years. It had already been seven years since I'd animated Rip, using more of my power than I ever had before. I still remember the metallic taste in my mouth as blood had poured from my nose, the way it felt like something inside me had fractured and split.

As Rip pushes on, putting some distance between us, the invisible tethers follow him like long marionette strings. He only turned because my own soul responded to itself. That's all.

The mark. I shake my head and spit a thick glob of mucus into the snow. I need to focus on the mark now. He's right over that ridge, I tell myself. Get the two shadesilver nuggets for the foreman. Steel enters my bones again. I've got a job to do.

The drifts are lighter here and Rip no longer has to push our path through. We move quietly up to the edge of the ridge, and I make him stop and stay behind me as I crawl up on my belly to the crest, peering over into the ghost shanties below. Gray rags flutter in the light wind, partially torn loose from the crudely cut-out windows. There were seven of them in all, the shanties. The mountain stream still garbles and gurgles along, a dark vein against the white.

At first, I'm disappointed. No sign of life. My eyes pick apart the scene for anything out of place. There's a small stack of wood near the side of one of the middle shanties, tucked away and almost out of sight. The wood is fresh cut.

Got you.

Relief floods me. But now isn't the time to feel the soreness in my knee and shins or to curl up in one of those shanties and sleep until the sun goes down and comes up again. My fingers slide beneath the muslin shirt inside my jacket and brush against the little cross, warm next to my neck. With the storm, Cutter would have no reason to crawl out of the slight warmth that the shanty provides. Most likely, he is still inside. From what I gathered in my conversation with the other miners, he's got some kind of iron on him. Even a man who isn't used to handling a gun can be deadly in close quarters.

I breathe deep through the damp wool of my scarf. There's a tremble in my hands and faint buzzing beneath the surface of my skin. A little tremble in me is alright, keeps me sharp when I'm hunting, closing in.

We skirt the ridge on the left side, sliding into the settlement behind the farthest shanty, hidden and quiet. This time, Rip is behind me, and I push my own way through the shin-high drifts that pull away in a natural scoop between the buildings. Within striking distance now, I pull the pack from Rip's back and leave it next to the shanty wall, along with my outermost furred coat. I can fight in it but I don't like the way the bulky sleeves slow me down. I ease my new long knives free of their sheaths.

Moments later, I'm kicking in the door of the middle shanty, the dry, worn wood splintering beneath my boot. Despite the force, the door doesn't open. I frown. Setting my shoulder to the remaining boards, I shove, and the door creaks in an inch or two. There's something blocking it. Clever mark. I hear nothing from inside, but I'm standing in front of the only way out. Likely he's hunkering down, hoping whatever blockage he's constructed will hold. The foreman told me he's a coward, but I've learned not to always trust the word of one man about the character of another.

I shove the door harder this time, keeping myself well away from the crack that is opening so I don't get an unexpected knife to the face. It's clear that I'm not going to be opening it alone.

"Rip."

The big Animated lumbers up to the door as I step back. Pushing against the threads of magic, I set him at the door, his massive hands spread out against the planks. His shoulders push forward and he shoves. The door gives, breaking away from its top hinge. Rip pulls back as I draw my knives. There's no motion from the shanty. I step through the door, the long clean blades guarding my front.

The inside is dim with a dusty haze in the air from the efforts with the door. My eyes dart everywhere, ready for sudden movement. The little makeshift fireplace in the corner has charred logs in the bed of ashes. Next to it, a hole has been cut in the wall to the outside as a second entrance. Across from me, a shelf with a tin plate, cup, and utensils sits above a table made from stacked crates. In the far corner a low cot supports a ragged pile of blankets. On top of those blankets sags a motionless form.

Cutter.

I approach carefully, still expecting him to suddenly leap from the cot and attempt an escape. His dirty wide-brimmed hat is tipped low over his eyes, and he's slumped forward, hands lying limp and stiff in his lap. Reaching out with one knife, I tip the hat off his head and his dead eyes stare down at the floor. The front of his collared shirt is stained dark around his chest. One wound, but it looks as if something was tearing at him.

"Stars almighty," I breathe, taking a step back. A chill runs through me, and it's not from the winter air this time. Studying the hole in the far wall again, I notice something resembling claw marks around the edges. My necromancy doesn't react to the dead man on the cot. It's different than the unnatural emptiness I feel with Rip, the strange underlying current of something being held alive when it shouldn't. Cutter's dead. Well and truly dead. But one ravaged wound straight to the chest like that? Something was after his soul.

Shades don't usually come down this far. The evidence is right in front of me. Cutter hasn't been dead more than a day or two at most. Probably less. I stalk toward the hole in the wall and examine the marks, then step out into the snow. There are prints everywhere, the drift that had been blown up against the outside wall was packed nearly flat. More than one Shade. My blood goes ice cold in my veins.

I look across the dark stream, still flowing briskly down from further up in the mountains, and the trees in the distance. The Cathedral peaks are unsettlingly close. The tracks around my feet lead back toward the trees. I squint at them.

No. None of them lead back, they're all pointed toward—

I'm knocked on my face in the packed snow, the wind rushing from my lungs in one big whoosh as something rock hard hits my back. The sharp toe of my boot anchors me in the ice and I roll sideways, knife coming up to defend my face and neck. The shadesilver blade slices across the Shade's chest as it scrambles after me, its rotten breath washing over my face.

The first glimpse I get is ash-colored skin, shredded clothing and a wide, flat face with nothing but the hues of the Dark After flooding its black eyes. The Shade screams. It's not like any scream from a natural living body. This one sounds like the sharp whistle of the coldest northern wind, a shriek straight out of some hellish abyss. If sound could cut you, I'd be lying on this packed snow deader than a butchered pig.

My knife leaves a gaping slash across the Shade's chest, but no blood spills out, just a thin weeping of black smoke. The magic in the blade is enough to do the damage I need, the properties of the shadesilver proving their worth against the dead. I scramble away, kicking at it, my thick boots battering away at its face. Back on my feet, I grip the knives with white-knuckled fingers. I reach out to Rip and pull him toward me, but he's got to go around the line of shanties to reach us.

I run toward the stream, trying to put some distance between me and the Shade, but I'm not fast enough. I hear a crackling, blubbering growl right behind me and spin to face it.

Another Shade leaps at me, the broken line of its mouth revealing black teeth. I plunge my knives up and into its gut as we fall. I'm driven backwards a few steps and then trip, the stream rushing up to meet me. The freezing water splashes into the back of my shirt beneath my jacket and soaks my pants. The Shade rips at the front of my clothes like a rabid dog, hissing and growling as the foul black smoke weeps from its body and spills down over my face.

My long knives are buried in the Shade, and I can't pull them free. Panicked, my mind keeps screaming at me to get a blade through its heart before it can drive its claw-like fingers through mine. I hold one arm in front of me in a weak shield and snake my right hand down. Grasping fingers catch hold of the tip of my tiny shadesilver boot knife and pull.

I'm sick of the sounds the Shade is screeching into my ears, and I yell back at it with my own scream of fury, flipping the boot knife around in my hand and burying it hilt deep under the Shade's arm. The wretched thing jerks and flails, and its weight disappears from my body as it flops backwards like a boned fish.

Twisting around in the water, I get myself up, almost falling back in as I shake with the adrenaline burning through my limbs. And then I hear the shrieks. Not from the blackened shape in the water in front of me, but behind me toward the line of trees.

There are five of them, the sunken eyes fixed directly on me, drawn like flies to blood as my living soul pulses, vibrant in the silent landscape. Rip lumbers through the snow toward me, slow and steady. I have a minute or less before those Shades reach us. Rip is deadly against single opponents, but the concentration it takes for me to fight through him and keep myself alive is… well, Pops would say we had as much chance as a chicken in a fox hole. I pull my knives free from the Shade on the ground and back away. I can't run. There's nowhere to go.

I set Rip in front of me like a shield, standing a couple steps back from him. They'll have to get around him first, which will slow them down and at least give me a chance. Rip crouches slightly on his thick legs, arms outstretched to grab the way I've told him to. I push a calming breath between my lips.

I don't think the Shades will damage him too badly. They're not here for him. They're drawn to the only soul for dozens of miles. But I'll be bloody fluxed to the After if I let them take it without a fight.

They hit us, scrabbling and slavering and shrieking. Rip manages to grab two of them and a third scrambles straight up onto his shoulder. I duck beneath the embrace of a fourth and jam a blade into the heart cavity. The Shade drops, fizzling black smoke and grasping at the air with its bone-thin arms. The last one claws at my ribcage and cuts through my jacket just enough to leave scratches before bouncing off into the snow, falling with the momentum from its mad lunge.

It's all I can do to keep Rip focused on holding the two Shades caught in his grip as the one that climbed over him leaps at me, catching my shoulders and sinking those rotting teeth into the flesh above my collarbone. My clothing keeps the worst of it away, but the pressure of those undead jaws is way stronger than it should be. With a yelp, I swing wildly with my knives. The one behind me drags me down to the snow, clawed fingers hooked on my pant legs. Pain explodes through my back as I land in a twist, trying to fight off two Shades at once, my arms locked tight to protect my chest.

Sharp claws shred past my jacket and shirt, hitting the shadesilver cross with a sizzle as the metal burns the dead flesh. The Shade at my back sinks teeth into my shoulder, scrawny legs and arms wrapped around me like a vice. I struggle, but the arm around my neck is beginning to squeeze the breath right out of me. The Shade above me tears at the silver chain around my neck, shrieking as it burns.

I feel gashes open in my neck and chest as the Shade frantically digs for my soul. He can't have it, but the wanting of it is all that's in that rotting brain. It's going to kill me. I'm going to die. I feel the magic holding me to Rip stretch, fray, and snap as my vision begins to go blurry. He cannot help me now. I do not have the strength to repair the tethers. The After pulls at me.

I DON'T WANT TO DIE.

I can't choke the words past my restricted vocal chords but the scream inside shakes every organ, every corner of me.

Somewhere in the white beyond me I hear a roar like a great mountain bear charging from its den. The Shade clawing at my throat and chest is peeled away like a leech, and through bleary eyes I watch as Rip tears it in two, black smoke erupting as he tosses it away like a twig. I suck in a glorious gulp of air, staring at the Animated, who should be lying motionless without my direction. He reaches for me, pulling me out of the snow and dragging the Shade at my back loose. He grasps it around the neck and throws it down, pounding it into the ground with one massive, booted foot. The snow stains ash black.

I am dropped to the ground like a rag doll, and the quiet of the little hidden valley pulses through my ears with my roaring blood. I curl there, hacking and sputtering the life back into my lungs. Rip stands over me like a looming statue, still and silent.

Gasping and wincing at the pain in my chest and back, I squeeze my hands closed around fistfuls of snow. My mind whirls like a storm. "Nuggets…" I whisper. "We have to bring back the silver."

The short distance to stand up on my own feet feels further than the trek over the Bard's Thumb. I feel small in front of Rip.

His dark eyes look down at me, not out into the distance. The blank expression that he usually wears is gone, and there is a strange sentience in his face. I realize that he is holding out one hand, and two shining lumps glitter on his gray palm.

I am afraid to touch them. I shiver with cold and pain and fear as my fingertips brush over the shadesilver and Rip's lukewarm skin, impervious to the temperatures of the peaks. I reach for the magic tethers, and when I do, I feel the soft pulse of my own soul mirrored back at me, vibrant.

CHAPTER EIGHT

BRUISES

I'm bruised like a bad apple. Unbuttoning my vest is a slow process and I wince as my shoulders twist just enough to pull it off. My shirt is next, but I sit next to the fire and try to pretend nothing else exists beyond the snapping flames. My mind disappears for a while, something I've been good at since I was young. I learned how to let it drift into daydreams, imagining stories of wild heroes. And I learned to let it go when I need to pretend like something wasn't happening.

That's what I'm doing now. When we left the abandoned settlement, Rip quit watching me as quick as he'd started, and now he just stares like the corpse he's meant to be. I'm afraid to feel along the magic tether between us, afraid of what I'll find.

As soon as Rip had pulled the Shades apart, I hustled back up that mountain like the Devil himself was on my tail. We found the little cave on the other side of Bard's Thumb easily enough. I knew I'd never make it all the way back until I'd seen to the wounds the Shades had left me.

Pulling my shirt away from the caked blood over my chest and neck is the kind of pain that makes you wish you were somewhere else. I don't let out more than a grunt in front of

Rip, though. He doesn't care, but I do.

I find a roll of bandage in the rucksack and set it over my thigh while I clean the wounds with water from my canteen. They are deep, nothing life-threatening, but they burn like hellfire. I've never had Shade wounds like this, but I've heard tell they're not likely to get infected. They just won't heal for a good long while, longer than a usual wound. I wrap the bandages around my chest and over my shoulder and neck carefully. I'll need some looking after when I reach the foot of the mountain. I guess I'll be sneaking into Reverend Ambrose's forge again when I get back to Paradise.

I don't want to think about Paradise. So I don't. I pull my bottom lip between my teeth and worry it until I get a piece of skin free and ripped away. It's a bad habit. But that doesn't stop me. When I get this awful anxious feeling twisting my guts around in knots, it won't stop until I give it a little piece of me. Life's been ripping little pieces of me away for years. A bit of skin off my lip isn't going to kill me now. Rip just stares at nothing.

There's a sharp pain building in my core, deep in my chest. It's not as strong as when I animated Rip, but sometimes it comes out of nowhere like this, stealing away my breath and closing my lungs in an iron vise grip. I try to hold it back but I gasp, hunching over. Somewhere inside, my soul is pulling at itself. Miles warned me about this years ago, told me that the longer I hold on to the corpse beside me, the higher the cost of the magic that keeps him bound.

It's not natural, my mind reminds me in a voice that sounds an awful lot like Gerdy. In spite of the ache, I manage to sass back.

"Nothing's natural in this broken-up world," I wheeze, defiant. I grab a fistful of my shirt and squeeze my eyes shut.

Shallow breaths don't hurt as bad as the deep ones, so that's how I breathe for several minutes until the worst of it passes on. I think of Reverend Ambrose in his forge and match my breaths to the memory of the bellows.

"That's alright," he used to tell me. "In and out, just like the air blowing into the fire. The Almighty gave us breath to keep us alive."

For a moment, I get real small again, hiding in the corner of the smithy and trying to breathe like the bellows. And Rip just stares like the hellish abomination he is. Hate fills me like a deep well, hot and sharp and mean. I reach for one of my shadesilver knives and make my way over to him. The closer I get, the meaner I feel.

I stab the knife straight through his chest. And then through his arm. And then through his face. There's no sound. It's silent, no tearing flesh or spurt of blood, just a slow leaking of black smoke. The knife disappears into his body and reappears, and after a few seconds the skin just knits itself right back up. Unlike the Shades, he's not truly dead, so my knives do little to nothing.

But with every stab, my body shudders a little. I feel them like a dull punch through the tether linking us together. There's no one to stop me. Finally, I get myself under control. I toss the knife over to my belt with the other one. My wounds bleed under the bandage.

"Damn you," I whisper under my breath.

The rest of the trek down Bard's Thumb and back to the little stable where I left the roan mare is slower. Deep snow hampers my progress even though I'm picking my way down the trail we left. The wind has blown deep drifts back over a good length of it, and I push my own way through this time. Rip shuffles after me. My body resists the strain, pushing back, and I stop more than once to catch my breath. Blood trickles slowly from beneath my bandage.

Pops pipes up in my head, telling me to "quit being so stubborn, girl." But I ignore him and my body and the silent lumbering corpse behind me. By the time we finally reach the base of the Little Sister with the old hunting cabin in the distance, the snow is around my ankles instead of my knees, but I'm blinking stars away from my eyes. If I stop moving, my legs will give out on me.

The roan mare sticks her head out of the little stall and whinnies loudly, ears perked forward. I reach the building and grip the top of the stall door, leaning hard against the wood. Dimly I realize that her stall is not as dirty as it should be, and I smile. Reverend Ambrose did come check on her. She nips at my sleeve and blows a glob of saliva and grain bits all over the side of my face.

"Alright, alright," I mutter. It takes me three tries to get the saddle on her back. My arms feel weaker than a newborn's. Strangely, she doesn't act up with her usual antics. I manage to pull myself into the saddle and take a moment to blink away the darkness at the corners of my eyes. Rip stands to the side. I wait for him to look at me like he did back over the Bard's Thumb, but he doesn't.

The mare lurches into a trot, and the jostling nearly makes me pass out. I slow her to a walk and grip the saddle horn with both hands. Just a little further. Just a little further now. I don't know how much time passes then. I ride into the night, and somehow I know where to go. Somehow, I keep heading toward the thought of that tall chapel steeple and the warmth of the forge. Lights sparkle in the distance like a swarm of fireflies on a summer night.

I wake up in warmth. The crackle of a hearth fire feels like a mother's caress. My eyes don't want to open, and I think I'd rather stay in the quiet dark. Something cool and wet rests against my chest and neck, and a blessed numbness has spread beneath it. I blink, fully coming back to the world.

"Praise the Almighty."

I blink again through the crust around my eyes and turn my head. Reverend Ambrose sits on a stool next to me, his sleeves rolled past his elbows and his glasses slipped down his nose a little. He looks like he hasn't slept a wink. He gives me a tired smile and reaches for a glass. He helps me sit up a bit so I can drink. My throat feels like a desert.

"Hungry?" the reverend asks.

"I could eat," I croak, wincing at the sound of my own voice.

The eggs and ham taste like some feast from the Almighty's own table. The saltiness sticks around on my tongue after every bite. Reverend Ambrose eats his own plate of food nearby and watches me like he's expecting me to topple over. I'm in his house next to the forge. It's a small building. Clean and humble. Reverend Ambrose never cared much for fancy trappings.

"How long was I out?" I ask.

He finishes his last bite of egg. "Three days. The horse is in the barn, and so is your Animated." He gestures toward my neck. "I gather those didn't come from your thief."

He's covered the wounds with an herb poultice. I peel away

the corner just enough to see the edges. They are clean, but there's no sign of scabbing. The edges glisten, wet and red. I set the plate on my lap. I guess I owe him some explanation since he saved my life. He won't push me, he never does. But I figure he'd like me to tell him.

"Shades. A bunch of 'em by that old, abandoned settlement on the other side of Bard's Thumb. Seven of them in the pack that jumped me. I found the mark ripped up in one of the shacks. He was dead a day or two at least. Maybe less. Hard to tell."

The reverend frowns. "There haven't been more than a couple stragglers that far south before. A pack of Shades…" he mutters darkly. "And they all attacked you at once?"

"More or less."

"You been up that far north before?"

I meet his eyes. "Yeah, I have. Pops took me up there a long time ago."

He remembers when I came back down the mountains before, torn up and bloody and with a freshly animated corpse dragging along behind me. I told him Pops was dead, and then I didn't say another word until I hightailed it south. I never told anyone what happened in those mountains. I don't know that I ever will.

"That was a fair way further north though," I admitted. "I've seen a Shade before, but never in a pack like this."

I tell him everything from the moment Rip and I came down the last bit of the Bard's Thumb to the ride back and passing out when I saw the lights of Paradise. I leave out the bit about Rip moving about of his own free will. I'm still deciding on whether I want to tell him that part. I watch the reverend press the knuckle of his right forefinger against his lips as he thinks. Then he taps it a few times, staring off toward the window.

"Hunter."

"Mm?"

"Do you think the pack of Shades killed your mark?"

I think on it a bit before answering, remembering the way Cutter looked. "No. That wound was from one Shade. He wasn't torn up enough for a pack."

He turns toward me then, leaning forward on his knees and fixing me with the look he used to give me when I was a little girl and he had something important to tell me. "You've got a strong soul. No, I don't want to hear it."

I close my mouth, surprised. He's never used a tone like that with me, and I figure I should probably hear him out.

"Anyone with enough power to animate a man like that for as long as you have… you're probably brighter than a beacon to the Shades. They're servants of the Dark After, and they feed off the strength of any soul they can kill. It's no surprise to me that they wanted yours."

All the thoughts in my head are complicated, and I don't like any of them much. I met other necromancers when I went South. Miles Lightfellow, Danny Bridges, Marlena D'Jannes. None of them had kept an Animated as long as I have. Danny Bridges hadn't animated anything in years. I know the cost, and that someday I'll drop dead or whatever happens to necromancers that use up too much of their soul. The longer Rip stays with me, the closer that day comes. I realize I've pressed my hand against my chest to calm the pace of my heart.

The reverend's voice is softer when he speaks again. "I've known you since you were toddling along after your mother into that chapel. I don't know the whole story of what happened up in those mountains, but I know a lot of what happened before that. The Dark After is chasing you, girl. And I'm afraid it always will. But the Almighty walks beside you. I can see that clear as day."

"The Almighty don't seem to bother much with me," I say. I offer him a wry smile. "I think you always see him because he's more interested in you."

Reverend Ambrose leans back, gets more comfortable in his chair. "Someday you'll run out of road to run on. We all do, sooner or later."

"And your road ended up here?" I ask, raising one eyebrow.

He laughs. "I'll admit that Paradise wasn't my first choice. But the people here have taught me a good many things that I needed to learn. And so have you." The wrinkles around his eyes disappear with the smile. "Whoever that man out there used to be, he's gone. And what's left of him is poisoning you."

I imagine Gerdy and the others surrounding the house with their muskets and garden spades. Reverend Ambrose's road may have ended up here, but mine won't. Every time I come back he hopes I'll stay. But I'll be taking my leave of Paradise just as soon as I can stand up on my own two feet. Reverend Ambrose has always been kind to me. And that kindness is something I don't rightly know what to do with.

"Thank you for seeing to me, Reverend. I won't trespass on you any longer than I need to."

He looks sad, then, and I've never felt so far away from someone so close to me. He takes my plate and washes up our breakfast dishes.

"I've got a few things to see to out in the forge," he says. "There's more ham in the larder if you're hungry. And some peach preserves. Loaf of bread on the table." He looks around the room and nods to himself. It feels horribly empty when the door shuts behind him.

CHAPTER NINE

CIRCLES

Walking in circles around the small house has me feeling like a caged polecat. I do a fair bit of thinking while I circle, and I have a plan. I'll head back down to Silver City to let Mr. McBride know that his man Cutter has passed on and return one of the two shadesilver nuggets in the pocket of my duster. I'll pay Tabitha to keep my room for me and then ride over to Grand Junction to pay Addy a visit. Addy has a good head on her shoulders, and it's been too long since I rode up to her porch. It'll help clear my thoughts.

Reverend Ambrose stays in the forge until well after dinner time, and I finally cook up a bit of potatoes and the leftover ham and take him out a plate. I'm a bit steadier on my feet now and try to ignore the weakness in my limbs. The fresh air will do me some good.

There's guilt riding my shoulders. I should've told him about Rip by now. He's the closest thing to a father I have left, and I trust him. But something in me can't abide the thought of telling him what happened up north. I've never known what to do with the reverend's particular brand of kindness.

He's working on a pair of horseshoes when I walk in with

the plates. His arms are shiny with sweat, and the forge apron is smeared with soot. His gray hair is trapped beneath a dirty bandana, and he squints down at the shape of the shoe held in his iron tongs. He sure doesn't look like a preacher when he's in the forge. Not like the crisp, white-shirted preachers in the south, anyhow. They've got a different kind of grease in their hair.

I set the plate of ham and potatoes on the table amongst the metal shavings, pieces of iron bar, and wood forms. The reverend finishes the last few gentle taps on the horseshoe and sets it aside to cool. He scoops up a bite of potatoes. I take my own bite and pause. Too much salt. I'm sure my mama is up in the Holy After clutching her apron front in horror. I watch the reverend carefully as he eats another bite, and then another. Fool man won't tell me my cooking isn't any good.

"Mighty salty," I say.

He grunts around the last of his potatoes and then blows a thin line of air between his pursed lips. "They are a bit salty," he admits, and then tucks into the ham. He goes to the bucket of drinking water in the corner and lifts the lid, downing two full dippers before offering it to me.

I drink, chasing the salt away from my tongue. There's nothing better than good clean water when you've had some salty potatoes. I stack the plates and dig in the dirt a little with the toe of my boot.

"I figure I'll clean out of here in the morning."

It's a darn near stupid idea, and Reverend Ambrose looks over at my bandaged shoulder and chest. He doesn't agree, I can tell that much, but he doesn't say anything to stop me. I think I want him to, but I'll still say no if he does. It's a hard thing, trying to understand your own mind. Whenever I try to tell him that everything he's done for me means a hell of a lot, the words get stuck somewhere behind my teeth. A simple 'thank you' never quite seems good enough.

"Those shadesilver knives you made for me," I say. "They saved my life up there. Fine piece of work, Reverend."

He looks pleased at that. "Shadesilver is tricky to work with. It's harder and stronger than iron, but if you get it too hot in the forge, it'll crack. Not on the outside where you can see it, but under the surface. It takes a lot longer to make anything of it, but with patience, it'll come out alright."

I'm not sure he's just talking about the shadesilver, but I say nothing. He puts away his tools and wipes his hands on the front of his apron.

"Chapel service is in the morning. I'd like it if you came."

"I doubt Gerdy would feel greatly inspired by the Almighty to let me sit with her in the chapel, Reverend."

He shakes his head. "It's not her chapel."

"I appreciate the invitation. But I'd like to move on before I'm even more unwelcome. I can get fresh bandages in Silver City, and I'll have Addy see to them again when I get to Grand Junction," I tell him, so he'll know where I am. I gave him the address to Addy's hotel years ago, and the one at Tabitha's. He's sent me dozens of letters over the years, and truth be told, getting a letter from an old friend can sure brighten a person's day.

I think of something else to say to break the silence, but it disappears before it reaches the air. That happens sometimes, the words appear in my head but I can't remember long enough to say them. Somehow I need to make him understand that I can't stay, even if the rest of the folks in Paradise weren't trying to put lead through my chest. Some part of me doesn't breathe until I leave, until the town fades away behind my roan mare and I can't see it anymore. Paradise will suffocate the life right out of you until you're less human than an animated corpse. Reverend Ambrose is the only real beating heart left in this town. The rest of them are so shriveled up with hate and fear that they might as well be buried in the ground already.

The more I think about it, the angrier I get, so I just walk out of the forge and back into the house. I've said my piece, and I don't reckon I need to repeat myself.

Reverend Ambrose never touched my supplies, they're sitting in the pack on the floor next to my cot. I sort through them and figure I can make it back to Silver City on what I have. I won't need to show my face in Paradise, and I won't need to take anything from the reverend. It'll be lean eating for a couple of days, but I've survived on less.

When he comes in for the night, he sits in his rocking chair next to the hearth and bows his head, gnarled and weathered hands folded in his lap as he prays. I know he's praying for me, and something about that is comforting. I figure if the Almighty listens to anyone, it's him. Something changes in his face when his hands finally unfold - a sort of peace. He catches me watching him and smiles.

"First thing in the morning, then?" he asks.

"I reckon so."

"I'll send some of the smoked ham along. Too much for an old man like me to eat anyway. Have some extra potatoes too." He is speaking to himself by the time his voice trails off. He heaves himself out of his chair and digs into his pantry cupboard. As he busies himself wrapping the smoked ham in a bit of brown paper, he fumbles with the string. His blacksmith's fingers are clumsy with the bit of yarn.

"You'll stay with Addy a while then, I imagine," he says.

I hadn't really considered it, to tell the truth. When I'd come down the mountain, I'd been so bloodied and rattled from Rip's strange behavior that I hadn't thought of anything much except living long enough to get to the reverend's house. I can't shake the feeling of nausea sitting in the pit of my stomach, or the memory of Rip's eyes looking straight into mine. I need to talk to Addy. She always helps me get my mind set to rights. I look at the old man wrapping potatoes in brown paper at the table.

I keep too much from him. But he's too close to home, too close to the memories of a past I turn my back on every day. And he's a holy man. He'd shake his head at that, but if he's left his demons behind him to find peace, I sure as the Dark After don't want to sully him with mine.

"I'll stay with Addy a while," I agree finally. "She can always use the extra help around her place, and an extra gun to keep the dandies from slipping a ring around her finger."

He nods. "You're still working for that mining man, McBride?"

I'm surprised by the question. "He pays well."

"Don't get yourself tied to men like him."

"Alright."

He hands me the packages, and we tuck in for the night, the last embers of the fire glowing and spitting in the hearth. The old cot creaks every time I shift, so after a while I force myself to quit trying to get comfortable and lay there like an undertaker's stiff. The bed is more comfortable than the silence.

I wake the roan mare early the next morning, long before the early birds in Paradise start opening their shutters. I buckle my guns and my knives around my hips just in case. The first shreds of sunlight creep over the mountains as I open the door to Rip's stall. My stomach nervously twists a little, but he's staring at the ground. I let out a long breath. Even days later, the anxiousness crawls around under my skin like a nest of bees.

The wounds in my chest and neck are still red and fresh, but they're not bleeding anymore. My shirt and vest cover the bandages, so I'll not have to answer to Tabitha when I show up at her doorstep again. I mount up with a wince as the torn muscles give under the strain. My fingers scrabble a little at the leather, and I pull myself into the saddle through sheer force of will. Rest and food and Reverend Ambrose's kind healing have done me a world of good, but my body's limits struggle to keep up with my demands.

Skittish, the roan mare dances to the side and blows big breaths out her nose while she kicks out with her hind hooves. I pull back and forth on each rein until I've got her attention and spin her in a tight circle. Done acting up, she stands quiet, glaring back at me and worrying the bit between her yellowed teeth.

Something catches my eye – the shape of someone hidden behind the corner of the smithy. My right gun is in my hand real quick, and I cock the hammer back with my thumb. The roan mare skitters forward a few steps. A young boy peers out at me, eyes like an owl's as he sees my gun trained on him. He's not any more than eleven, maybe twelve years old.

He stutters out, "Soulless heathen!" and turns to run, kicking dust behind him as he high tails it back into town. I mutter a word under my breath that my mama would've disapproved of and then set my heels to the roan mare's sides, sending her in the opposite direction.

By the time we've made it around the other side of Paradise, I can hear shouts in the distance as news of my being in town spreads to less friendly ears. But I'm far enough away now, they won't come after me. I tell myself that because if they do, I'll be hard pressed to fight 'em off in the state I'm in. But the idea puts a bit of excitement in my tired bones. Someday I'll come and march back into Gerdy's saloon and order whiskey, nice as you please.

I lean over the saddle horn as the mare settles into a brisk trot. Rip lumbers along behind, surprisingly quick for his size. Something wild grips me through the rush of leaving Paradise, and I grin to myself as I look back, raise my gun, and fire a shot into the sky.

CHAPTER TEN

TWO SHADESILVER NUGGETS

"T he state of you!"

Tabitha has her hands planted firmly on her wide hips as soon as I walk through the door of her boarding house, tutting like a mother hen. There's a smudge of flour across one of her plump cheeks, covering the angry flush of red coloring her skin as she looks me over. I don't think I look as bad as all that, so I offer her a tired smile. It's been a long ride from Paradise, and I'm ready to hunker down in my bed upstairs to get some shut eye before I turn myself in at McBride's office to give my report.

"Sit on that chair before you fall in a heap," Tabitha orders. "I'll fix you a plate."

I do what I'm told, and the hard seat feels sort of uncomfortable after hours in the saddle. But when Tabitha puts a plate of grits and carrots in front of me, I eat like a woman starved. The warm texture of the grits takes me back to the cabin up north and morning breakfast with Pops.

"This is mighty good, Tabitha," I say, and she looks pleased despite herself. Tabitha's a fine cook, and she knows it, but she enjoys hearing it again just the same. I shovel the mound of carrots in and notice the light honey flavor. When I finally push the plate away, I'm ready for a long nap. Tabitha takes up my plate and disappears back into the kitchen. I don't hear Jo Farstep until she's pulling out the chair next to mine and sitting with a soft grunt.

"Fair warning, you've made some enemies here, girl."

I raise one eyebrow. "Hadley?"

She nods. "He's been getting loose lipped around his card tables since you left. Says he's going to clear you out of Silver City."

Some folks don't know when to leave well enough alone, I suppose. But something in Jo's expression tells me that I have more to worry about than Hadley's big mouth. And when Jo Farstep thinks a thing is worth worrying about, I figure I'd be smart to listen.

"He planning something?" I ask her.

"Not alone. He doesn't have the balls or the brains. But he's got Torrence's ear now, got him thinking maybe McBride is taking too much of a shine to you. Word is you got a big payday coming in for that Cutter job."

Paulie Torrence. A McBride bounty hunter with fast guns and a sly ease about him that reminds me of a fox. I snort. "Any one of them that wants to trek out to the Bard's Thumb and do it themselves is welcome to it. They just want the pay without the work."

Jo's eyes are harder steel than the gun at her hip. "If I were you, I'd go out and get that pay before anyone has a chance to cause mischief."

"I was going to get some shuteye before I turn myself in."

"I think you'd best go in now."

She's got the same tone that Pops used when he was done talking about something and I'd better just do as he said. I don't know if Jo Farstep would call me a friend, but we've built some respect for each other over the two years I've been in Silver City. And truth be told, if Paulie Torrence and Hadley have tricks up their sleeves, I'd be a fool not to heed her warning.

When I push myself up from the table, I put too much strain on my wounds, and a grunt of pain escapes me. Jo doesn't miss much, and she reaches out and pokes a finger against my shirt and the bandaged collarbone beneath. I hiss through my teeth.

"Cutter put up a fight?" she asks.

I shake my head. "Shades."

That lifts her eyebrows right into her graying hairline. "Bugger me, girl. Did they kill him or did you?"

"He was dead when I found him," I admit. "Bastards tore a hole right through him."

"How many?"

I look her dead in the eyes. "Seven or eight."

"You're either the luckiest sod I've ever met or you've got a curse on you that would scare the devil himself," Jo says grimly. "Go on and get your pay and be careful."

I haul Rip out of his stall behind Tabitha's, and we head down the street toward Kinney's office. Jo didn't tell me exactly what it was that Torrence and Hadley had in mind, but Torrence is the type of hothead who might step out in broad daylight to wave guns around. Hadley is dumber than a bag full of rocks, and he's got a misplaced sense of pride.

The good folk of Silver City buzz around like bees in a hive. It's usual assortment of everyday passersby. The general store shopkeeper entreats a pair of ladies to come in and see his latest shipment of cloth as they saunter beneath their tasseled parasols. A muscled driver hoists two trunks up to the rear boot of his stagecoach while their owner, a middle-aged gentleman with a long coat, steps through the door into the cushioned seats. Ms. Jennings, the schoolmarm, leads her gaggle of children out for a brisk walk. A firm believer that bright minds took their fair share of fresh air and exercise, was Ms. Jennings. I always had a bit of admiration for the way she was able to pin her golden hair so tightly to her head that not a wisp ever looked out of place.

On the other side of his barbershop window, Mr. Thomas bends over the open mouth of some unfortunate man, dental tools scraping away at an offensive tooth. I wonder if the man will have any teeth left at all when he leaves.

Paulie Torrence leans up against the side of the office building, chewing on a wad of tobacco. Nasty habit. My mama had seen to it that Pops didn't have any of his chew around after they got hitched. I'd tried it once when I found a little stash that Pops had hidden away under a floorboard but didn't much like the taste.

Torrence grins at me. He's a mean little man, a few inches shorter than myself, with a scattering of reddish blond hair on his face that makes up about half of a mustache and beard. His eyes are bluer than summer sky, and they look real out of place in the rest of his face. Makes him look boyish. There's something unsettling about the way he grins.

"Paulie," I say with a nod.

"Welcome back, necro." He looks a little too comfortable, one leg cocked up behind him against the board siding. His holster is tied around his thigh. He's looking for trouble, sure enough. "Heard you got a big payout coming."

"Maybe. Big job."

"Leave some for the rest of us, yeah?" he spits to one side and fixes me with another grin, his teeth stained a yellowish brown.

"Sure, Paulie, sure."

Rip stays outside to block the doorway as I step into Kinney's office. July's sitting behind the counter, scowling away at a ledger. The floor has a fresh coat of wax. He's not happy to see me, probably was hoping I'd rot away up in the Cathedrals.

I reach into my pocket and pull out the two shadesilver nuggets. They're each about the size of a rifle bullet, and worth close to a hundred bills each. They tingle against my palm, pulling at the magic in my veins. Kinney grabs them out of my hand and makes a show of holding them up to the light to make sure I've brought him real shadesilver. Even a half-blind beggar can see that they're real, but I let him feel his moment of power.

"Aye, these are the ones," he finally tells me, and makes a note in a second ledger that he pulls off a shelf behind him. "Cutter?"

"Dead," I say. "Shades got to him before I did. He's up in an abandoned mining camp north of Bard's Thumb."

"Is he now?" Kinney looks pleased at that. "Sure he didn't slip away from you up there?"

I let my voice get real soft and low. "I got close enough to pick his pocket. You want to trek up there into the Cathedrals to see his body rotting in a shack, you're welcome to it, July."

He doesn't push me. Picking up one of the shadesilver pieces, he hands it back to me. "The payment, as agreed. Mr. McBride sends his thanks."

I doubt Hector McBride even knows my name, but I appreciate his generosity. Kinney watches me, his eyes glittering like a weasel. I lean for just a moment more on the counter before turning to the door with my right hand on my revolver. A glance out into the street shows not a single person in sight. It's too quiet.

The moment I step out the door, I duck to the left as the sharp report of a fired gun meets me. The bullet lodges in the planter box a few feet away. A poor shot. Not Paulie Torrence, then. He's nowhere to be seen. Rip stands like a statue right where I left him.

I've already spotted Ulysses Hadley hovering behind a building down the street. He fired the bullet, and it's a small wonder he got as close to me as he did. But he's not out here by his lonesome. I don't see Paulie, and that concerns me more than a little bit. I glance up and down to make sure that the street is clear before I start shooting.

I jerk my guns from their snug homes and cock the hammers, waiting for Ulysses to show his ugly mug around the corner again. Something flickers to my left and I throw myself back against the building just as another gunman appears from around Mr. Thomas' barbershop, guns blazing in my direction. The quick movement pulls at the wounds beneath my bandages, and I force out a harsh breath between my teeth, head swimming. Bullets snick into the boardwalk as I get my revolvers up.

I fire once. The man jerks backwards and grabs at his shoulder, stumbling out into the street and yelling in pain. He's not Paulie. I pull Rip toward me, and he lumbers away from the office door. I set him in between me and Ulysses' guns. He's not likely to hit me, but I don't want to take chances.

Another ragged face peers out behind the water trough at the Red Diamond Saloon's hitching rail, and one more up on top of the roof. I'd like my chances a whole heap more if I knew where Paulie Torrence was.

I jam my wide-brim down further on my head and roll my fingers over the butts of my guns. Pulling Rip tight against my back, I take three big steps into the dusty street and then drop to one knee. Bullets fly over my head, and one buries itself in Rip's chest.

My first shot rips through the corner of the water trough and snicks into the man's arm. The second skims over roof trim on the saloon, narrowly missing the man who ducks back behind it. Ulysses is firing again, but he shoots wide, and it disappears harmlessly into the street. A mustached face appears above the roofline again, taking aim.

A deeper crack booms over my head and the man on the rooftop scrambles up and then pitches down over the front of the building to land with a crunch over the hitching rail. I spin, ready to fire again, but it's Jo Farstep, levelling the barrel of her rifle over the edge of the office roof and loading another bullet.

I turn my attention to Ulysses. The bullets have already fallen away from Rip's shadowy skin, and he moves in tandem with me, protecting my back as we advance toward the drunk man standing at the corner of the tailor's shop. He's fumbling bullets into the cylinder of his revolver. Two fall to the ground at his feet, his hands shaking. The cylinder clicks into place, and he fires at me. It's a blank round. He pulls the hammer back again.

Eight strides bring me close enough to pick his pocket, and I fire my left revolver into his chest at point blank range.

There's nothing hard about shooting a man. A pull of the trigger, easy as you please, and one little piece of lead will stop him deader than a butchered pig. Ulysses drops like a stone with his eyes rolled back in his head. A strange feeling comes over me, something that makes me wish I'd eaten a few less grits.

He was looking to kill me. A man gets too big for his britches if he thinks he's got to prove he's not weak. But he was weak, too weak to make a trip over the Bard's Thumb to kill a man. And too weak to kill me. Cold necromancer magic courses through my arms, urgent, reaching for the dead man at my feet. The pull never gets easier. He's the only one drawing my magic, so the others are still alive.

I don't like the taste in my mouth. I holster my guns and look back over the street to see Jo descending the steps from the roof of Kinney's office, rifle over one shoulder and her pistol trained on Paulie Torrence. He saunters down the steps with his thumbs in his belt loops like he hasn't got a care in the world. When he sees me watching him, he gives me a wink.

"Nice shooting, Hunter!" he calls out. "Clearing out the drunks."

I look at Jo, and she looks a bit confused herself, as if she hasn't quite figured Paulie out yet either. She keeps her pistol pointed somewhere around where his kidneys are.

"Boss wants to see ya," says Paulie.

I stare at him. "I suggest you start talking plain."

"Mr. McBride sent me to fetch you when you come out of Kinney's." His blue eyes sparkle like it's all a good joke. "I should'a said something when you first come down the street, but these gentlemen seemed to need a bit of your time."

It wouldn't take more than a second for my fist to find his jaw. I imagine the satisfaction of seeing his smile punched right off his lips. I let myself imagine it for a good long minute before I answer.

"Alright, Torrence. Let's go see Mr. McBride."

CHAPTER ELEVEN

REGENTS AND SECESSIONISTS

Hector McBride's house is about a mile outside of Silver City. It's a real pretty place, like the big houses in the south. Painted green with shutters on the windows and a cobbled walkway leading to a carved front door. Paulie Torrence wipes his boots off on a rug outside and points at it like I'm to do the same. I scuff my boots over the rough cloth a bit and call it good enough. Jo doesn't bother. I leave Rip outside on the porch, knowing he's likely to break something expensive by accident.

A stern looking butler answers the door. "Mr. McBride is expecting you. Please go up to the library directly. Leave your firearms and any other weapons here on the table."

I notice his thick southern accent, all proper and dandy sounding. Looks like Mr. McBride really did build himself a southern palace in the north. Paulie unbuckles his holster, but I glance around the grand entryway first, noting the two gunmen sitting in the parlor to my left. I'd wager a good stack of coins that they aren't the only ones.

"Your guns, miss."

The butler watches me from behind the little round

spectacles he's wearing. I unbuckle my guns and lay them next to Paulie's. I feel naked without them, and my hands itch to take them right back. I leave my second belt with the shadesilver knives firmly buckled around my waist. The butler points at it.

"I must ask you to remove your blade weapons as well, miss."

"Not these," I say. I don't like how Paulie has taken notice of the knives. "I'll be pleased to walk right back out that door if Mr. McBride won't see me with them."

The butler's mouth opens in a strange little 'o' shape, and his face turns a bit mottled and red like Tabitha's canned beets. He's about to give me a piece of his mind, I expect, when Mr. McBride himself appears at the top of the staircase.

"Now, now, Robert. Those knives are likely worth a bounty hunter's life savings, I wouldn't be parted from them either. Let them come upstairs."

The butler gives me a stiff bow and looks a bit like someone curdled his milk. Jo sets her shotgun and holster on the table with mine and I feel better knowing she's behind me as we walk up the staircase. I also wish I'd wiped off my boots a little more. The carved banister is made of dark wood that is polished up like a mirror. I bet if I leaned close enough I could see my face in it. Hanging over the entry is a crystal chandelier sparkling with hundreds of tiny baubles. At the top of the staircase there's a big painting hanging on the wall. A general in a long blue coat points out over his brigade of riflemen as they charge a group of ruffian soldiers on the other side of a ravine. I frown at it.

Mr. McBride nods to the painting and touches the gilt frame affectionately. "A piece by a famous artist called Arthur Yarbrough. He went onto the battlefield with the men during the war and wrote to the papers that he was 'capturing the soul of the conflict.' Of course, he was a Regents man through and through. But a fine piece."

I don't know what to say to that. Pops fought on the Secessionist side of the war, and he was bitter about it all right up to the end. Always said that folks will get to fighting over the darnedest things and will kill each other over less. I look back at Arthur Yarbrough's ruffians, brought to life with a few strokes of brown and sandy colored oil paints. They look mighty fearful. Not like my Pops. I look at the general. A nice blue coat with fancy brass buttons doesn't make any man a hero. Jo studies the painting with a shadowed expression and I realize I don't even know what side she fought for.

Mr. McBride's library has more books in it than I've ever seen in my life. Shelves line three of the four walls in the same dark wood as the staircase, and the leather and cloth spines of the books line up in proud rows. My mama would've thought she'd died and gone to heaven in a place like this, the Almighty rest her soul. I never did have much time for reading, but there was a book or two that tickled my fancy as a child.

The desk in the center of the room is too big for one man, but Hector McBride seems to fit behind it with ease. Paulie stands to one side while Jo and I shuffle into the middle of the room. I feel as out of place in it as a pauper in a palace. I hope Mr. McBride isn't long-winded because I'm ready to lie down on this nice woven rug and take a nap.

Mr. McBride pulls the stopper out of a glass bottle and pours Jo and I each a little whiskey in a crystal glass. I'm not much for drinking this early in the afternoon, but the smooth fire poured down my throat wakes me up enough to be respectable. Jo holds hers but doesn't take so much as a sip. Mr. McBride settles himself comfortably in the leather armchair behind the desk and sips from his own glass, giving us a look over. I've never been this close to the man, and he's a dandy, sure enough. He's got a fitted waistcoat and a gold pocket watch chain tucked against his side that matches the links in the cuffs of his crisp white sleeves. A brown mustache and trimmed beard on his face that match the wood of the bookshelves. Uses some grease in his hair too, all slicked back. He's maybe forty years old, if I had to wager a guess. Not much more than that. And he looks at us with the confident eyes of a man who knows his place in the world, and how much his money can buy. I don't much like the idea of being bought by this man, and I have a suspicion that he may intend something of that nature.

"I imagine Sheriff Brady will have a bit of a mess to clean up when he arrives back in town later this afternoon," says McBride. "Two men dead in the street, two others wounded."

"They fired first."

"Undoubtedly. Word has it that you've been giving Mr. Hadley a rough time of it lately. Now, I know the sort of man Hadley is, so don't imagine that I place any blame at your door for what's happened. I'll say as much to the sheriff. You needn't worry."

It hadn't occurred to me to be worried. But if he believed he was doing me a favor, let him think so. He seems to wait for me to say thank you, but I don't, so he continues.

"It's a delicate business, shadesilver mining. Hard to keep order in a big outfit like this. I work with surveyors to find promising pieces of land, and buyers who purchase it on my behalf. I speak to the sappers and engineers about where to dig mine shafts and where to build rigs on the rivers and streams. I hear reports every week from the foremen in all fourteen mining outfits I own. Then the clerks come in and show me their ledgers so that I can discuss prices and market opportunities with my lawyers and investors…" He pauses to sip at his whiskey. "Now you might understand that a man's mind can get overwhelmed with so many details all at once. But I've built a living out of it and I take on the responsibility that comes with having so many lives tied to my own. Part of that responsibility is keeping order. Which you've been exceedingly helpful with lately, Hunter."

"It's fair work and generous pay, Mr. McBride."

"You don't seem to need the generous pay, if you don't mind me saying so."

I frown at the strange gleam that comes into his eyes when he pointedly looks at the shadesilver knives at my hips. They draw too much attention. Down South, there are more people with more money, so a pair of shadesilver knives of that size doesn't warrant so much as a second glance. Especially not on a bounty hunter. Here, I'm taking a risk. Given the fact that I'm still standing and not a shredded mess up in the frozen Cathedrals, I'd say it's been worth it.

"Everybody needs to make a living."

"That's a fine pair of weapons. How did you come by them?"

"Begging your pardon, Mr. McBride, but is that the reason you asked to see me?" I ask. "They're not stolen, if that's what you're getting at."

His good-natured smile fades just a little, and he sets his empty glass on the too-large desk. "I asked to see you because you seem to be a person of integrity. And because you have a specific set of skills that I find useful. Torrence, don't touch the encyclopedias."

Paulie pulls his fingers away from a shelf of books that look more like foundation bricks for a house than something to read. Mr. McBride steeples his fingers on the desk.

"I hope you'll pardon my curiosity, but I find myself intrigued by the concept of necromancy. It's a rather vulgar style of magic, you'll allow, but the potential in such a gift has certain charms." He leans forward. "I understand that animating a corpse as long as you have requires a good deal of such magic."

I shift on my feet, not much liking the conversation. "So they say."

He smiles. "You've done some difficult jobs for me that only a select few people would take on. You know the north better than most. I'd like to hire you on permanently. You'd still be doing the same work you are now, but I might require your services for more delicate business, you understand. Some that may require you and other hired guns in my employ to work together. Travel more."

"I like working on my own, Mr. McBride. Never did get a taste for running in a pack."

He nods and does a bit of thinking. "I can understand that more than you might think. I also understand that necromancers are rare in these parts. You're the first one I've seen this far north. I can't imagine it's an easy life. Folks get a bit jumpy around you and your corpse."

"Folks get jumpy around a good many things that aren't out to do them any harm," says Jo. The way Mr. McBride looks her over is probably the same way he's looked over a fair bit of shadesilver, determining its value. All the same, I'm glad she's saved me trying to come up with something to say.

"Jo Farstep, isn't it? You've worked for me for a year or so now."

"That's right."

"I don't believe my invitation to this conversation extended to you." He taps his fingers on the desk, and the air gets a bit tense for my liking. But then he smiles. "Ah yes, Farstep. I knew I'd heard the name before. A sharpshooter for the Regents, weren't you? St. Albane Seventh Infantry. A decorated company, so I'm told. I'm intrigued enough to say that I'm happy to extend my offer to you both. No need to decide now. I'll leave it on the table, and if either of you choose to accept, just come back, and tell Robert you wish to see me."

Jo's face didn't change a bit when he mentioned the Seventh, but I couldn't hide my surprise. I wouldn't have guessed that she fought for the Regents, not if someone had bet a hundred shadesilver nuggets on it. I get the feeling that our visit with Mr. McBride is over as he starts to shuffle through some papers on his desk. Paulie steps away from the bookshelf to lead us out of the room.

"Wait a moment, Hunter."

He walks around the side of his desk and places something cool in my palm. The shadesilver nugget looks familiar, and I realize that it matches its twin in my pocket.

Mr. McBride pats my shoulder. "Call it an incentive if you want. I have another job for you."

The shadesilver feels heavy in my palm. But there's an opportunity here. I don't much need the money, but I also don't fancy wandering around the country trying to find work. I try to hand the nugget back to him.

"I have some business to attend to directly, Mr. McBride. But if you have work for me when I come back, I'd be obliged to you."

His mustache twitches, and he leaves the nugget where it lies on my open palm. "I have a job for you right now, Hunter." He pauses, noticing when I tense. "Call it a fair trade. A day or two of your time, and in exchange I'll put in a good word for you with the Sheriff. Wouldn't want to have him thinking you were at fault for Hadley's murder."

Reverend Ambrose was right about this man. I meet his eyes,

both of us weighing the danger in the other. I reach out through the tether, feeling Rip on the other side of it. Nothing was amiss, the faint thrum of magic tying us together was as it should be. Sheriff Brady will do whatever McBride tells him to, and if he is told to string me up by my neck in a tree, he'll do it. I close my fingers over the shadesilver.

"One job. I'll stick around a day or two."

"And I look forward to your return once your business elsewhere is concluded. Pleasure doing business with you, Hunter," he says. "Good day, ladies."

Jo and I collect our guns back down at the table, and Robert the butler shows us out and shuts the heavy door solidly behind us. Jo's been awful quiet, and I get the feeling that she'd have been happier if I'd turned down Mr. McBride's offer and walked out of his fancy house for good. I don't know what makes me care so much about her opinion, but I think she's a decent sort of person.

Rip lumbers after us as we turn back toward the main street of Silver City. Paulie tips his hat with a roguish grin and jogs away toward Mr. McBride's horse pens.

"He didn't pull a gun on you?" I ask Jo.

She shakes her head and spits into the dust. "He's a rat. Told me where Hadley's boys were sitting in the street. I didn't trust him, so I brought him up to the roof with me."

We walk in silence until we reach Tabitha's. Right before we part ways, Jo stops and sets her shotgun butt on the ground. She's got something to say, so I wait.

"The last time I signed on as a hired gun, I killed a lot of people I had no business killing," says Jo, real quiet. "You be careful, Hunter. He's not interested in letting you go."

Then she shoulders her gun and walks away, leaving me with a mix of feelings in my gut. None of them are pleasant.

CHAPTER TWELVE

THE HOGSHEAD BANDITS

When Paulie Torrence arrives at Tabitha's and interrupts my breakfast the next morning, I begin to regret agreeing to the job. He pulls out a chair, watching me eat with that devil-may-care grin he always wears. The eggs turn sour in my belly, and I push the plate away, dabbing at my lips with the cloth napkin.

"Well?" I ask.

"There's a group of ne'er-do-wells making off with some supplies from the Hogshead camp. Boss doesn't want things to slow the work down there, see? Wants us to clear 'em out. Ten paper bills a head."

I toss the napkin over the plate. Ten bills a head, like cattle. "Deserters?"

"Bandits, more like," says Paulie. He rolls his neck from side to side. "Shouldn't take us more than a few hours to get out there and find their camp if they have one. They've hit the Hogshead supplies four times in the past couple of weeks, so they're probably holed up nearby."

It strikes me as a bit odd that bandits would only take supplies instead of hitting the clerk's office for some of the nuggets and shadesilver dust from the mine. I say so, and Paulie scratches the blond peach fuzz on his jaw.

"Supplies… silver dust… a handful of dirt. Stealin' is stealin', and Mr. McBride doesn't take kindly to it."

Mr. McBride doesn't take kindly to much he can't control, from what I can tell. But the silver nuggets I left behind in a false floorboard in my room aren't paying me to take things kindly. I stand, leave my plate on the table, and follow Paulie out to the stables. He disappears around back to get his own horse from the hitching rail. My roan mare is in a particular mood, laying her ears flat and nipping at my duster as I try to saddle her without catching a bit of my skin in those mean teeth. I tell her that someday I'm going to turn her into a pot of good strong glue.

I open the stall door next to the mare and pull Rip toward me. He unfolds his long legs and lurches to his feet in that unnerving way that looks like all his bones are held together with a bit of wire. His black eyes stare, and I silently dare him to look my way. He doesn't. I'm starting to wonder if that moment over the Bard's Thumb was just my mind playing a bit of fancy on itself. Wouldn't be the first time. Pops always used to tell me that my brain lived out in the clouds somewhere.

"That really is the most unnatural thing I ever did see," says Paulie from a nearby stall, watching Rip shuffle out into the aisle.

Ignoring him, I jam my boot in the stirrup and swing over the saddle, gathering my reins and sending the mare on her way out of the long barn. Rip lumbers after me like an uncomfortable shadow. The temptation to let him go and watch him disappear into dust doesn't strike me often, but this is one of those times. I focus on the brisk sway of the mare's walk, relaxing my hips into the familiar motion and ignoring the dead man behind me. Paulie's riding his garishly golden palomino gelding. He's not done too bad for himself in the bounty hunting line of work either, if his horse and the silver-trimmed saddle are anything to go by.

He flashes me his tobacco-stained grin, and I fight the urge to scowl at him. Does he ever stop doing that? If I'm going to have to see Paulie Torrence's face more often, I don't know that Mr. McBride has enough silver to pay me that cost. We set off down the road away from Silver City toward the closest and largest of McBride's mining outfits.

It doesn't take more than a few minutes of silence for Paulie to start talking. He turns in his saddle and looks back at Rip. I ignore him, hoping he'll just leave well enough alone. But hope doesn't seem to get me far in life.

"I'd ask how you killed him, but that hole in his chest tells its own story. Shotgun blast, I'd say. That'd put you, what… ten feet away from him, a shot like that? Had to have been pretty damn close. You're not bad to look at, you know. Is that what happened, tried to sneak a hand under the skirts? Or the trousers, in your case."

I say nothing. I wonder if Hector McBride will give me ten bills for Paulie's head. Blast the money, I wouldn't even need pay. Paulie seems to take my silence as an invitation to keep right on talking.

"Or maybe he sold you out. I hear necros aren't welcome in some places up north. Where are you from, anyway?"

I fix my gaze on the grassy bluffs ahead. Paulie turns back around in his saddle, still wearing that stupid grin on his face like he's always telling himself a joke that only he thinks is funny. I'm used to his type, and I learned a long time ago how to pretend they don't exist.

"Alright, alright. Keep your trousers buttoned, then. But I

gotta ask you one thing. How does it work? You know, bringing a dead man back like that? Almighty, I bet it's a sight."

Memories are the devil. Even when you tell them to stay away, they take any opportunity to whisper in your ear. Sometimes they come back when I see a fresh set of bones or hear the ring of a pickaxe on stone. Sometimes it's the smell of cheap cigar smoke, or the tug of magic that happens whenever I'm around something that's recently died, tempting me to reach out and bring it back to life.

And then it creeps in, the feeling of magic crackling in a burst like gunfire through my chest and down through my arms, out the tips of my fingers. I remember Rip's eyes when they were brown, not black, and his dying breath right before the magic hit him, dragging him back from the After. I remember the pain, white-hot and blinding, ripping through my body like a thousand knives. And then the nothing before waking up to see the pitch-black veined eyes of a corpse watching me as I came back to the light.

I'll be bloody fluxed to the Dark After before I tell Paulie Torrence a word.

The Hogshead Mine shaft drills into the rocky caves near where the Mule and Hogshead Rivers join and start wandering their way south. The shaft struck a decent vein of shadesilver, and a good amount of the stuff was found in the riverbed itself. It was McBride's first big payout and filled his pockets with enough money to start additional operations in other parts of the Territories. Somehow, they're still finding enough dust and chipping out enough of a vein in the caves that McBride can afford to hire on twenty or thirty miners with two foremen, a weight clerk, and a couple of hired guns to keep an eye on things. I have a hunch that the hired guns won't be keeping eyes on things at Hogshead much longer if there are thieves making off with supplies right under their noses.

The path out to the mine leads us through some short, rocky bluffs, and then we finally see the freshly painted wooden sign: Hogshead Mine, Hector McBride, proprietor. There's a small bend in the pathway, and then the bluffs fall away and the river, dark and sludgy, crawls along up ahead. There are small wooden structures everywhere, sluice gates and troughs, panning bays, and a small village of mining huts. Every man or woman working the riverside operation wears the same clothing: a simple shirt with the sleeves rolled to the elbows, trousers, and a worn pair of suspenders. The hats always look like they got thrown underneath a herd of charging cattle at one time.

A woman with a face that looks as sharply edged as the rocky crags of the Cathedrals comes over to us. She wears a bronze foreman's pin on the front of her shirt. Brown hair is pulled back under a brown hat that matches her brown trousers, brown shirt, and brown suspenders. Her skin is rubbed brown with dirt, and her green eyes look weirdly out of place. After fixing Rip with a curled lip of disgust, she squints at us.

"You the bounty hunters?"

I touch the brim of my hat. "That'd be us. You Foreman Hills?"

She nods. "I expect that you'll clear out the ruffians so my men can do their work in peace. Those hired guns McBride sent us aren't worth a damn. Never seen lazier slobs in my life. They keep telling me they're paid to guard within the boundaries of the mining outfit and no further." She hawks a bit of phlegm and spits.

"Ruffians?" I ask.

"Never did get a good look at 'em. The one we did see last time was a short fella, real ragged. Saw him from the back. They never pulled any weapons." She points to the woods across the river. "They come from the woods and leave the same way."

I look around again and pick out the two hired gunmen. One stands on top of the mine shaft entrance, making a big show of watching across the river. The other lounges against the clerk's small cabin, his rifle leaning easy on his shoulder. He watches me and pinches the brim of his hat when he sees me look his way. I don't have much time for lazy slobs, so I turn back to Foreman Hills.

"What did they take?"

"Food crates mostly. But last time they took some tools and a few of the new blankets Mr. McBride had sent for the miners."

I frown at that. But Paulie seems to be done with the chatter. He nudges his palomino forward toward the bridge leading across the water. "Don't worry, Foreman," he calls back. "We'll have 'em put down before you stop for lunch."

The bridge looks like a pile of sticks held together with ropes of braided twine. It's wide enough for the horses, but the roan mare plants her feet on the shore in front of it and refuses to move another step. I pull Rip close behind her and use him to push her forward, but she bunches the muscles in her haunches and digs in. She kicks out at Rip, knocking him back a step or two. His gray skin swirls as the hoofprint disappears from his thigh. I pull harder at him, and finally the mare takes a shaky step onto the bridge. It feels more solid than it looks.

One more step, and then the mare takes off, her hooves skipping across the bridge as she hops and jumps her way to the safety of the shore on the other side. I haul on the reins, pulling her in a circle as soon as she hits the dirt. Rip silently follows, his ragged spectral boots making no sound on the logs. Paulie is grinning at me like a fool by the time the mare settles.

"Lively one, ain't she?" he says. His palomino stands quietly, grinding the bit between his teeth and behaving himself. I dismount and lead the mare along the edge of the woods, looking for any clue as to where the "ruffians" might have entered. I find it after only a minute of searching. About ten feet into the trees and knee-high layer of underbrush, there's a small channel of broken branches and a boot footprint in a little dip of mud. Whoever they are, they're not skilled at covering their tracks.

"Leave the horses," I tell Paulie. The roan mare is too easily spooked, and the brushy, root-broken ground inside the woods isn't going to help us any. Once we have the palomino and roan tied to a pair of young birches at the edge of the forest, we make our way in. Now Rip is in front, carving us a path through the brush the same way he did through the snow on the Bard's Thumb. I peer around him and keep my eyes on the trail we follow. It's not much, but now and then I catch a broken branch, a footprint, and once we even stumble across an apple core that was tossed aside.

I have an uncomfortable twist in the pit of my belly. Whoever these thieves are, they don't seem all that worried about being followed. Either they're just plain stupid, or they're not fearful of anything that might come after them. The air in the forest is close and thick, and a trickle of sweat runs down the back of my neck. The late autumn weather hasn't quite reached this region yet. I find myself missing the cold of the Cathedrals. I'll take a cold wind over thick, hot air any day.

We walk about a mile before I hear the first sign of our ruffians. The clank of a cookpot comes from somewhere up ahead. I slip my guns free of their holsters, and Paulie does the same. I notice the smooth ivory grips on his guns. Like everything else he owns, they're expensive. Small wonder he can feed himself with the money he's shelled out for a fancy set of poppers and that circus pony and saddle.

I push Rip to the side so I can see what we're heading into, and creep quietly through the brush, more careful now to keep my steps from giving us away. There's a little stomped-down clearing about ten yards ahead of us, and as I sink down against the trunk of a big granddaddy oak tree, I make out about five or six all wearing old or baggy clothes that don't seem to fit them. When the first one turns in my direction, a few things snap into place. That's a young face. Fourteen, sixteen at most.

The others aren't much older. There are a few blankets strung over ropes to make tents, and a small fire in the middle of the circle. The ruffians are all boys, tough looking. One of them sits on a tree stump at the edge that seems a mite out of place, his shaggy black hair hanging like tattered curtains over eyes that dart nervous-like around at the others. The biggest boy, maybe eighteen, has a holster belted around his scrawny hips, but the gun's grip looks worn and old even from where I sit. He bends over the cookpot to inspect the other boy's cooking and gets loud and angry about it smelling burnt.

"I get you better food and you still can't cook nothing good," he barks angrily in the face of the boy who clearly has drawn the short stick of cooking for the rest. One holstered gun is the only weapon I can see. This is just a bunch of vagrant boys acting like they know a thing or two, stealing from one of the richest men in the north because they don't know any better. I start changing my plan. Lengths of rope lay coiled up on the food crates on the other side of the camp. Paulie and I can take them by surprise, shake things up a little, and tie them all in a line. They'll pay for what they stole, or maybe Mr. McBride will take it out of them in labor. I doubt we'll get ten bills a head for this lot, but it's an easier job than I bargained for.

I turn to whisper my plan to Paulie. He's not there. I look around, but the only body nearby is Rip's, hidden behind a twisted pine. A twig snaps somewhere on the other side of the camp, and the boys startle. The biggest pulls the old revolver out of his holster, and the sharp snap of gunfire echoes through the trees. A bullet goes straight through the boy's forehead and out the back as he topples over into the fire.

CHAPTER THIRTEEN

NECROMANCER

The boys scream, running in every direction like spooked cattle. One pistol shot barks from the trees, and another 'bandit' jerks and crumples to the ground, howling and trying to reach around to his back as he dies. I pull my guns and walk forward into the clearing.

"Paulie Torrence!" I shout. "Hold your fire, you bastard!"

I snag the collar of a boy who runs close enough and yank him back to the ground. I point my gun at his forehead, and he freezes, hands held in front of his face. The body of the boy with the revolver is close enough that I feel the tug through my hands, pulling, beckoning. Magic in my veins simmers the way a racehorse chomps at the bit, muscles gathered to burst forward as soon as its rider gives an inch of rein. I ignore it. Then I feel something else.

There's magic in the clearing, and it's not mine. The body of the boy at the edge of the clearing, the one with the bullet in his back, twitches a little. He's dead and gone, but something is tugging at him. Necromancy. I hear Paulie's gunfire again. I fire three rounds into the trees. I won't hit him, but if my bullets get close enough, maybe that'll be enough to convince him I mean business. The boy at my feet scrambles up and runs for it, crashing into the brush.

He leaps into the clearing, madder than a hornet. For a minute, I think he's going to level at me, but he goes after the running boy. I spin on my heels and reach out with my own magic, thin strands creeping out through the air and curling around the dead boy's body. I learned a long time ago how to resist pulling at every dead body I crossed, but the strange traces of foreign necromancy left behind on this boy feel wild and raw. Whoever I'm after, they're dangerous, unskilled. I pull Rip into the clearing to guard my back.

Like a bloodhound, I memorize the feel of the other magic and follow the trail of it back into the trees. My necromancy feels smooth like a river stone, but the traces I follow are sharp edged. It's gritty, like sand in my teeth. When I finally find the culprit, he's huddled like a newborn under the boughs of a pine tree. I pull the branches away, keeping the business end of my gun trained on the boy inside. He's got his hands pressed to his ears, eyes squeezed shut. It's the shaggy haired kid I saw setting on the stump earlier.

His breathing is too fast. Little wheezes and sounds like a kicked puppy come out of him as he tries to control the magic rolling off his hands and arms. He's strong. Too strong.

"Kid," I say.

He yelps and scrambles backwards. Hits the trunk of the tree with his back, staring at the end of my revolver pointed at his face. His hands come away from his ears and he holds them up, palms out.

"Please don't, please don't…" he begs.

"Hush up and come on out of there." I pull the branches further away and lower my gun. "By the Holy After, breathe, boy. Your magic is wild as a rock viper. Pull it back, through your fingers and up your arms."

He stares at me, and I think he's going to stop breathing for good. His face goes all ghostly pale, and I can tell he's realizing that there's magic in the air that isn't his. He stays put, a frozen rabbit caught in a trap. Gunfire cracks again somewhere in the woods, distant.

"You're Soulless?" he whispers.

"Depends on who you ask," I say. "Now are you going to come on out of there or do I need to reach in and drag you out by your ears?"

He pulls himself out, pine needles stuck all over his clothes and hair. I keep my gun handy, but I'm not pointing it at him anymore. Kid's more likely to faint than come after me, especially when he catches sight of the giant corpse standing a few feet behind me.

"Almighty preserve us!" he cries out, scrambling back toward the pine tree. I grab hold of his arm.

"He's not dangerous unless I tell him to be. Get a grip, boy. You're in a world of trouble already, don't make it worse for yourself."

Still staring terrified at Rip, he twists his hands in the hem of his coat, which looks like it was made for someone twice his size. A green and yellow bruise colors his left cheekbone, and his bottom lip has a wicked split in it. Something crashes toward us in the brush. My revolver comes face to face with Paulie Torrence. He's holstered his guns, but I don't trust him not to do something else stupid.

"What the Dark After was that, Torrence?" I spit at him. "They're a bunch of kids."

"A thief's a thief. I got to run down the last one before we head back. You going to put this one down?"

Paulie Torrence will never know how close he came to death

right there in that forest. My finger twitches on the trigger of my revolver, and I imagine a dozen ways I might leave him here, dead. I could tell McBride that he was killed by that boy with the gun. But that's a lie, and Pops would come back from the Holy After to give me a whipping if he heard me tell one. I wish he'd just let it slide one time.

"No, Paulie, I'm not going to put him down. And you're not going to either, or I'll lay you out in a coffin right here in these trees. You clear on that?"

He pulls a wad of chewing tobacco from the pouch on his belt and shoves it in the side of his mouth, the stringy red clump still sticking out between his lips.

"Sure thing, Hunter. Boss will probably want him anyway."

The boy's eyes are flicking back and forth between Paulie and me and Rip, and he looks like he's ready to run. "Mister, I didn't steal anything. I just came here two days ago, honest, I swear. Big Tom said they weren't really hurting anybody. 'They got lots of money and they wouldn't miss it,' he said."

"Big Tom, eh?" asks Paulie. He points toward the body laying in the scattered fire. "That him?"

The boy swallows. "Yes…yessir."

"You know who you were stealin' from?" Paulie leans in real close to the boy's face and puts a hand on his shoulder. I watch him squeeze just enough to make it hurt, and the boy shrinks away from him. "Mr. Hector McBride. You know who that is?"

"Yessir. His name is on the sign," the boy whispers back. "The mine sign."

"Well, we got ourselves a boy can read!" hoots Paulie, straightening up and cuffing the side of the boy's head. "Smart boy like you ought to know better. You know we hang thieves 'round these parts?"

The boy pales under the darker shade of brown that's been

burnt into his skin by a decent amount of time in the sun. Whatever stutters out of his mouth is gibberish. When he tries to pull back, Paulie's fingers dig in harder to his thin shoulder.

"That's enough, Torrence." I wait until he lets go. "Where are you from, boy? You got folks somewhere around here?"

I can tell by the way his eyes get dark and his lips stick together real tight that he doesn't want to tell me the answer. If he's running with a pack like this, it's unlikely he's got much of a family. They're probably dead and gone. I feel the sharp-edged magic around him. Or maybe he does have a family that doesn't want a Soulless dirtying up their house. Whoever he is, nobody ever taught him anything about animating, or he wouldn't have been trying to resurrect every dead body in the clearing. I glance at Paulie. As far as I can tell, he's got no magic, so he can't tell that the boy is simmering with it like a neglected cookfire pot. But if he finds out, I don't know what he'll do. So I figure I need some insurance if I'm going to get the boy away from him and Mr. McBride.

I pull Rip closer and face him toward Paulie and the boy. The horrified sound the boy makes reminds me a bit of a dying brush shrew. He's frozen, rooted to the spot. No need for Paulie to keep him from running now. I'm half surprised he doesn't soil his britches.

"Paulie, you said there was one more on the run. Why don't you go on ahead and see if you can find him. I'll pack this one back to Silver City."

He eyes me, and if there is one thing that I hate to admit about Paulie Torrence, it's that the man might be a twisted little weasel, but he's not stupid. But he twirls his revolver back into its holster without raising a fuss. "Alright, Hunter. If you say so. Another ten bills sounds good to me."

I stare what I wish was a bullet hole right between his eyes.

"Alive, Torrence. You already got three murdered boys on your record, and I intend to let Mr. McBride know what happened here."

"You do that," he says. "If it helps you sleep at night, you do that."

And then he's gone, disappearing through the forest toward the horses. I reach out and gather up a good handful of the coat behind the boy's neck and push him forward. He's shaking like a wet leaf.

"Almighty… save us," he whispers under his breath, squeezing his eyes shut tight like he can make Rip go away just by pretending he doesn't exist. I feel disgust. Little feather-bellied sap, that's what Pops would've called him. Too soft to walk outside of a comfortable house. I notice that he doesn't have any callouses on his hands. I put him at about fourteen years old. Not a single hair grows on his smooth chin, just black, shaggy hair on his head with a bit of grease in it. Big dark eyes with eyelashes longer than they should be.

"Are you going to hang me and bring me back as a…?"

I thought he'd lost his voice somewhere back in the clearing. I look at him from under the brim of my hat. There's no use trying to scare him worse than he is.

"I'm not intending for that to happen, no."

He glances over his shoulder at the skulking giant behind us. I can see a book's worth of questions in those dark eyes, but he says nothing. I don't much like the idea of handing him over to Mr. McBride. Paulie Torrence may not be able to tell that this boy is a necromancer, but something tells me we won't be so lucky with McBride. I'll bet money on it.

Torrence will tell McBride that I have one of the boys from the gang of thieves. McBride will want him to answer for his crimes. Maybe he'll let the boy off with a rap on the knuckles, but I doubt it. And I don't know what's gotten into me, but I realize that I'm not easy about the idea of McBride getting his hooks into this kid. An untrained necromancer with this kind of strength isn't something I want in the hands of a power-hungry businessman.

But that means that I better have some kind of plan to get me and the kid out of Silver City without a noose around either of our necks. If I can take him to Addy, she'll get him fixed up quick. Give him a home. She's always taking in strays.

I grimace at him as he stumbles along next to me, my hand still firmly gripping the back of his coat. He's not worth my trouble. I've already got one iron ball and chain around my ankle, and it's walking behind us. But the truth is, the boy doesn't have a chance. World like this? It'll chew him up and spit out his bones. Especially if he goes around with this untethered magic flying out every which way. He's likely to animate something eventually, and the Almighty only knows what it'll be. Or who.

I could let him go. Paulie would never believe that he got the drop on me. Maybe I will take my chances with McBride and tell the kid to go back wherever he came from. Can't be worse than here. He's too far north, and while Silver City mostly lets me go about my business, it only takes one person who doesn't like what he is to take his life in a dark turn. And it's clear he doesn't know his hind end from his front when it comes to being out on his own.

We come out of the forest and back onto the riverbank. Paulie and his horse are gone, and the roan mare spooks at the sight of us, flaring her dumb nostrils and stamping her foot like she's just seen a snake come out of the grass. The boy spooks a little at her too, and I think about leaving the pair of them tied to the tree and walking on home by myself.

"You been on a horse before, boy?"

He gives a little shake of his head, he and the mare both watching each other with the whites of their eyes. "I sat on a pony once."

"Can you mount up to the saddle, or do I need to boost you up there?"

His shoulders hunch forward a little. "No, I can do it."

It surprises me when he does, pulling himself up while I hold the mare's bridle. She stands perfectly still as soon as he touches her. Well I'll be darned. I untie her reins and yank the boy's foot out of the stirrup so I can jump into the saddle behind him. The roan mare is sturdy enough to carry us both back to Silver City as long as we don't need to leave in a hurry. The surly foreman meets us at the other end of the bridge.

"The other bounty hunter says it was nothing but a bunch of kids," she says, eyeing the boy sitting in front of me like she's thinking of roasting him on a spit. "Vagrant bastards, never amount to nothin'. You take him on back and see he gets the lickin' that's coming to him. I hear Sheriff Brady might have a bit of rope just his size."

The boy shivers, and I look down at the foreman. "I'll see he gets his due."

"You best." She steps well out of Rip's way as we move on.

We ride down the path, away from the mine and the sluice troughs and the good-for-nothing gunmen still standing exactly where I left them guarding the exact boundaries of Hector McBride's property. The boy clutches the saddle horn like his life depends on it. When the mare settles into a swaying walk, nothing but the grassy bluffs out ahead of us, I decide to get some answers.

"You're not a farmer's boy. And you're not a smith or tradesman's apprentice. Hands are too smooth to have seen any kind of real work. Your coat's old and dirty, but the shirt underneath it isn't. That's quality cloth. You're not used to sleeping out in the woods either, I reckon. So as I see it, either your family is dead and gone, or you're a runaway."

His shoulders go stiff. I don't wait for him to respond, just keep on talking the way my Pops always used to when he had something to say and I was going to wait for him to say it.

"When we get back to Silver City, Mr. McBride is going to want to see you. I don't know how merciful a mood he's going to be in when we get there. You're a necromancer, but nobody has taught you a thing about what that means or how to use it. Or not use it, in your case. I don't know where you come from, but up here, people aren't friendly to our kind. I can help you get somewhere safe, but you're going to have to do exactly what I say. If McBride finds out you're a necromancer, he might just keep you on a leash for the rest of your life. And if not, you can strike out on your own and see if you can slip the noose yourself."

I let him think on that for a while. The mare sways, ears pricked forward. Rip shambles next to her hip, and for once, she's not bothered by his being there. In fact, she's been close to angelic since the moment the boy got up in that saddle. Fool horse. The boy still says nothing, and I know what Reverend Ambrose would've said the moment he crawled out from under the pine tree.

"What's your name, boy?"

The silence stretches thin like a piece of taffy. I wait until it finally breaks, quiet-like.

"Johnny. My name is Johnny."

CHAPTER FOURTEEN

TEN PAPER BILLS A HEAD

Tabitha gives me a suspicious look when I bring the kid into her boarding house, and then promptly fetches him a plate of food and tells him to sit himself in a chair before he falls over. He's still all curled into himself, hiding his eyes under his hair like he hopes he might disappear into Tabitha's freshly waxed floor. He relaxed a little when we left Rip in his stall, and his magic has quieted down some, but I still feel it pulsing through the air like a heartbeat. The kid's a walking hazard, it's only a matter of time before he drags something back from the grave. Best case scenario it's a dead chicken or alley cat. Worst case…

My presence in Silver City with Rip has been tolerated by most, and McBride seems to have taken a particular interest in my talents since I arrived. Necromancers aren't accepted in most polite society up here, but I remember the way McBride's eyes got greedy when I stood in his office. A boy like Johnny would be snapped up like a fish on a hook.

I watch as the boy nibbles at a bit of toast and bacon. He avoids looking at me, even when I pull out a chair and sit next to him. He goes rigid like a dead possum, and his fingers freeze on the plate. I grimace. Maybe he's not worth my time. Maybe I just let Hector McBride take him off my hands. Johnny glances at me lightning quick from under that curtain of black hair. Something pulls at a bit of me from the past, wide eyes on such a young face caught in the world's spinning current. I sigh.

"Finish your food. Mr. McBride will be wanting to see us, and you and I got some things to talk about first."

"Please let me go," he whispers around a mouthful of bacon. "I'll never come back here again."

"Too late for that now, kid."

He only eats a few bites, and then I'm pulling him out of his chair and marching him up to the second floor of Tabitha's boarding rooms. Once I've pulled the door shut and locked it, I point to the chair in the corner.

"Sit."

He slumps into it, and I ease onto the edge of the bed. I'd like nothing more than to pull the boots off my sore feet and rest for a spell, but I face the kid and try to talk to him, skittish creature that he is. "So. You're a necromancer."

There's a little shake of his head. "No, I've never… I still have my soul."

My mama used to say that patience was a virtue. Unfortunately, it's not one the Almighty saw fit to bless me with. I take off my hat and set it aside, rubbing the ache out of my temples with my fingers. I count to three before I answer.

"Doesn't matter. You're a necromancer with or without an Animated. It's clear nobody taught you anything about your magic. But that doesn't mean you don't have it. And it sure as the bloody flux isn't going to save you from people who find out."

"I don't want to use it."

I nod. "Fair enough. But there are people who will want you

to use it. And there are people who would rather see you buried six feet under instead of walking around breathing."

His jaw shifts at that, and he glances out toward the window. "Maybe we should be. Buried, I mean."

"Speak for yourself, but I like breathing just fine." I wave my hand in the general direction of his coat. "I know you came from somewhere, kid. You may not like me, but I am trying to help you. Where's your family?"

He goes tight-lipped and looks down at his grubby hands.

"Look," I say. "If you want me to turn you over to Mr. McBride or the sheriff, I'll do it right now. You'll either spend some time in a jail cell, get real close and personal with a gallows rope, or end up working for Mr. McBride. I got no problem riding out of here on my own. Now I'd be willing to bet a good deal of money that you've been through some rough times, but you're not the only kid who had to grow up with the power to bring a corpse back to life. You got two choices. You can decide who you want to be, or you can let someone else do the deciding for you."

"You're Soulless," he says, and finally a little spark of something lights his eyes. "And you want me to be Soulless too. Necromancers are cursed by the Dark After, and we must resist the urge to reach into the darkness, or else we won't ever come back!"

I laugh. He looks shocked and leans away from me in the chair. I get up off my bed and crouch in front of him, so close that he can feel my breath on his face.

"You seem to know an awful lot for a snot-nosed kid drowning in a big man's coat," I tell him, real quiet. "Let me tell you something. You can't control your magic. When I found you under that tree, you were lit up like a bonfire with it. If you don't learn how to control it, and how it works, you're going to do something that you'll regret. Or it's going to get you shot."

The spark's gone right out of his eyes again, and he picks at the dirt under his cracked fingernails. I notice the impressive, yellowed bruise on his cheekbone again.

"How long you been with those other boys?" I ask.

"Three days."

The bruise isn't from them, then. "When did you run away from home?"

He swallows and closes his eyes. "Nine days."

"Do you want to go back?"

"No."

"Alright. If you want to learn how to control your necromancy so you never animate a single soul, I'll take you to someone who can teach you. Is that what you want?"

He hesitates a good bit before he nods. He doesn't really trust me, but the list of folks who do is powerful short anyhow. There's a knock at my door, and Tabitha's voice comes through the wood.

"Hunter? Paulie Torrence is downstairs asking for you."

I look at Johnny. "If you want to come with me, keep your tongue behind your teeth. No word about your magic. Let's just hope McBride doesn't employ anyone who can sniff out what you are."

The butler's expression looks as if someone told him there was a speck of mud on his polished shoes, but he still opens the door for me when I knock. Johnny hunches along behind me, still wearing that ridiculous coat. I figure it makes him look young and helpless. Not that he needs much help with that. I left Rip behind. Better I seem as innocent as possible for this conversation.

Robert the butler leads us up the grand staircase and I glance back, expecting to see Johnny in awe of the fancy house. But I'm a bit surprised when he doesn't even look around. His eyes stay glued to my boots as he follows me up the steps. He does manage one look at the Yarbrough painting before we step into McBride's office.

Paulie Torrence is already there, leaning against the wall to our right this time. Nobody ever looked more like a cat that caught a canary than Paulie Torrence. I'm tired of seeing his face everywhere.

Hector McBride looks up from his desk and pulls a gold timepiece from the front of his red brocade waistcoat. "Eight o'clock on the dot. I trust Tabitha saw you fed when you returned?"

"She's not the type of woman to let anyone go hungry if they walk through her door, Mr. McBride," I answer. He talks about everyone in the town as if he owns their establishments as well as his own. He looks past me at the boy standing awkwardly in the doorway.

"This must be one of our thieves. The other one is sitting in one of the good Sheriff's jail cells. But I expect there's a reason you've brought this one to me." He pulls open one of the drawers in the big mahogany desk. "Ten bills a head, split between the two of you, as we agreed. Good at any bank in the Territories."

He holds out twenty-five paper bank notes over the desk. I eye it, but I don't want a single copper pithing's worth of that money. "Begging your pardon, Mr. McBride, but I can't rightly take that money for what we did today."

Both of his eyebrows lift a little. "Torrence reported to me that there were three thieves killed in the gunfire, and these two boys were brought back in to be turned in to the law."

I curl my lip in disgust. "Those three dead thieves were boys. Not one of 'em over eighteen years old. Torrence fired on them, and two of them weren't armed with anything more than a cookpot ladle."

 "Now just a minute," Torrence says, holding his palms up toward me. "The first one I saw had a big old revolver strapped to him. Didn't think you'd get squeamish about pulling a trigger, Hunter."

I turn on him. "You killed two unarmed boys in cold blood. And that Big Tom had as much chance of beating you to the draw as Ulysses Hadley. But I suppose you get off on the idea of pulling your guns on a bunch of boys. Easy cash, no chance of you lying in the dirt at the end."

Torrence's smile is long gone. "Maybe you shouldn't be a bounty hunter if you lose your nerve at the sight of a few boys. Why'd you keep this one with you? Gonna teach him a few tricks back at Tabitha's?"

My right hand goes to the hilt of a shadesilver knife. Paulie's got a knife in his boot, and if he pulls it, I know I've got him.

"Enough."

Hector McBride rises from his chair and gestures Paulie away. "I will have no uncivilized discourse in my home. Keep your temper or I will have no use for you, Mr. Torrence. If indeed these thieves were not grown men, shooting them down in the woods was terribly indecent of you. I will speak with Hunter alone and get to the bottom of this."

Paulie looks like he still wants to stick me with the business end of a boot knife, but he storms out of the room. Johnny has shifted toward the bookshelves, avoiding the gaze of the man behind the desk. McBride sits back down in his chair and pulls a silk handkerchief from his breast pocket. A quick sweep over his forehead, and then it is tucked back in its place. He tugs the waistcoat down with a sigh.

"My apologies. Mr. Torrence has his talents, but he is not without his faults. I will address this further with him when he is in better control of his temper." He narrows his eyes at me. "But I must admit, I was not expecting to see him get under your skin. I would've thought you impervious to such vulgar talk. Now, I can respect your hesitation to accept your pay, all things considered, but I intend to compensate you for your efforts on my behalf."

"That's not necessary."

He sets his hand on the twenty-five bills. "A woman of principle. You're a rarity in these parts."

"I'm no saint, Mr. McBride. But I don't use bullets on children."

"Of course I would never have suggested it had I known," he says reassuringly. I don't like that I can't tell if he's telling the truth. Most people I can tell just by looking them in the eyes, but McBride confuses me sometimes, and I don't care for it.

"I hope you have given some more thought to my offer." He pulls a sheet of paper from the drawer and sets it on the desk, turning it so I can read the writing. "I took the liberty of drawing up a contract, offering you a stake in my company and a percentage of its income in return for your services. I need more people of principle in my employ, and as they are rather hard to come by, I trust you will understand my eager interest in securing someone with your particular talents."

"I appreciate the offer," I say slowly, letting the words come to me the right way. "I have some folks to look in on. I'll be leaving Silver City for a spell, and I'll think on it while I'm gone."

There's a little flash of irritation in his eyes, right before it disappears back behind the cool businessman's mask. But he nods, the picture of understanding. "Of course. And the boy? There must be a reason you brought him here."

I reach behind me and pull Johnny forward by the shoulder of his coat. "His name is Johnny. I found him hiding under a tree while Torrence was shooting up the rest. He was only with that band of boys a couple of days. I figure he's got a whole life ahead of him, and maybe I can set him on a better path. I know some folks that might take him in, and I intend to take him there."

Hector McBride watches me say my piece, and as I talk, his eyes drift away from me and onto Johnny again. I can see him assessing, dissecting everything he can see. He believes me a woman of principle, and I think it will be enough to convince him that I am taking the kid on as an act of charity to relieve my burdened conscience. He knows I'm not afraid of walking away from his money, and it puts him in my debt. He settles back into his chair and his neatly trimmed mustache curls upward.

"Johnny, is it?"

"Yessir."

"Where is your family, boy?"

Johnny twists his hands together. "I'm on my own, sir. I apologize for the thieving. I didn't have anywhere else to go."

I don't know if he's trying to sound pathetic, but it works. McBride nods and picks up the money, folding it neatly in half before extending it to me again. "Very well. I admire your generosity, and I'd like to make a small investment in this boy's future. See that it is put to good use."

The cash makes it into my pocket, and I tip my hat. "Much obliged, Mr. McBride. I'll stop in when I come back to Silver City."

"Please do. I look forward to future business with you, Hunter. The contract will be here when you return."

I grab the back of the boy's coat and push him out of the office, back down the stairs and out of the front door nearly before the butler can open it for us. I buckle my holsters around my hips as we walk. Johnny stumbles a little and might have fallen on his face if I hadn't reached out to steady him. He'll need a horse. The roan can't carry us both all the way to Grand Junction. But the first order of business is elsewhere. I hustle us both onto the boardwalk and toward Miss Halloway's Seamstress and Mercantile.

CHAPTER FIFTEEN

A CLEAN SHIRT THAT FITS

Miss Letitia Halloway is the type of woman who speaks her mind freely and often. As seamstress and cloth merchant for the town's respectable folk, she knows more about the goings on than the Sheriff and spends her days sharing the latest gossip over fine thread and buttonholes. She's a Weaver, and her magic is of a far more practical kind. With no family of her own to occupy her time outside of her work, she inhabits the gable room above the shop sparingly. Silver City's most successful spinster sits on a mountain of secrets bigger than any of the Cathedrals, and most of the folks in the town come to her for the latest news. They usually end up going home with more than a fair bit of advice as well. And she's one of the few people in town that doesn't seem to find me intolerably offensive. At least, not enough that she'd turn away my money on the rare occasion I need a new shirt.

When Johnny steps through the doorway into her shop, she fixes him with a stare that would put Hector McBride's calculation to a fair bit of shame. Her small gold-rimmed spectacles sit exactly halfway down a hawkish nose. Wisps of salt and pepper brown hair have pulled loose from the bun at the back of her head and frame her sharp cheekbones. I wouldn't have ever said she was a particularly pretty woman, but she's as regal as a queen. I imagine she's seen more than her fair share of curiosities in her forty-six years. And now she's seen Johnny.

She pulls the measuring tape from her neck as she's striding toward him, her heavy black shoes clacking against the floorboards. He's a head shorter than her, and she peers at him like a great bird of prey.

"You're a lucky young man," she tells him tartly. "I assume since you are not in a jail cell or hanging from a gallows, you've been given a chance to make something of yourself."

As expected, news gets around quick in Silver City. I tip my hat to her. "I need you to fix him up with some proper clothes."

"A new coat, it would seem," she says.

"A simple duster will do fine. Something that fits."

She sniffs and touches the front of his stained shirt with her thumb and forefinger. "Something that fits…" she mutters to herself, offended that I would specify that. Of course it will fit. "Tell me you intend to order a clean shirt as well."

There is money in my pocket, so I nod. "Two clean shirts. Have anything on hand?"

"Of course. I have several in his size. Blue, gray and cream."

The sweaty, dirty state of the shirt he's wearing suggests that the cream might be out of its depth here. "Blue and gray, I think. And a wide-brim hat."

She scribbles something on a slip of paper from her apron pocket and gives me a once over, tapping her pencil on her fingers. "Perhaps a new hat for you as well."

There's not a chance in the Dark After that Miss Halloway is going to part me from my hat, so I run my fingers over the worn brim. It's familiar, comforting.

"No thank you, ma'am. Just his."

She tsks but bustles away toward the back of her shop and the shelves of shirts, pants, and coats. I wander toward a rack of satin and touch a bolt of deep green with the tips of my fingers. I've always enjoyed the smoothness of satin, the way it feels cool even on a hot, dusty day. That said, I haven't got a lick of time for the skirts, waists, and capes made from the stuff. How Miss Halloway and the other ladies of Silver City can breathe through their corsets is a mystery I've never solved. Addy swears they're comfortable, but I'm not sure I believe her. My mama used to wear them, of course, but she died long before I was old enough to be squeezed into one. Small blessings.

There's a half-finished corset lying on Miss Halloway's worktable in the back room. She's finished some of the boning, and the rest waits to be sewn in and used to prop up some respectable bosom. I feel the itch of sweat beneath the simple cloth contraption I wrangled up for myself to wear under my shirts. I've never been well-endowed, and that suits me just fine. I eye several fine pairs of black stockings and wrinkle my nose.

Johnny waits by the counter, peering into a row of glass jars full of buttons. Brass buttons, bone buttons, cloth covered buttons, wooden buttons plain and carved, and even a small assortment of ivory buttons imported from the country of Maneira far to the southeast. Pops used to read stories about Maneiran elephants to me when I was a sprout, and I'd always thought that maybe someday I would catch a ride on one of the big steam ships to see them. Years ago I'd gone south planning to earn enough for a ticket, but I never got around to buying one. The cities in the south had kept me busy enough until Pops' last letter had brought me back north in a hurry.

I hear a clink and see Johnny putting the lid carefully back on the brass button jar. When he catches my eye, he shoves his hands in his pockets and keeps them there instead of examining any more of Miss Halloway's wares. And just as well, too, because she comes bustling back over to him with an armful of clothing and shoos him away into a curtained dressing room at the back of the shop. As soon as he's out of sight, she takes several meaningful steps toward me.

"I hear tell you and Paulie Torrence found a few thieves up in the woods by Hogshead."

I remove myself from the ladies clothing section and sidle back to the safer center of the room. "You always did have a fast ear, Miss Halloway."

She lowers her voice to keep the young man behind the curtains from hearing our talk, but she's not much good at whispering. And she can't abide a mystery. "So he's an orphan runaway, then? How charitable of you to take him in. I hadn't thought of you as the type of woman to…" she eyes my figure in a way that makes me squirm inside. "To take in a child."

"I'm only taking him as far as Grand Junction. I know some folks there that will give him a good home and see that he's raised decent." There is one flaw in my plan, of course, and that is the fact that I haven't asked Addy if she'll have him. But if there's anyone I know well, it's Adelaide Sterling. She'll get sore at me for taking advantage of her kind-hearted generosity, but she'll take him in.

Miss Halloway rearranges a neatly folded pile of trousers that doesn't need rearranging. "You'll be leaving Silver City, then?"

"For a spell, yes."

She smooths her hand over the stacked trousers. "If you don't mind me asking, Miss Hunter, and you'll forgive my curiosity, should someone with your particular malady be taking on a child? I would imagine your influence might be a danger to such a young soul."

I ignore the way she pussyfoots around the word necromancer.

"Bounty hunting certainly isn't a life for the faint-hearted, Miss Halloway. But as I said, he'll be with me as far as Grand Junction, and then he'll be handed over to someone else. There's no need to worry yourself about him."

"Yes of course," she says, clearly disappointed. She's been trying her darnedest to get me to tell her my life story since I first stepped foot in Silver City and took a room at Tabitha's. Not knowing a thing rankles her like a burdock under a saddle blanket. I'm spared any further questions by the reappearance of the kid, who emerges out of the dressing room with a crisp new blue shirt tucked into a pair of brown trousers. His bruised face and shaggy hair still need some working on, but Addy will see to that. He looks a darn sight closer to respectable.

Miss Halloway crowds him like a mother hen, pulling and plucking at the fabric. She fusses over the waistband of his trousers and makes a proclamation that he's in need of a few good meals. Johnny lets her fuss and then says a quiet 'thank you, ma'am' once she's satisfied that the clothes fit him right. She seems pleased with his manners and rounds the corner of her merchant's counter to add up our total.

"Give me enough of that dark green satin for a skirt and bustle," I say. "And some of the black lace flounce to go with it."

Her fingers pause over the sums, and she blinks rapidly a few times in my direction. "I… yes of course, Miss Hunter."

"Just Hunter."

She cuts several yards from the bolt of satin, tucks the black lace inside, and wraps it all up nicely in some brown paper. I buy the package separately from Johnny's new things and fold the rest of his money back in my pocket. It's late by the time we walk out of the mercantile, and the shops along the Silver City main street are closing. My stomach gnaws at itself, and the thought of Tabitha's cooking makes my mouth water. Before we reach the boardinghouse, the boy finds his tongue.

"Thank you."

I look down at the kid. "What for?"

"For helping me."

He still doesn't look me in the eyes, but we've got time to sturdy him up some on the ride to Grand Junction. I shrug. We return to the truce of silence as we step into Tabitha's, but I make sure he wipes his boots off before we walk in.

Jo Farstep is waiting for us at a table. Three more of Tabitha's boarders sit around eating their suppers after getting back late from the mines and the cattle herds. They all give us a good stare when we come in. Tabitha sets steaming plates of okra and pork belly in front of us, and Johnny can't ignore his stomach anymore. He tucks in, and I notice the way he carefully cuts the meat into neat squares.

The pork belly melts in my mouth, savory meat mixed with a spicy Ferenese dressing. My Pops was never one for spices on his food, always said if he wanted his mouth to burn, he'd swallow a lit candle. I wasn't much for it either until I went farther south. The whole world was a big place, I found, and folks have found more ways to cook their food than I had ever imagined. I'd eaten Maneiran sticky rice and herbs, smoked spearfish fresh from the nets of the fishing boats in St. Albane and then coughed my way through a deep red curry from Ferensia. It was an illuminating thing, eating all those different foods, and the most important thing I learned through it all was just that I liked to eat. I'll eat nearly anything that's put in front of me. Except for octopus. I took one look at those limp tentacles and swore I'd rather go and starve in a desert. Everybody has got to draw their line somewhere.

I savor the pork and okra down to the last bite dragged across my plate and gathered onto the spoon. Johnny dabs his lips with the napkin. Most of Tabitha's boarders don't know how to use one. A sleeve is as good a thing as any. Tabitha clears my plate and then asks Johnny if he wants seconds. He shakes his head no with a 'thank you, ma'am'. I hide a smirk. Women do seem to get real motherly around Johnny.

I sit there a little while until the room clears and it's just me, Johnny, and Jo at the table. She straightens her bum leg out, giving her belly room to work through all the good cooking she just put in it.

"So you got yourself a kid. I didn't believe it until you walked in the door."

"Not my kid. Just taking him down south a ways."

"Got a name, son?" she asks the boy.

"Johnny."

"Where you from?"

He presses his lips together like a stubborn mule. Jo nods with a sort of easy understanding and folds her hands over her belly.

"Fair enough. Man's got to have his secrets. You've more than a few, from the look of things. I'd be willing to bet this month's pay you kept a few from Mr. McBride." She narrows her eyes at him like she's trying to answer a question for herself. Then she grins. "Ah. I see." She turns back to me. "When are you leaving?"

"Tomorrow morning."

She pushes her chair back and stands stiffly, rubbing one hand down her thigh. "I'd make it the crack of dawn if I were you. Secret like that isn't going to stay secret for long."

How she's figured out what Johnny is, I couldn't say. But she knows, and I'm sure of that. I always suspected Jo Farstep had a bit of her own magic, and I'd wager my shadesilver knives that it has to do with her decorated history as a sharpshooter. It's probably the Sight. Sometimes the tall tales that folks tell have more than a grain of truth to them.

I reach out my hand to her, and she shakes it, the callouses on our palms the silent bond of our profession. She leans in.

"Goodspeed to you, friend."

"You're welcome to travel along with us," I say. I wouldn't mind Jo's company and the company of the six-guns strapped to her waist. "You'd be welcome in Grand Junction."

"Just signed on to help move a herd of cattle to Barnesville and then one more back here to Silver City. Got a hankering to work with beasts instead of hunting men for a spell. Our paths will cross again, and when they do I won't be opposed to riding with you."

I grip her hand tighter. "Much obliged to you, Jo."

She points one finger at Johnny. "Take care of yourself, young man. Stay clear of thieves." With a scraping sound, her chair slides back under the table, and she leaves without another word. I push my own chair in and wave at Johnny to follow me. There's an empty room next to mine, and I show Johnny to it. Tabitha won't mind. I tell him to get some shuteye, and then pull the door closed and retire to my own quarters. A stale smell hovers in the air, so the first thing I do is open the window to let in some of the cool night air.

The bed creaks a bit when I sit down, and I toss my hat onto the chair. My neckerchief is stiff with sweat, so I toss it to the floor. I try to wash my face a bit in the washbasin and turn the water a light brown color as the dust and dirt from the day's ride drips into the bowl. I unbutton my shirt and gently remove the bandages from the Shade wounds. They're starting to heal, finally. I close my eyes as the outside air hits my skin. My gunbelt hangs around the footpost of the bed, and I wonder, not for the first time, what my life would've looked like if I had gotten on that steam ship to Maneira all those years ago. If I'd never gone south at all. If I'd been like Mama and married a man with a stern look and a rare smile like Pops.

After thinking about it a bit, I figure that Pops was right after all. It's a fancy thing to imagine yourself in a place different than you are. I'm right here in this room, sitting on a bed with a few broken springs, hanging up a pair of guns and shadesilver knives. I touch the magic tether to Rip, and it hums softly down to the stable behind me. I pull the little silver cross away from my chest and run my thumb over the smooth metal. It prickles against my skin, pulling a tiny bit of necromancy to the surface with a pulse.

The desk in the corner still has some paper in the drawer, so I light a candle and pull a sheet out. A few dips of a pen into the little black inkwell, and I'm writing the familiar words on yet another letter to the man I left behind in Paradise.

Reverend Ambrose,

I hope you are well. I'm leaving Silver City to head down Grand Junction way. I'll be with Addy there for a while. I've got a boy traveling with me. A job from Mr. McBride to clear out some bandits went south, and some boys got killed. I hope your Almighty forgives me for that, and for the rest. I'm taking the boy to Addy so she can make something of him. He's too good a kid for Hector McBride. His name is Johnny. He's a necromancer, and I aim to see he gets to make his own choices as to what that means. You're more for praying than I am, so if you could put in a good word for him, I think that would be kind of you.

Yours truly,

Hunter

P.S. Those shadesilver knives you made for me are mighty fine.

CHAPTER SIXTEEN

A WELL-BROKE HORSE

When Mr. Hiram Gentle tries to sell me the sorrel gelding for twenty-five bills, I throw my hands in the air and head for the gate. He leaves the beast standing quietly in the middle of the pen and hurries after me, his short legs shuffling to keep up as his rounded middle strains at the waistcoat he buttoned lopsided when I woke him at a quarter past five o'clock.

"Now see here, ma'am, you asked me for a well-broke horse and that gelding is a fine animal for any new rider. Twenty, then. We'll say twenty. It's less than I would ask from anyone else."

"I paid twenty-five for my roan mare when she was four. That sorrel is well over twenty years old, and he sure as the flux ain't as fine a beast as she is."

"He's got good hooves, not a lick of lameness in him. Teeth are good, no sores on his legs or back. And I'll even throw in the saddle and bridle over on the fence."

I lean against the fence next to the hulking dark form of Rip and make him sweat a little bit while I think it over. Hiram glances at the corpse several times, nervously wringing his hands. Johnny stands on the other side of the gate, and he watches the horse with some curiosity. Hiram is a good judge of horseflesh, and I won't find better animals anywhere else in town. But twenty bills would take up everything Johnny has left from Mr. McBride and then some.

"Eighteen. That's my final offer."

Hiram takes off his bowler hat and scratches at the black curls that ring the bald spot on top of his head. For a minute or two I think maybe I pushed him too far, but then he slaps the bowler back on his head and extends his hand. "That's highway robbery, Hunter. Eighteen it is then."

I smile and hand him a wad of paper bills. "Pleasure doing business with you again, Hiram. Go get your horse, boy."

Johnny climbs over the gate as awkwardly as he does everything else. He walks toward the sorrel gelding and holds out his hand, fingers rigid. The horse looks half asleep, but his ears perk up a little and he snuffs at the boy's palm with his whiskery upper lip. Johnny brought him a little bit of grass from outside the corral.

I figure now is as good a time as any to teach Johnny how to saddle and bridle the gelding. I make him carry the big hunk of leather over to the sorrel and throw it onto the horse's wide back. He misses the first time and only gets it about halfway up the gelding's side. I wait for him to try again while his cheeks flush red. The second try works, but the saddle horn is right smack in the center of the horse's back.

"Loop the back stirrup over the horn and get that saddle above his withers, here," I say, pointing. "Then slide it back a little so it's not dragging his hide the wrong way."

Johnny bites his lip in concentration and this time he gets the saddle in the right place. The gelding stands so still he might as well be a statue except for the occasional whisk of his tail. After a bit of confusion about all the straps, Johnny also manages to get the bridle over the gelding's ears. He hesitates a little when I show him how to stick his thumb in the side of the sorrel's mouth to get him to open for the bit, but soon discovers the smooth space in the gums between thick teeth.

"Alright, get up there."

He sticks his booted foot in the stirrup and swings up over the saddle. He's real proud of himself for a minute before realizing that he left the long leather reins hanging on the ground below the gelding's face. I hide my smile and pick them up for him.

"Don't do that again. If that had been the roan mare, you'd be halfway to St. Albane by now or lying in a thicket somewhere."

His knuckles turn white as he grips the reins. "Does he have a name?"

"Pardon?"

"The horse."

"You can call him whatever you want. He's your horse."

"General."

I look at the sleepy sorrel gelding standing with one hind hoof cocked. "Bit fancy for a horse like this." Whatever else I was going to say about it disappears back behind my teeth when Johnny's face falls. Little feather-bellied sap. "But I suppose it's a good enough name. Let's go."

His expression stays a little downcast as I tie the second bedroll behind his saddle and move some of our supplies into the saddlebags. I've made a blunder, somehow, but I'm not sure how to fix it. So I leave it alone and pull the roan mare's reins from the hitching rail to mount. She circles her nose around and nips at me, but she only gets the tip of my boot. I mutter something about the spawn of the Dark After and touch my heels to her sides, pulling on the tether for Rip to follow. Johnny rides a few paces behind me with his new General. The sorrel seems to have perked up a bit now that we're leaving the corral, and he has a smooth, easy trot. Still, Johnny might be a little bowlegged when we stop for the night after his first full day in a saddle.

The sun is starting to flood the valley with some golden glow as we reach the edge of town and ride past McBride's house. I won't lie, I'll breathe easier once we're out of sight of it. My letter will be on its way to the reverend with the morning coach in less than an hour. I left three months of pay with Tabitha for my room, and she just pursed her lips together and reminded me that she would not keep it a day longer.

I slow the mare down to a walk, keeping a strong hand on her reins. She tosses her head and gets mad at me but finally matches the sorrel's pace. I tell Johnny to keep his hands lower when I notice them bobbing wildly up and down in front of his chest. Heels down, look between the ears. After a few miles, he starts to look like he knows what he's doing.

"How far is Grand Junction?" he asks.

"Four days ride. A bit longer since you're not riding as fast."

He stews on that for a bit. "Is it bigger than Silver City?"

"About twice the size."

"Twice? But it's in the middle of the Territories."

I take a guess. "You from Lamarnais?"

He immediately goes quiet and loosens his fingers on the reins, eyes on the saddle horn in front of him. I nod and push him a bit further.

"Big city, family with some money. Never been further into the Territories. Lamarnais has old blood in it, even some Ferenese nobility from back in the Settlement era. Lot of manners in Lamarnais, good and proper. Maybe too proper for a necromancer like you."

"I'm not going back there, so why does it matter?"

"Just like to know the folks I ride with, is all."

"You said the people we're going to see can teach me how to control it?" he asks, ignoring my questions.

The first thing this kid needs is a bath and a haircut and someone who can keep him out of the way of men like Hector McBride until he's old enough to look after himself. Addy is the best person I know for the job. I'll leave money with her, enough to cover his expenses for a while. And I'll need to send a letter to Miles. The thought makes me wince a little like I got something sour on my tongue. There's nobody better to teach Johnny how to be a necromancer than Miles Lightfellow. Nobody better to teach him how to be a scud-bottom vagrant either. When I left Miles, he was drunk in a whorehouse in Gallington. I didn't leave him on good terms. In fact, the terms were bad, and he may have been pointing the barrels of his famous Weeping Angels in my direction. I don't want to talk about Miles. The kid might turn his horse right around and go back to Silver City. But I can tell him about Addy.

"We're going to see a friend of mine. Her name is Adelaide Sterling, and she owns a hotel in Grand Junction. She's got magic. Not our kind, but she knows enough about it that I think she can be helpful. Besides, she'll do something about that scrub brush on top of your head."

"She's not a necromancer?"

"Addy has a Charm. A rare good one too. Best businesswoman in the Northern Territories. No one leaves her tables with a full wallet."

Johnny frowns at this. "She swindles people out of money?"

I imagine the look on Addy's face at being called a swindler. "I wouldn't say that too loudly where she can hear you. Folks come from a long way to stay at the Blue Moon Hotel. It's the best night's sleep most of them have had in their lives. She makes people feel comfortable, takes the edge off their worries for a bit."

I never got used to sleeping in Miss Addy's featherbeds. When a bed is too soft it starts to feel like you're sleeping on nothing but a wisp of cloud, and that's mighty unsettling. If my guess about Johnny is right, he'll feel at home in a fancier room. But tonight, he'll be sleeping in his bedroll on the ground with roots and rocks digging into his back.

We make decent time despite the kid's green riding. There's a good spot to settle in for the night on the ridge of a shallow canyon. The road will lead us closer to the river tomorrow, and I can already hear the water tumbling along in the distance. A copse of scrub trees gives us some shelter, and I dismount and pull my saddle from the roan mare's back. She had a good day's ride, so she's blessedly calm and doesn't even try to pinch my skin in her teeth. I set the saddle down inside the copse of trees before I notice that Johnny is still sitting on his sorrel.

"You can get down now, we'll stop here for tonight."

He looks a mite embarrassed as he shifts in the saddle. "I don't know if I can."

"Won't know until you try."

His face flushes bright red, and he stubbornly grits his teeth and leans over the saddle horn to slide off General's broad back. Once his boots hit the ground, he takes a step or two like a stiff old man, then realizes he's within a few feet of Rip. He flinches away and shuffles back toward his horse.

"He won't bite," I say. "Pull the saddle down and rub the sweat off General's girth with the cloth in your saddlebag. If we take care of them, they'll take care of us. That's one of the first rules about horses."

I leave out the fact that the roan mare is an exception to the rule. The kid seems to have run out of words, and he fumbles with the cinch strap on his saddle. He pulls on the strap, leveraging it over his shoulder, and the buckle frees. Then he scrubs at the dark sweat line down the gelding's side with the thick cloth. The sorrel lets out a patient sigh and flicks his tail from side to side. The roan mare doesn't seem to mind him, but she flicks her ears back when Johnny ties the gelding next to her on the brush. He drags his saddle over a little way off from mine and copies the way I sit with my back against the sturdy hunk of leather. I pull Rip toward me and make sure he walks as close to the kid as I can get him.

Johnny scrambles back when the giant corpse's tattered boots whisper a few feet from him and his eyes go round as saucer plates again. Rip awkwardly crumples down to the ground next to me, and the look of disgust and fear on the boy's face as he watches us is the same look I've seen hundreds of times. Means nothing to me now.

I set some pieces of the dried brush on a bare scrap of dirt and get a fire started. The flames crackle, small at first. The warmth feels good. Autumn weather isn't as bad here as it is in Paradise yet, but the cold is enough to take the feeling out of your hands after a full day of riding in it. The kid manages to get down some of the pork and beans I cook over the fire and then nods off with his chin drooping against his chest.

Fool kid. His bedroll is still tied to the back of his saddle. I untie the laces and drape the thick cloth over him so he doesn't freeze during the night. Nine days in the wild sure hasn't taught him enough to survive yet. I settle in, resting my head against the seat of my saddle and my boots crossed nearest to the fire to keep my toes warm. It's peaceful out here on the prairie, the stars glittering above me like the diamonds at a rich lady's throat. I take a deep breath. I always sleep better out here, far away from the gaze of other folk. Nature is a simple place with simple rules. If you're smart and know your way about things, you live. Some people find the vastness of the world a heavy weight, but looking up into that black ceiling of stars, I feel comfort knowing the world is far bigger than the two of us lying by a small fire in the midst of a grassy ocean.

I shift down a little, get comfortable. As I begin to drift off, my hand resting on the butt of one of my revolvers in the holster lying on my stomach, the magic between Rip and I ripples and hums. When I sleep, the nightmares come.

CHAPTER SEVENTEEN

HOLY ORDER

"You won't pull that trigger, girl. You're not a murderer," he says, dark eyes glittering like obsidian under his sweaty hair. He curls his lip and the silver tooth glints. His hand inches toward the pickaxe lying on the wooden crate, and I know that he will kill me if I don't kill him first.

I pull the stock of my Pops' old shotgun against my shoulder and fire.

I'm drenched in my own sweat when I wake out of that dream, and struggle to get my breathing back to a normal pace. It's hard to get air into my lungs, they feel like a giant's foot is pressing them flat into my spine. It's still dark, and the horses whicker and snort softly at me, still sleepy. A quick slap to my face brings me out of it some. I won't look at Rip. The sounds of the night keep me company for the last hour before dawn.

The boy tosses and turns in his sleep. By the time first light is creeping over the prairie and turning everything a deep gold color, he's curled up like a baby mouse under his blanket. Even when I rise and start cooking a tin of beans, he doesn't wake. I eat half the tin and kick at his boots to wake him. He startles, sitting up with his hair an awful mess. But when I hand him the beans, he eats like he hasn't seen food in days. Growing boys sure can put food away.

It isn't even full morning yet when we mount and ride off, the last faint tendrils of smoke drifting up from the pile of dirt I kicked over the fire. Mounting his sorrel gelding proves to be even more of a challenge for Johnny after a night of sleep. The stiffness in his legs will have settled in good and proper now. He doesn't complain, but by the time we reach Grand Junction, he'll be sore in places he'll wish he wasn't.

The Hogshead River appears just before noon, a great black snake carving a canyon through the reddish dirt. The water tumbles along in a rush, little caps of white popping up here and there in the waves as they run south. A fast current, today. A few miles ahead the river widens out and slows to a steadier pace.

I'm not one for a bunch of talking, and Johnny doesn't seem to have anything to say either. The sound of the river is the only thing that breaks the silence. The horses pick their way easily through the soft dirt and knee-high grass. Every now and then I hear the clop of a hoof striking smooth rock. The quiet of the wild is something I love. There's enough space to hear your own thoughts and the only eyes on you are the occasional ranging coyote or a brown jackrabbit frozen against the brush. Most of the time, I like to be alone with my thoughts. But I feel uneasy and restless today, like there's a raging current of fire prickling under the skin of my arms. The tethers between Rip and I feel strained, which I try to ignore as he shuffles along behind the horses. The tattered remains of his shirt swing around him, and my eyes are drawn again to the black hole shredded through his chest.

An echo of my finger squeezing around the shotgun trigger courses through my hand, and I try to swallow through a dry throat. Rip's eyes flicker toward me.

I want to run, to drive my heels into the mare's sides until she's flying far away from the evil, soulless thing behind me. The soul fragment I splintered out of myself to animate him pulses out in a broken, maddening rhythm. Something is wrong. I pull up the mare, and she wrestles with the bit. The saddle horn feels comforting under my palm as I grip it to stay in my seat. My head swims.

"Hunter?"

The boy.

I blink fast, hoping to clear my senses. The swig of water from my canteen isn't cold, but it brings me back enough to notice the boy's face all scrunched up with worry. He's pulled General to a stop just ahead, his fool hands holding the reins to his chest again.

"Drop your hands."

He does, a bit confused. "Are you alright?"

I clip the canteen back onto my belt and ignore the way my voice sounds a bit choppy when I finally answer him. "We'll reach the river soon, let the horses have a drink and refill our canteens."

He doesn't much like my answer, I can see. But I spur on the roan mare and send her into a brisk trot toward the river, pulling Rip into his disjointed run as he follows. The magic between us calms. Johnny bounces uncomfortably on General's back despite the gelding's smooth pace. By the time we reach Grand Junction, he'll have a better seat. There's a wide slope down to the river's edge that cuts through the sharper angled walls of the gully it carves through the land.

A small collection of wagons is circled a few hundred yards from the water, each pulled by a team of yoked mules. The big animals twitch their overlong ears at us as we approach, and one lets out a deafening bray. I've never understood how the creatures can bellow and squeak all at the same time. The wagons are sturdy, and by the looks of them, they've traveled a fair distance already. A man tends to the leading team, carrying a darkly polished walking staff.

Merenessans.

It's too late to leave Rip behind, they'll have already seen us approaching. Their Holy Order would label me just as soulless as the folks in Paradise, but for different reasons. The founder of their faith, Saint Merenessa, taught that magic in any form taints the purity of the world. Anyone born in their order with a magical talent is labeled an outcast and forced to leave the sanctuary of their isolated people. They will do us no harm, but I doubt they'll be thrilled to see me.

A woman climbs down from the wagon behind the man, carefully keeping her simple shift dress clear of the dirty wheels. She shades her eyes as we approach, and she whispers something to the man. There are at least five men and women between the wagons and the river, gathering water and washing clothing.

"Good day to you!" calls the man. I ride close enough to get a good look at him, and he offers us both a smile that is amiable enough to be considered friendly. His hair is slicked back against his head and immaculately combed, and his mustache and beard are cut close to his face. Everything about the Merenessans is clean, and it seems strangely out of place in this dirty wilderness. The woman's smile is less friendly, and she eyes the guns at my belt.

"Afternoon." I try to sound pleasant, which usually means raising the tone of my voice a bit and softening out some of the gravel. "My name is Hunter, and this is Johnny."

"I am Tulo, and this is my wife Betta. We welcome you to our wagons."

The welcome isn't purely out of the goodness of his heart. It's an obligation to their saint. Merenessans follow so many rules that it makes my head spin. One of the few I know is that they must welcome any stranger to their home, but not inside it unless you're one of their own. A Merenessan house is only open to those who share their faith.

Two small girls run through the wagons and behind Betta, each clutching a small ragdoll in their hands and giggling as they clamber up the steep bank beside the river to look out over the water. Betta turns to watch them with the eagle eyes of a mother.

"Where are you folks headed? Looks like you're loaded up for a long journey," I say, motioning to the packed wagons.

"We are going to New Prania to join the Holy Order there."

"New Prania?" I want to ask him if he's barking mad. "That's a dangerous road to travel even if you're armed and familiar with the land. But with wagons and children?"

He smiles at me as if I'm simple. "Our Lady Merenessa's will is that we travel to New Prania, and that is where we travel. We cannot come to harm if the souls of these penitents are pure. It is difficult for outsiders to understand."

The two girls are still playing at the river's edge, and their mother eyes me like a cat would a dog. "We won't trouble you much longer," I say. "Just stopping to water the horses before we move on."

I slide off the mare's back, and Johnny follows suit. I notice he's not quite as slow getting out of the saddle this time. I tip my hat to Betta as I walk by her and lead the mare down the soft slope to the river. The water still rushes, but the little pool near the shore where we stand ripples around the rocks visible in the shallows. The roan mare and General drink big thirsty gulps, their ears twitching to the side with each swallow. Cold water feels like a bit of heaven after the dryness of the morning.

Soft giggling reaches my ears, and I look up to our left along the riverbank, where four bright eyes peer at us from the edge of the gully. The two girls have crawled out on a gnarled tree leaning over the river, and their skinny legs dangle in the air as they watch us. They point at us, whispering in the secret language of curious children.

Betta calls out to them to come back to the wagons, and just as the first girl turns herself around on her perch, the long trunk cracks and falls toward the water. A terrified scream fills my ears, and my legs move before my mind catches on. Strong currents move the water swiftly through this part of the channel. The riverbed carves deep and would close over my head within a few paces of the banked walls.

I'm the closest. Duster and hat drop to the dirt as I run up the bank, unbuckling my gunbelt and tossing it onto the gully's edge. One of the girls is only a little way into the river, hanging on to a short log pinned between two rocks. The water rushes over her head, turning her screams into choked, horrible sounds. Someone jumps into the water behind me, and Johnny's black hair disappears briefly as he swims toward the trapped child.

The other girl has vanished. I keep running and catch a glimpse of flailing hands and a gasping, white face. She's being carried downstream by the rushing current. It's at least two or three miles before the river widens and slows. She won't last that long. There's a point where the gully extends over the rushing water below just enough to give me a better leap.

The Merenessans shout behind me, and the chilling screech of a terrified mother pierces straight through my chest as I throw myself off the ledge into the river.

CHAPTER EIGHTEEN

A MERENESSAN'S DEBT

I've always been afraid of dying. As a necromancer, I breath death in like smoke every day as it chips my soul away, pulling me closer and closer to a hole in the ground with a little wooden marker stuck over it. I told Reverend Ambrose once that I wasn't scared of death at all, honest. He didn't believe me, but he nodded and put his hand on my shoulder the way he always does. Dreams of death chase me every night. Some are memories, like Rip's death, or the vague recollection of my mama coughing up her throat and lungs with the bloody flux. Pops wouldn't let me in with her at the very end.

But when the memories don't plague me, I dream death in every form. A mark catching me off guard, sending a bullet through my chest the way I did Rip. Trapped in a house on fire. Falling from a high cliff and watching the ground rush to meet me. And drowning. I dream of drowning.

The river water closes over my head and tries to claw its way into my nose and mouth. I scramble to the surface as I'm dragged along in the current. The girl isn't that far ahead, I can reach her. She's still fighting the water, her mouth open in a round O to suck in precious air. I learned to swim in the creek behind our cabin almost as soon as I could walk, and my shoulders remember the strong strokes that Pops taught me, pulling me through the water even faster than the current. Up ahead, there's a good tumble of branches and tree trunks caught against big rocks jutting up from the riverbed. The girl is headed straight for them. I push myself harder, barely lifting my head for a breath until my hand lands on something soft.

I wrap my body around the girl, pulling her to my chest and trying to hold her head out of the water. She coughs and sputters in my face, the screams shocked right out of her as she clings to my sodden shirt. If I can't get us to the riverbank with that mess of trees and rocks, I don't know when the next chance will come. No chance better than the one in front of your face, Pops always said.

Holding the girl and with her pushing and clinging to me, my head stays under the water more often than it comes up for air. I kick as hard as I can toward the left side of the riverbank, ready to snag a good solid grip on one of those branches. The rocks loom large, and even though they are worn smooth by the rushing water, we're moving too fast. If we hit one of those, we'll be hurting. A small hand hits my face and water pours past my clenched teeth. I grab blindly for something, anything to pull us nearer the bank. Something sharp catches against my leg down in the water and slows us down just enough that I can grasp a branch nearby. I pull with all my might, turning so that my body is between the large rock rushing toward us and the fragile girl in my arms.

I feel the crack in my ribs as we hit. My back crushes against the boulder as the water pins us there, swirling around my head and the girl's shoulders. The branch is a lifeline, and I grip it with all my strength. I'm not about to die in this river. I pull myself further out of the water and get the first breath of real air since I jumped from that ledge. The breath burns and I stop short as splintering pain stabs through me. The girl scrambles to the top of the boulder, a good foot away from the current. Her golden hair is plastered to her face, and her cheeks are whiter than an ancient ghost, but she's alive. Voices reach us from the riverbank, and the three Merenessan men clamber into the branches and rocks to reach us.

The rushing river still pins me against the boulder. If I let go of the branch, I'll be pulled under, and it'll be the last day of my life. The girl crawls across the rickety bridge of branches until she reaches her father, who snatches her from the river and hands her up the human ladder to safety. Then he turns to me and holds out his walking staff. It's not close enough.

I pull on a different lifeline. Rip appears over the edge. I stopped dragging him alongside us on the riverbank when we hit the rock. The big corpse steps past the gully and slides down toward the water. The Merenessans withdraw from him in horror as he clambers over the rocks and tree trunks. I pull him until he's kneeling on the rock nearest to me, an arm's length away. He sits there, waiting. Gripping the branch is becoming a nearly impossible task. I have one shot. Responding to me, Rip's thick arm reaches out over the water until I can see the broken fingernails on his huge hands. I push off with my legs and reach out. His hand closes around my arm and hauls me free of the water with a compulsive jerk.

Pain nearly blinds me as the mostly healed wounds in my neck and shoulder and my cracked ribs are pulled nearly to a breaking point when Rip lifts me clear. The pressure from the current is gone, and I fight the need to gasp for air with the agony ripping through my chest. The ringing in my ears renders me nearly deaf as I climb toward redemption at the water's edge. Living hands close around my arms and pull me upward until I am standing on solid ground. I understand now why some folks kiss the earth after a long ride on one of those steam ships.

The Merenessan man holding me upright is forced to let go as I lose control of my legs and sink to the grass. Rip claws his way up the embankment behind the men and stands motionless a few feet away, staring into the distance. Someone speaks to me, but the words bounce away from my ears. All I can hear is the rushing water. I clasp one arm protectively around myself and force my breath to be shallow, looking for the little girl.

She's safe in Tulo's arms, and he is crying and kissing her cheeks as she wraps her arms around his neck as if she'll never let him go again. She's crying too. Good, I think. Good to let it all out now. I cough up some water.

"The other girl…?" I croak.

"The young man got her out," the man next to me says. "They're both alive, praise the good Mother Merenessa!"

I don't say a word of thanks to his saint, but I do manage a begrudging nod of gratitude in the Almighty's general direction. I guess he saw fit to leave me here another day. I still can't manage to stand on my own two feet, so the man helps me along on the walk back to the wagons. It's too far, and I just want to sit down and go to sleep so I can forget the pain and the exhaustion settling into my bones. But I make my brain go somewhere else and take one step, and then another. I go back to a good memory, the way the reverend and I always did when I ran into his forge after the kids of Paradise had their fun.

Mama always loved flowers. Our cabin wasn't much to look at, but Mama saw to it that Pops made her some little wooden boxes to hang under our glass windows so she could plant some wild purple daisies and creeping holly. Brighten up the place a bit. She loved ferns too, feathery green ones that grew in the forest. I remember the time she brought some back and she was going to plant them along the path to our front door. Pops had never heard of such a thing, and he argued about it. Didn't see the point in clearing out the forest just to bring it right back in, he said. But in the end, Mama set her lips in a stern line, and those ferns got planted.

"A little bit of the forest by our cabin is beautiful too," she told me as we pushed dirt around the fragile stems of the plants, my chubby hands settled on top of her soft big ones. "People in the big city, they don't ever get to have this little bit of forest by their houses."

And she was right. When I saw a big city for the first time, there wasn't a single green thing. Everything was brown and gray and black, like all the green had been chased out. I didn't much like that, and for all the years I spent in those cities, I never stopped missing the forest.

The roan mare had spooked as soon as I let go of her reins to run after the girl in the river. Betta says she took off back north. General, like the well-broke gelding he is, stayed put. Johnny is sitting next to a woman starting a fire, wrapped in a thick blanket from one of the wagons. Water drips over his face and neck, and he stands up in a hurry as soon as he sees me.

"Hunter!" he says. "You alright?"

"Sure. Just went for a little swim," I say. A cough has me doubled over in a hurry, pressing my hand tightly against my side. It's so tender that even the wet waistcoat over my shirt feels too tight. I barely sit down before a blanket is thrown over my shoulders, and Betta is grasping for my hand.

"Thank you, thank you, thank you," she sobs, pressing her face against my palm. For a minute, her distrust of an outsider falls away, and her overwhelming relief is the only thing between us. "I owe you a great debt."

My skin prickles at the closeness of another human being, and I pull my hand away. "Ma'am, I'd be a poor excuse for a living being if I stood by and let a little girl drown in a river. You don't owe me anything. But I'd greatly appreciate a cup of tea to warm my insides, if it isn't too much trouble."

And so Betta makes me a cup of tea, warm and smelling of earthy herbs brewed over the campfire. I sip slowly, my teeth still chattering from the chill. Then she brings me a small pile of clean, folded clothing.

"I found an extra waistcoat, shirt, and trousers for you," she says. "Please take them, you'll catch your death of chill in those wet clothes."

I hide my surprise, but only just. Merenessan women never dress in trousers or shirts like their men do. But I suspect she knew I'd refuse one of their simple white shift dresses. I couldn't ride anywhere in one of those. She hesitates.

"Do you… can I help you out of your things?" she offers. Her eyes flicker to my partially open shirt front and the red Shade marks laced across my collarbone.

I shake my head. "No, thank you. I'll do just fine on my own."

Standing as straight as I can manage until I'm out of sight, I round the corner of the furthest wagon and then sag against the wood planks to catch my breath. Rip stands at the edge of the circled wagons where I left him. He stares at nothing, and the magic is blessedly numb. I've exerted myself, and it, further than I have since that day on the north side of the Bard's Thumb.

I unbutton my waistcoat with trembling fingers and drop it to the ground. The shirt is much harder. Lifting my arms out of the sleeves nearly sends me into a black oblivion, but I manage to strip down to my skivvies and the bands wrapped around my breasts. If I tighten those a bit and add another strip of the cloth around my ribcage, that'll bind up the cracked ribs good enough to make it to Addy's. A dull pain throbs through my left leg, and when I pull down my trousers I'm greeted by a deep gash curving along the meat of my calf. Whatever caught my leg in the current was plenty sharp. It's not to the bone, but it's an ugly wound. I'll need more than a bandage for that.

The clean, dry clothes make me feel like a whole new human. I leave the waistcoat unbuttoned and walk back to the fire, wringing the water out of my hair weakly. Johnny wears new clothes as well, and his wet things are hung on sticks near the fire to dry. Betta bustles over to take my sodden pile of clothing. I pull off my boots and leave them tipped open end toward the crackling flames. They'll dry out by morning. My socks smell like a dead dog, and I wrinkle my nose as I carefully peel them off my feet. Leave your feet in wet socks and boots for too long and they'll get to rotting.

I ask Betta for some clean bandages and a poultice for my leg. At first, she insists that she can do the doctoring herself, but I manage to convince her that it's not that bad. From the bloodstain already seeping through the side of the trouser leg, I can tell she doesn't believe a word of it. Tulo approaches me and pulls his hat from his bald head.

"I cannot offer you any worldly possession that will pay for the lives of my daughters. But I can offer you shelter and rest for the night, if you will stay with us. I sent my brother on one of the mules to look for your horse. He is a good tracker; he will find her by morning."

There's still plenty of daylight, but we won't get far with me in the state I'm in and Johnny sniffling under his blanket by the fire. If the roan mare is halfway back to Silver City, Johnny and I are too much weight for General to carry all the way to Grand Junction by himself. So I agree.

The two women cook river trout that night, and the crispy, flaky fish is some of the best I've ever eaten. I suppose not dying makes anything taste better, but Betta and her sister-in-law are fine cooks. They don't use as much spice as Tabitha would, but Merenessans are known for a blander palate. I don't mind, and from the looks of things, neither does Johnny.

When night falls, Tulo and his brother pull small corn shuck mattresses out of the wagons and make Johnny and I beds outside near the fire. Betta even brings out a genuine feather pillow for me to lay on. They won't let us inside their wagons, but they bring the comforts of their travel outside. I try to refuse the feather pillow, but Betta will not hear of it.

As soon as the Merenessans disappear into their wagons for the night, I sit with my back turned to Johnny and begin seeing to my leg. I roll up the trousers and wash out the wound with a little water from my canteen. Merenessans don't touch liquor, so there's no chance of me cleaning it out with anything stronger. I have Johnny get my little doctoring kit from the saddlebags. He tries to look over my shoulder, but I wave him away. I've stitched more than a few wounds with horsehair and needles, and this one closes up decent. I nearly bite a hole through my lip and sweat runs down the back of my neck into my shirt by the time I finish. The poultice starts to numb the area immediately, pulled tight against the angry skin with fresh bandages.

Johnny and I lay on our mattresses, staring at the flames. I'm so exhausted that I couldn't move an inch if I wanted to. But my mind still whirls with the sound of the river's current behind us. Johnny has his blanket tucked up under his chin, his eyes owlish in the dark. He's chewing on his fingernails.

"Say, kid."

"Yeah?"

"Jumping into the river after that little girl like you did… that was real brave of you. Maybe you're not always a feather-bellied sap."

He pulls a bit of hangnail from his thumb and looks at me in that unsure way he has. "You think I'm a feather-bellied sap?"

"I did find you hiding under a pine tree like a scared rabbit."

"Oh."

A bit of silence then, but it's warm with the fire's soft snapping. I feel my eyelids getting heavier, the throbbing pain in my body giving way to the need for sleep. Just before I nod off, I hear Johnny one last time.

"Hunter?"

"Mmmm."

"What's a feather-bellied sap?"

I fall asleep before I can tell him.

CHAPTER NINETEEN

OLD WOUNDS

Tulo's younger brother proves to be more than a decent tracker. The little camp is awake and bustling, preparing a bit of breakfast when he trots in on his seal brown mule, leading the roan mare behind him. She broke one of her leather reins, but the saddle and my saddlebags are in good condition, which surprises me. I ought to sell that horse and have done with her. She's got a few brambles stuck in her mane and tail and holds her head low like she knows good and well that she's in a heap of trouble.

I can barely sit straight to eat breakfast, taking shallow breaths against the pain in my ribs. Betta cooks some potatoes in a cast iron pan over the fire, and they're good. But even chewing and swallowing down potatoes must be done carefully and without much moving around. We're still a good two and a half to three days out from Grand Junction, and I don't relish the thought of bouncing around in that saddle. Tulo and Betta say nothing about moving on upriver, but they look ready to leave. Johnny seems a bit better this morning, though he's still sniffling. Betta lets him keep the blanket. I retrieve extra wraps from the saddlebags and tie them around my ribcage as tightly as I can manage. Bruises the size of a dinner plate have bloomed across my ribs on the left side. I can already imagine Addy clucking over me like a mother hen when we arrive in Grand Junction.

My boots are dry, at least. Small blessings. My socks are stiffer than a corpse in a coffin, but I manage to wrangle them over my feet. Tulo fixes the roan mare's rein with a length of rope, feeds his mules and then walks over to me, his face all scrunched with thinking.

"Betta does not think you should travel today. Take a day of rest with us. Our journey is not so urgent that we cannot stay one more night."

I'm not much good at laying around and being lazy, and I think a whole day of setting on my dusty behind waiting for the sun to set would be one whole day too much.

"I appreciate it. But we best be getting on."

"I expected so. Betta put extra rations in your saddlebags, and some fresh bandages." He twists his felt hat around in his hands. "If you ever come to New Prania, you will find friendly faces there."

It's as much as he can offer a Soulless like me, but I figure he means well. "Stick to the road at the foot of the West Cathedrals," I tell him. "The forest road is a faster journey, but more bad folk hassling travelers. You ever been that far north?"

"No."

"Then you make sure you stock up on heavy wool hats and socks when you get to Silver City. Go see Ms. Halloway and tell her Hunter sent you. She'll see to it you have what you need," I tell him, and then lower my voice. "Do you carry any shadesilver?"

He looks mighty offended at the idea. "It is forbidden."

"Forbidden by somebody who never saw a Shade, I reckon. If

you stay at the foot of the mountains, you'll be safer. Don't forage any further up than that." I manage to get on my feet, and give him a long, hard look. "Shades will claw the heart out of your chest while you're still breathing, and the cold will kill you in minutes just for spite. If you're leaving the south, you best start thinking about how you're going to protect your family."

Shades are just rumors where he's from, nothing but smoke and vapors. I've seen it before, the confidence in saints or guns or plain old stubborn determination. The north doesn't care much about your confidence. So when Tulo tells me that Mereressa will lead them to safety, I don't argue. Reverend Ambrose once told me that the Almighty protects us even when we're stupid. But that doesn't mean we can't die if we try hard enough.

I shake Tulo's hand and tip my hat to Betta. Johnny holds the roan mare's reins while I climb the impossible height to the hunk of leather that will cradle my aches and pains the rest of the way to Grand Junction. The mare is quiet. Maybe her little run for freedom yesterday tuckered her out.

We ride away from the circle of wagons. Tulo and Betta and their little girls and the rest of their family are the kind of people that appear in my life for a moment and then vanish faster than a cool wind in summer. But if this one day of knowing them meant that their little girls got to live a longer life, I guess that's worth it.

The white canvas wagon tops are still visible for a long time after we start riding south, until finally they are swallowed up by the land. The river speeds along beside us for a good while before it slows and widens out further. The closest real crossing now is Grand Junction. Our horses might make it across here, but it would be a risky swim. Johnny pulls his coat collar up around his neck, looking miserable. He's shivering a bit in his saddle. Addy will throw a royal fit at the state of us both. At least the wind doesn't bother me, not after the deep chill of the Cathedrals. Feels like a regular heat wave down this far. But the weather isn't my concern. I'm already hunching my shoulders to lessen the stabbing throb that flares in my cracked ribs with every breath. Almost makes a person not want to breathe at all. I gingerly keep my leg held away from the stirrup fenders until my hip aches with the effort. At least the wounds that the Shade left in my neck and shoulder are finally beginning to close and scar over.

We pass some other travelers on the road, but they all give us a wide berth. Johnny seems to shrink into himself a little every time someone sees us. He's so jumpy he's starting to make me jumpy. We'll spend one more night out on the prairie before we reach the town, and then maybe Addy can calm his nerves a bit. He still hasn't told me anything new about himself, and I can understand that. The more someone else knows about you, the more danger you're in. I guess if he wants to keep his story to himself, that's his business.

The roan mare spooks a little at a black snake that weaves its way across the dirt road, and I come out of my thoughts to see the sky getting dark. There's a little grove of trees about two hundred yards away that'll do us just fine for the night, and I head toward it. Johnny steers General off the road after me. I need to change the bandage on that leg and get something in my belly before it eats itself. We've got enough food left in the saddlebags for a decent dinner by traveling standards, but I can't help the way my mouth waters at the thought of what Tabitha might be cooking back in the boarding house.

Johnny dismounts before I do, tying General's rein to one of the tree branches. I grit my teeth a bit before I attempt to swing my leg over the back of my saddle. Getting up this morning was hard enough. I could bring Rip over beside the mare for help, but she's as likely to spook as stand still if he comes any closer. What would Miles say if he could see me now? I shake my head at the imaginary mockery and grip the saddle horn with both hands, whispering to the mare that she'll be deader than a corpse if she moves while I get down.

Landing on my good leg still feels like my whole body was put through a sawmill twice. I hold on to the stirrup for a minute to catch my breath, and blessedly the mare stands still.

"Kid, come over here."

Johnny shuffles over. I don't know what my face looks like, but based on the way his eyes get big, it's not good. I pat the leather.

"I need you to tie up this mare for me and help me pull the cinch buckle. You think you can handle that?"

He nods, solemn as a gravedigger, and leads the mare next to General while I limp after him. He manages to pull the cinch up far enough to release the buckle, and the mare blows out her nose as he drags the saddle off her back. She's got a big rectangle of sweat where the saddle blanket was sitting. Johnny gets the horse rag out of the saddlebag and rubs her down a bit without me asking.

"I think you're getting the hang of horses," I say.

He looks pleased. "You said we have to take care of them, so they'll take care of us."

"I did indeed. Even for persnickety nags like this one." I pat the mare's reddish shoulder, and she pins her ears back just a little. I mutter a curse at her as she side-eyes me. Johnny watches us curiously.

"Why do you keep her if you don't like her?" he asks.

I give the mare another pat on the neck just for spite. "Most people don't much like me either, so we've got that going for us. But probably just because I'm stubborn."

Johnny hauls both saddles to a good spot for the campfire. I settle down on the ground with some difficulty. I've had a cracked rib before, but I was younger then. Rip lumbers over as I tug at him and sit him far enough away not to spook the kid. Johnny still watches him, face lit by the first flames jumping out of the pile of kindling and sticks.

"What's it like?" he finally asks, quiet. "Having your soul… in a corpse, I mean."

I pull a clean roll of cloth from my saddlebags to fix up my leg. "Most of my soul is still right here in my chest. I just splintered off a piece of it to pull him back from the Dark After."

Questions swirl around on his confused face. "Why did you do it?"

"That's a question I've only answered for one person, kid. We've all got bits of our story that we don't much like to share. Let's just say I wasn't ready to let him rest in peace and leave it at that."

The big Animated hunches over, his hands limp at his sides in the dirt. The black hole torn through his chest looks like an unearthly void against the light of the fire, and I see Johnny really looking at him for the first time.

"Did you kill him?"

"Yes, I did."

"How long ago?"

"Seven years."

His gaze shifts back to me quickly. "Have you killed anyone else?"

I frown at him. "You were there when we found that gang of boys. Three of 'em died."

He shakes his head a little. "Yeah, but that man Torrence

killed them. I watched you, and you didn't fire on any of them."

"I don't kill children."

"But others?"

"Yes." I fix him with a hard look. "You want me to be a killer, boy?"

"No, I don't."

He says it so innocently that I don't know what to say back. I shift back against my saddle and turn away from him to roll my trouser leg to the knee. There's a deep brown stain over the cloth on my calf, and when I unwind it, the wound seeps a little. But it doesn't smell rotten, and I don't feel fevered. Small miracles. Bending over to wrap it tightly again is going to put a good strain on my ribs. So I rest for a minute, closing my eyes.

"Can I help you with – "

My eyes fly open to see Johnny standing beside me, staring down at my leg. Adrenaline surges through me, and I barely keep myself from yanking the trouser leg back down. I know the ugliness he sees, and I'm surprised by the shame that creeps up on me. The river's wound cuts through skin already broken up by dozens of finger-width scars covering my legs from just above my knees down to my ankles. Words come out of my mouth before I even know the anger is there.

"You'll get away from me if you know what's good for you," I hear myself snarl at him. "I'll kill you right here and go on to Grand Junction by myself."

He goes pale and retreats to his saddle. I grind my teeth together to keep myself from saying anything else. I don't want him to be here, and I sure as the Dark After don't want to take him to Addy. Every curse I know makes its way through my head as I strangle the cloth in my hand. For a minute, I think I might reach for my gun belt. Across from me, Rip slowly rises from the ground, facing Johnny with dead eyes.

The bellows. Remember the bellows, in and out.

"I'm sorry!" Johnny gasps as Rip takes a step forward. I bite down on my lip and dig my fingernails into my palms. I let myself sink into the pain in my leg, in my palm, in my ribs. Back into the peace.

Rip crumples to the ground like a marionette with cut strings, still staring at Johnny. I quietly wrap my leg and pull the trouser down to cover the bandage. Leaning back, I see the boy gripping his saddle with white knuckles. It's not his fault, and I should tell him so. But I don't, because if I open my mouth, the anger will come out again.

We sit there for a while until I trust my voice. "You've got a quiet step."

He's carefully studying the tips of his boots and says nothing. His wide-eyed curiosity goes away somewhere, and his eyes look as empty as the corpse across the fire. Neither of us say another word.

CHAPTER TWENTY

ADELAIDE STERLING

Addy has a powerful kind of magic, and it has nothing to do with the Charm. She sees into people, sees the truth of things even when they don't want to say it. The first time I wandered into her hotel, she sat me down and got me a glass of cold water when I asked for whiskey. Knowing her better now, I'm surprised she didn't splash it in my face.

As soon as we come within sight of Grand Junction, the weight of the past few months seems to drain away from my shoulders. I know that her Charm doesn't reach that far, but the thought of walking back into the Blue Moon Hotel and handing my current problem over to Addy takes some pressure off my chest.

It's a bustling city, named well as a junction between the major roads along the river. From Grand Junction, you can catch a stagecoach bound for just about anywhere in the Territories. The hotel is on the eastern side of town, a big grand building painted a warm blue color with white trim. Smoke rises from the buildings, signs swing on their hooks in the light breeze, and respectable folk walk and ride through the main street. I pause by the sheriff's office and tip my hat to the deputy setting in the chair under the overhang. He looks between me and the boy, and then over to the Animated behind us.

"Deputy Skinner," I say.

"Well I'll be derned," he answers, pulling on one end of the gray mustache that droops below his chin. "It's the corpse raiser from Paradise."

"I'm staying with Addy for a spell. Let Sheriff Molby know, will you?"

He spits into the dusty street. "See to it you don't cause no trouble while you're here, especially with Miss Sterling being so hospitable to you."

Pretty much the whole town loves Addy. She's only made one mistake in her entire life as far as they're concerned, and it just rode into town. I spur on the roan mare and lead the way toward the big white sign on Addy's railed porch. BLUE MOON HOTEL. Her stableboy, Owen, runs out to meet us so fast I'm surprised he doesn't trip over his own feet. He pulls the cap off his head and waves it in the air.

"Hiya, Hunter!" he calls out. He grabs the reins of the mare as we reach the hitching rail, and I look down at him and pretend to do a bit of thinking.

"You're taller than when I saw you last."

He beams and puffs out his skinny chest. "Yes'm! Miss Addy says I've growed like the weeds in the garden!"

"Still skinny as a bean pole too," I say with a shake of my head. I slide out of the saddle and wince when my feet are reunited with the ground, holding my ribs with a shallow breath. "You take that mare on over to the barn and come right back for the gelding. Rub them both down. Just a half-ration of oats after they cool down a bit."

I flip a copper coin from my pocket into the air, and Owen snatches it with a wink. "You got it, Miss Hunter!"

He hurries away with the mare, his head reaching only to the middle of her shoulder. I squint after him, doing the math in my head. He must be about nine or ten now. Addy took him in after his mama died over at the brothel above one of the saloons. Johnny dismounts from the gelding and looks curiously at the hotel. If he was raised in Lamarnais, I doubt it's the fanciest place he's seen. But he pulls off the floppy hat I gave him and worries it in his hands for something to do. He hasn't spoken a word to me since last night.

"Come on in then."

The heavy wooden doors have etched glass ovals in them, and brass handles. Addy's always been a sucker for shiny things, and the hotel is as lavish as she could make it. Johnny trails behind me as I step inside. Paneled woodwork lines the walls below gold floral wallpaper from St. Albane. Woven Ferenese rugs lead into the lounge to the left and the dining room to the right. A crystal chandelier hangs from the ceiling above my head. Rip is an unfortunate stain on the grandeur, and I make sure he's planted firmly in the center of the room and far away from anything breakable.

A young woman with silver-rimmed spectacles sits behind the front desk, making notes in a ledger. She sees us and purses her lips tightly, drawing her features even closer together than they usually are.

I lift my hat from my head. "Mabel."

"You shouldn't bring that foul thing in with you," she says, pointing a thin finger in Rip's direction. "How long will you be staying with us this time?" Her voice is higher pitched than most and sounds as if someone just gave her a pinch.

"Where's Addy?" I ask.

She doesn't need to answer, because just then I feel warmth flood through my tired limbs and hear a familiar voice behind us.

"Hunter, darling!"

A rustle of satin precedes the sight of Adelaide Sterling hurrying toward us from the dining room. Her midnight black hair is piled atop her head in a chaotic but immovable mass of curls, gold combs tucked on either side. Bright blue satin skirts with black lace trim sweep over the carpets above the gentle taps of her shoes. The beauty mark on her upper lip sits atop a smile that lights up her whole face. She throws her arms around my shoulders and kisses me on each cheek, eyes sparkling with a saucy bit of mischief that only dims a little when she sees Rip hulking in the center of her lobby. To her credit, she doesn't say a word about him.

"Well, aren't you just what the doctor ordered! I was telling Mabel this morning that it's been too long since you came to visit. Though I must admit you do look like something my cats dragged in." Her nose wrinkles. "Smell like it too. I'll have the girls draw you up a bath first thing. And you must be starving! Miss Kay has a delectable pot of dumplings cooking for tonight."

She spins deftly on one foot to face the flustered boy behind me. "In all my days I've never seen you travel with anyone, Hunter. Who might you be, young man? What brings you to Grand Junction?"

Johnny's mouth opens like he's going to answer her, but nothing comes out. He's hardly the first man rendered speechless in front of Addy. It doesn't take her more than a few seconds to shift her tone to something calmer.

"There I go asking a bunch of questions before you've even properly settled in, do pardon me," she says. "My name is Adelaide Sterling, proprietor of the Blue Moon Hotel."

She holds her hand out to Johnny with a dazzling smile, and he takes it in awe. I smirk. I've always told Addy she doesn't need her Charm, she's a force of nature even without it. The kid finally finds his voice.

"I'm Johnny. From Lamarnais."

Her delicate eyebrows arch and she glances at me. "Lamarnais! A beautiful city. I'm just dying to know how you met Hunter, but I'll let you have some time to rest before I pepper you with more conversation. Come on upstairs and we'll get you settled."

Gathering fistfuls of satin, she leads the way up the broad wooden staircase to the third floor. There are exactly twenty-seven rooms in Addy's hotel. Not as many as the larger hotels I've stayed in, but no one keeps a cleaner and more comfortable place than Addy Sterling. Her largest even have clawfoot tubs with private bathrooms. She sends Johnny into a small room near the end of the right hallway.

"You go on in and freshen up. Ring the bell cord and Mabel will have someone send up water for your washbasin. Dinner is in an hour downstairs. Hunter and I will be across the hall in 204."

And into room 204 I am ushered with Addy's firm grip on my left arm. I pull Rip along with me, hoping none of her other tenants catch sight of him and ruin their evening. As soon as she closes the heavy door and locks the brass doorknob with a click, she turns to me, hands on hips.

"Don't you think for one second that I don't know what you're doing."

I pull the duster off my shoulders stiffly and toss it over the back of the desk chair, avoiding her piercing gaze like a chastised child. Rip hunches over in the far corner of the room. "What am I doing?"

"Who is that boy, Hunter?"

"His name is Johnny."

"Johnny," she repeats. "Is he a mark?"

I unbutton my waistcoat. With Addy's Charm thick throughout the hotel, I can feel my limbs relaxing, pain receding from the throbbing ribs beneath my bandages. The featherbed tempts me from the other side of the room. "No, he's not a mark."

"But you brought him here for a reason."

"He's a necromancer."

She pauses and brings one hand to her forehead, rubbing in slow circles. I sit down on the edge of the four-poster bed and start pulling my arms through the vest. I suck in a sharp breath as I pull too hard and get a stabbing pain through my ribs for my trouble. Addy throws her hands up and settles next to me, the featherbed sinking beneath us. Her hands are gentle now, and she helps me out of the waistcoat, folding it neatly in her lap and laying it aside.

"How badly are you hurt?" she asks, the sharpness gone from her tone.

"Not shot," I smile. "Could be worse."

She huffs. "That's what you northerners always say. 'Could be worse'. You'll be cold in your grave and I'll chisel that on your headstone, you stubborn…" she can't seem to think of anything cutting enough to call me at the moment, so she just sort of trails off. "Show me."

It takes us a few minutes to get the shirt over my head and the sloppy wrapping job I did with the cloths unwound. The bruising on my ribcage has turned dark purple. I nearly crack my molars as Addy presses her fingertips against the discolored skin. When she's done poking and prodding me like a sick calf, she makes a trip downstairs for some clean supplies. I roll up my trouser leg and wait for her to come back. When she does, she drops a handful of bandages on the bed and eyes the newly healing wound beneath my knee.

"Did you wrestle a Gallington bull?" she asks.

"A big boulder." I pull the soiled bandage away from the wound. "And a river."

She sighs. "Of course you did. Please tell me that at least you were doing something heroic."

"I saved a little Merenessan girl."

Her eyes soften. She settles on the bed next to me and wraps a bandage snugly around my ribs, then tucks the end into one of the strips. Finally, she speaks again.

"One of these days you're going to do something reckless and actually get yourself killed." She looks at my leg with a critical eye. "I'll have Miss Kay make another poultice. You should've stitched that better."

"One more scar on these legs won't matter any," I say. "I'm not trying to impress anyone."

She pulls her lips together, the way she always does when she wants to tell me what she really thinks, but she won't because she doesn't want to sound like a mother hen. Her three gold rings glimmer as she works. She's added a new one since I was here last, a band with leaves carved around it on her left forefinger. I catch a glimpse of the thin shadesilver bracelets she wears beneath her satin sleeves to boost her Charm. Addy always did like jewelry.

"Hunter, why don't you stay here in Grand Junction and settle down for a while? I could use the help around the hotel. There's a new cattle baron who bought Jack Spade's ranch west of town, and he's got big ideas for the way the town ought to be run. I could use some extra muscle around here."

"You're really scraping the bottom of the barrel if you're talking about me."

"I mean it." She nods toward the door. "Where'd you find

him, Hunter?"

I tell her the story, all of it. When I'm finished, she leans back against the bedpost and sighs, folding her hands in her lap.

"And you mean to leave him here," she says.

I don't like that she's cornered me so fast. I was hoping for a few more days before we have this conversation. "He'll need someone to clean him up a bit, give him something to do. I know he came from some posh family in Lamarnais, and that the bruise on his face didn't come from the other boys he fell in with." I fiddle with a bit of extra bandage. "And he'll need someone to teach him how to control his magic."

I don't look at Addy, because even as I say the words, I know how they will sound to her. She won't understand.

"Hunter Beckworth, I should've bandaged your head, it's clear you've cracked more than your ribs," she retorts in a furious whisper, ignoring my grimace at her use of the surname. "My magic is nothing like his, and you know it. If you're going to sit on this bed and pretend that there is someone better to teach him how to use necromancy than another necromancer, you can walk right out of my hotel this minute."

Once, when I was out running the traplines with Pops, we came across a female bobcat caught in one of the claw traps. She shrank back into the snowy brush as soon as she saw us, hissing and spitting and making all sorts of ruckus. In that moment, I'd felt more kinship with an animal than I had with most human folk. I'd pestered Pops until he finally agreed to spring the trap and let her go free. It took a bit of doing, and he'd had to knock her out cold to loosen her paw. Feeling trapped is something I like less than just about anything else in the world, and the sick knot in my stomach that goes along with it is mighty strong as I try to think of a way to talk my way out of whatever it is Addy thinks I ought to do.

"Well, I thought maybe Miles could…" I finally meet her gaze and the rest of the words die in the air between us as Addy gives me a murderous glare.

"The last thing this world needs is another living creature like Miles Lightfellow." She reaches out and takes one of my hands in hers. "Hunter, don't you think you've been running away from yourself long enough?"

I offer the only excuse I have left. "The world doesn't need another bounty hunter necromancer like me either. The best chance he has to be something better than me or Miles is to stay here and be taught proper by someone good."

"Ha! Don't you be putting me up on a pedestal, now." Addy squeezes my hand. "You're not so bad for a Soulless bounty hunter. That boy might be the best thing that ever happens to you. You can't go anywhere with your ribs the way they are. So you might as well stay and sleep in a real bed for a while and eat some decent meals. And while you're at it, you might as well teach him a thing or two."

There's no arguing once Addy has the upper hand. She's deadlier than a pair of revolvers, and she knows it. She smiles, real sweet, because she also knows I'm giving in.

CHAPTER TWENTY ONE

PORK RINDS AND BONES

The Territories are just a small spit of land in the ocean, surrounded by bigger, much older countries a decent three-- or four-- week steam ship journey away. Ferensia to the east, the Gandrin Republic to the south, and Maneira even further to the southeast. The few brave souls who meander further north than the Territories find themselves in endless miles of ice and black water. The north's tundra is a warm summer compared to the frozen end of the world.

Over a hundred years ago, the first settlers braved the temperamental sea to find out if life was better in an untamed wilderness than the crowded cities of their homelands. The Merenessans came to establish a holy sanctuary for their order. The Ferenese came to explore and tickle their sense of adventure, seeing as though the call of wild new land was a precious commodity in their civilized continent. The folks from Gandrin came to escape poverty and seek nature's bounty, promising to send back whatever they could find to fill up the empty coffers of the Republic.

Pops used to tell me stories of my great-great grandfather who came over the sea from the Republic. He was a young man with no wife, looking for a better future. Things were tense at first. No one knew if Ferensia or the Republic would lay an official claim on the land. They were allies, so nobody wanted to be the first to draw iron. I imagine the Merenessans were more than a little irritable at having company in their sanctuary. If they're allowed to be irritated, that is.

Before the two countries got around to a fight about who owned what scrap of land, shadesilver was discovered. And then it wasn't about who was Ferenese or Gandrin or Merenessan. It was about who had magic in their veins, and who didn't.

The Regents wanted to establish a government where the Territories were ruled by magic folks and keep all the shadesilver in tightly sealed vaults. The Secessionists didn't think that was such a fair idea, so they raised some hell about it, and before long a few angry words between two sides became stabbing and shooting.

The war went on for three years. It was mostly scrappy, ragtag bunches of militia led by men who just happened to have a louder voice than the rest of them. There were a few decorated officers on the side of the Regents, mostly from Ferensia. They saw a bit of something shiny and thought it would be nice to have the keys to the vault at the end if they won.

But those scrappy Secessionists gave them enough hell that eventually the Regents surrendered. The big mining outfit owners like McBride aren't magic folks, and that was one of the rules that the Secessionists demanded to make things fair. Nobody with magic can own more than a ten percent share of an established shadesilver mine.

They never made any rules for shadesilver still buried in the ground.

I sit on Addy's back porch, flipping one of my shadesilver

knives around in my hand and feeling the pleasant hum as it strengthens the magic in my veins. A good night's sleep did wonders, and I feel a little less like something that crawled out of a bog. Addy even convinced me to brush my hair, so now it sticks out all around my face like a lion's mane. Out in the yard, Johnny is hauling buckets of kitchen slops to the pigs and drawing water for the troughs. I don't know where Addy found clothes to fit him. Heck with the Charm, her real magic is being able to conjure things out of thin air.

Owen comes around the corner of the hotel, a dark smudge of dirt on his cheek already this early in the morning. He skips over to me.

"Mornin', Miss Hunter."

"That roan mare give you any trouble yesterday?"

"No ma'am, she's sweet as a peach around me. Just you she doesn't like," he says without a lick of a smile on his face. He looks out toward Johnny. "Well, I better go help him. Some folks ain't been around hard work much."

And with that, he swaggers toward Johnny with his chest all puffed out, sterner than a mine foreman. Johnny's a good sport and accepts Owen's instructions without any fuss, and soon they've fed and watered the pigs, the goats, the mules, and the chickens.

I don't relish the thought of talking to Johnny, but I know that if I go back in that hotel without trying, Addy will have my ears on one of her silver serving platters with the pork rinds. Johnny follows me out back to the stable, and I pull over wooden stool for him to sit on in the aisle between the stalls. The roan mare whickers at us. Mostly she whickers at Johnny and ignores me.

"Addy says I should teach you something about your magic."

I open a stall door and Rip lumbers out, black eyes staring at nothing. I crouch across from Johnny, who avoids my gaze and picks some dirt out of his fingernails. Not for the first time, I curse the fact that I'm not the one with Charm. Addy would say something to make him feel at ease. I'm good at making people feel less at ease.

"Look, I understand you not wanting to animate someone. It's your magic, and I'm not going to tell you what to do with it. But if you want to control it so you don't animate something by accident, you need to learn."

Johnny nods. "Alright."

"Shut your eyes."

He gives me a look and then turns his gaze over to Rip. I know he doesn't trust me, not after the night out on the prairie.

"As long as you aren't sneaking up on me, you've got nothing to worry about. Deal?"

He closes his eyes. I do too. I try to remember the time I explained my magic to Addy, but that was a long time ago.

"Trees have roots that reach into the ground, and they have branches that reach into the air. Necromancy is a bit of both. Our roots reach down into the space between life and death, and sense when something dies close by. Like when we were in the forest. You felt those boys die."

Johnny's face twists a little bit. It's not a pleasant thought to bring to mind. I wait for a minute to let him chew on that before I continue.

"And then, out come the branches. The Core of your magic is in your chest, and the branches reach out from that Core to attach to something and hold it between life and death. I call them tethers. Miles calls them strings."

His eyes open a crack. "Who is Miles?"

"Another necromancer. If you don't like me, pray you never meet him. Focus, I want you to see if you can feel the Core of your magic."

We sit there in silence for a bit before I interrupt him. "You have a concerning habit of not breathing. You can't reanimate yourself."

His breath stutters out, and his eyes open again, red-rimmed. There's a glaze over them, like he's seeing something else that isn't here, and he shakes his head.

"I know where it is. I don't want to feel it. I want you to teach me how to never feel it again."

I lock eyes with him. "When you're dead and in the ground, then you won't feel anything. I've seen a lot of folks try to feel nothing while they're still alive." Something pricks the back of my conscience, and I'm glad Addy isn't here to tell me that I'm talking about myself. "Seems to me that's a waste. Now focus."

He didn't like it, but he listened. "I have it."

"Now see if you can sense Rip. You can't animate him, but your magic should pull toward him, so he's good for you to practice on."

I settle into the faint hum of my own Core, and I feel the questing tethers of Johnny's necromancy reaching across the dirt floor of the stable toward Rip. They're erratic, jerking back and forth like spiders on a web.

"Focus."

The tethers smooth out a little until they reach Rip. They slow, quivering, as if frozen in the ground under the corpse's feet. Then they jerk back as if I'd cut them with one of my knives. Johnny trips over his own feet as he stumbles back toward the barn door and walks out.

"I won't!" he spits back at me. "Stop it, just stop asking me to do it!"

I leave Rip in the barn and follow him. He's burning up with something inside, just like I was when I ran into Reverend

Ambrose's forge and hid against the wall. Johnny runs out toward the wide-open spaces, his hat flailing behind him on its strings.

There's a lot of space out here, enough for a person to run away from a lot of things. So I let Johnny run, and I walk after him, one boot print in the dust at a time, breathing shallowly around my healing ribs. Grand Junction gets smaller and smaller behind us, and then it's just the prairie and the blue sky as I shuffle down the backside of a hill. Johnny isn't running now. He stops in the middle of a little dusty wallow and bends over, fists against his thighs. He yells, and it's a real mean sound from deep in his gut. I stop about ten yards away and loop my thumbs into my trouser pockets, shifting my weight onto the heel of my right boot.

"Stop following me!" Johnny yells. But he's not looking at me, so I figure he's talking to someone else inside his head. He stomps around a bit and kicks at a rock, sending it flying back up against the side of the hill I just walked down.

"Kicking rocks ain't going to fix what's eating you," I say, squinting at him from under the brim of my hat. "If you bottle that up long enough you could blow a new mine shaft for McBride."

"Yeah? What do you know about it?" He turns on me then, and the mousy little kid disappears behind his anger. "You don't want to talk about it either. And I don't want to be like you!"

"Who'd you run away from, Johnny?"

"Why don't you just leave me alone!"

"Who'd you run away from?"

"My father!" he shouts at me. Then he gets real quiet, and the anger drains out of him. "My father."

CHAPTER TWENTY TWO

SOULLESS

I've heard a lot of stories in my time, but not one ever made me as mad as the story Johnny tells me in that wallow. He is the youngest of three, and his father owns a printing shop in Lamarnais. As I suspected, they're well to do. His older brother and sister were born without a drop of magic in their veins, which suited their father just fine. Magic was unnatural and made a person greedy and wicked, as he saw it. Then Johnny was born.

"He couldn't beat it out of me, so he told me to keep out of his sight," Johnny says. "My mother had a library, and I read a lot of books. Some people didn't even know he had another kid. He told me that if I ever used my dirty magic that I would be Soulless."

Something changes in Johnny's face as he starts talking about his father. He looks younger, like I am watching him walk back in time to a place he doesn't want to go to. But it all pours out of him just like it needs to.

He sniffs and wipes his sleeve under his nose. "My sister Janey died two years ago. She got a fever and just… I didn't know a person could die so fast. I was in the library, and my father came and took me to Janey's room. He told me to bring her back or he'd send me after her. I tried. But when her skin turned gray and she opened her eyes all black and dead, I couldn't. I just couldn't and I let her go."

Johnny turns away from me then, shoulders all hunched around his crying. He drags his hat over his head and crumples it in his hands. My stomach turns as I watch him, and I know I would give every coin in my strongbox at Tabitha's to go back to that room and send Johnny's father to the Dark After.

"He said he'd never forgive me, and he didn't leave me alone after that." A scrape of his boot heel in the dirt as he twists slightly to look at me. "Are you going to send me back?"

Ten yards isn't much of a walk. I put my hand on his shoulder and feel the thin bone beneath his blue shirt. "Seems to me you don't much want to go back."

He shakes his head. "No."

"Lamarnais is too far of a ride in the wrong direction. I guess you might as well just stay on here. Addy won't throw you out as long as you help out and behave proper," I say awkwardly as I move my hand away from his shoulder. I roll some words around in my head a bit before finally deciding to spit them out. "Necromancy is in your veins, and that won't change. But you get to decide what to do with your life now, and if that means you don't ever use a drop of magic, so be it. If you want to learn, I'll teach you to control it. But it's your choice."

With another wipe of the sleeve, he meets my gaze. "I need to learn it, don't I?"

I shrug. "You might be able to keep yourself from using it, but you've a strong magic. It's not going to go away."

"I don't want it."

"I don't think any of us would've chosen it, if we could. But here we are. So what are you going to do?"

He runs his fingers over the brim of his hat, and then carefully settles it back on his head with one shuddery attempt at a deep breath. "I guess I'm gonna learn."

We leave the wallow and make our way back toward town and Addy's barn, where Rip stands silently waiting. Johnny still hesitates, but he pulls the small wooden stool over and eyes the big corpse. Rip stares back, and I feel a bit unsettled. I know what Johnny saw when he tried to bring his sister back, and it gnaws away at my insides. He'll never outlive that day.

The tethers of Johnny's necromancy creep toward Rip again, flowing along the floor like trickles of spilled water. My magic has always felt cold like the air in the Cathedrals, sharp and crisp. Johnny's necromancy feels quieter. And stronger. When the tethers reach Rip this time, they curl around his feet. I can feel the pull against the shard of my soul that resides in the Animated's chest. A dull ache spreads through me.

"Good. Now pull the tethers back toward you."

For a minute, nothing happens, and then the dull ache in my chest starts getting sharper, like something is tearing at me. The screams of the Shades echo in my ears, and I reach up to cover them. The magic tying me to Rip stretches and frays. I reach down and close my fists around the hilts of the shadesilver knives. My magic surges forward to push back against the intrusion. Johnny covers his own ears and squeezes his eyes shut. I push outwards as hard as I can.

"Johnny! Pull it back!"

He grits his teeth and yanks the magic back toward himself so hard he knocks himself right off the wooden stool and onto his rear in the dirt. The pull against my own magic disappears and takes my breath with it. I lean over and drag some air back into my lungs, taking short breaths with one arm clasped tightly to my ribs in agony.

"I'm sorry! I'm sorry!" Johnny says. "It's not supposed to do that, right?"

"You're real strong for a kid who doesn't want to animate anything," I say with a wheeze. "Almighty only knows how you haven't already brought somebody back."

"I won't do it again."

I shake my head and straighten up gingerly. "You most certainly will do it again. I told you to pull back your magic and you did, so we know you can control it some. It'll get easier every time you try."

Outside, the bell rings for lunch, and I hear Addy's voice calling out for us from the back steps. Chicken sounds real good, and my stomach growls. But I feel jittery, like a thousand ants are crawling under my skin. I roll my shoulders and force out a breath through my lips. The gaping black mouths of the Shades flash in and out at the corners of my mind. I wince and close my eyes, but that just brings me back to a damp cave and the memory of my soul fracturing in an explosion of blinding light. My next breath is less steady.

"Hunter?"

"Yeah, yeah. I'm good."

I pull my lower lip between my teeth and wrench a piece of loose skin free. But this time, the pinprick of pain isn't enough. A gunshot echoes in my ears. With a flinch, I reach up to cover them with my palms.

Stop it. Get out of my head.

Someone grips my arm hard, and the pressure pulls me back into Addy's barn like stretched taffy. I blink at Johnny, whose fingers are wrapped around my coat sleeve. And then I see why. Rip has taken two steps toward me, standing so close that I could reach out and touch the tattered hem of his vest. His black eyes are fixed on mine.

"Almighty," I whisper, and feel my knees buckle a little. "Johnny, get back away."

The tethers still feel frayed, but the soul fragment animating Rip's core beats back at me, steady, the same way it did out in the Cathedrals. It feels so familiar, and I hate admitting to myself that if I let Rip go, I don't know how much of me would be left. He doesn't move, but I can't move either. The tether starts to feel thick and unyielding. The barn disappears somewhere in a black tunnel that swallows me whole. I try to tighten my grip around the knives, drawing on the shadesilver to pull Rip's necromantic tethers back under my control completely.

"Hunter?" Addy's voice is closer now, and she swishes through the barn doors. "Y'all best come in for some lunch. You can't learn much on an empty stomach. Hunter, what in the Almighty's good earth…"

Her voice trails off. I feel her hand on my back, and she pulls me gently away from my locked stare with the Animated.

"Johnny, could you be a dear and get me a cold glass of water? Quick now."

The pressure on my arm disappears, and I hear Johnny's boots thumping back toward the hotel. Addy squeezes my hand several times in a distracting rhythm, and I feel her Charm wrapping around me like a warm blanket.

"Hunter, I'm going to need to you to breathe before you pass out. And then I'm going to need you to come inside and eat some of Miss Kay's good stuffed chicken. She even made the stuffing without raisins in it, just how you like it. Come on now."

I pull away, and the tethers relax like wet noodles. Taking several steps back away from Rip, I lean against the barn wall and wave away Addy's worrying while my head starts to clear.

"I'm alright, stop your fussing."

She plants her hands on her bustled hips. "You nearly scared me half to death when I walked in here. What's going on? And don't tell me nothing's wrong or I'll pack you up and send you right out of Grand Junction before dinner."

"I don't rightly know, Addy," I admit. "The magic got stronger when Johnny tried to reach out to Rip. And sometimes he moves on his own, without me telling him."

She gives Rip a long, hard look. "I don't feel a thing when I reach out to him with my magic. But I can feel you. There's a reason why necromancers don't hold onto an Animated as long as you have, Hunter. I don't want to see you go mad or run yourself into an early grave alongside that corpse."

Johnny jogs back into the barn with a glass of water, and hands it to me. It's not nearly cold enough for someone who grew up on the icy streams of the Cathedrals, but it brings me back to myself. Addy straightens out her skirts.

"You better figure out a way to teach him that doesn't involve you putting yourself in harm's way," she says with that tone of finality she always reserves for the times she's not interested in any talk back. "I've got a hundred things to do before the evening festivities, and I can't be worrying about the two of you. Now come on in and get your chicken before it goes cold."

Addy shoos us into the hotel like a schoolmarm, getting us set up at a table in the kitchen. Miss Kay bustles over to us with some freshly baked bread alongside the stuffed chicken. The first bite into the warm fluffy bread with slathered butter tastes enough like the Holy After that I know the Almighty must have been a baker.

"Nobody makes a loaf of bread like you, Miss Kay," I say through a mouthful of food. Her eyes crinkle upward as she smiles and cuts me a second slice from the cutting board. Her cropped hair is pulled away from her face with a floral handkerchief tied around her head, and she peers at me over silver spectacles.

"Sure, and you're just buttering me up, love," she answers, but she sounds pleased. Her soft voice and lilting accent are as warm and pleasant as her baking, despite the ladle that she shakes in our direction. "Don't you leave any crumbs on my clean floor, or I'll turn you right out."

"Yes ma'am," I smile. My hands are still trembling a little as I cut into the tender chicken and swish my fork through the meat and stuffing for a bite that my mama would've said was unladylike. The food does wonders for my grumbling stomach, but the dull ache in my chest doesn't fade. I glance over at Johnny, who is eating with a great deal more manners than I am. He's even tucked his napkin into the front of his shirt.

"Tomorrow, we try again," I say quietly once we've both slowed down and our plates are getting close to empty. "Don't give me that look, kid. The first time will be the worst. Besides, now we know what to expect."

He scrunches his face like he wants to argue with me, but he doesn't. "Alright. What happened?"

It was a fair question, and I was still sorting through it myself. "Your necromancy is stronger than mine, and it was pulling at the tether between me and Rip. I've never seen that happen before."

He chews on his last bite of chicken and scowls down at his plate. I push mine away and set my fork and knife neatly across the edge. "No need for a long face. And anyhow, you've got something far more serious to worry about for the time being."

"What?"

I grin. "A dance."

CHAPTER TWENTY THREE

SOUR NOTES

Addy sure knows how to throw a party. The hotel looks like the inside of a lamp, all lit up with glowing gold light. The chandeliers are dusted and shined to a brilliant sparkle, and the table of edible bits and bobs looks too fancy to eat. White tablecloths in the dining room have been traded out for some kind of black satin with tasseled trim. She's even managed to scrounge up the last of the autumn wildflowers from Almighty knows where for little vase arrangements on the tables. And just in the nick of time too, because a few snowflakes are just starting to fall outside the windows.

I tug at the collar of my crisply pressed white shirt quickly while Addy isn't watching. The black vest I'm wearing over it fits fine, but it's not worn in like my usual clothes. I feel like a display window dressing from Miss Halloway's tailor shop. Johnny looks less uncomfortable in black trousers and suspenders. Growing up in Lamarnais with well-to-do parents at least taught him how to wear nice clothes. Tired of the tight fit of my collar, I pull the top button until it comes free and blow out a good lungful of air, then wince and press my fingers against my bandaged side.

"Oh stop being such a baby," says Addy from where she sashays up behind me. It's an impressive feat how that woman manages to creep around in those heels. "You look nice. Those clothes of yours were in desperate need of a wash."

I feel the tips of my ears get a bit hot. "I wash them."

"Not enough for city life," she laughs. "I see you brought Rip in, that's good. That new cattle rancher Martin Price will be here tonight, and it would do him good to know there's someone else in Grand Junction who isn't afraid to run things a little differently."

Sure enough, Rip darkens the side of the room nearest the piano, the gray of his skin oddly warm in the lights. The tether between us has recovered from the strain of the morning, and Addy thought it would be a good idea to have him around for the evening. I disagree.

"Addy, none of these folks want to see a corpse while they're dancing a jig. Let me put him outside."

She glares at me. "I told you that while you were here I need the extra muscle. Martin Price is already throwing his weight around town, and I'm not about to have it in my hotel."

A dumber person might have reminded Addy that she is enough of a force of nature on her own and doesn't need any muscle from me. But I know she's not in the mood. I consider the hulking Animated on the far wall for a minute and then offer my thoughts.

"Maybe looping a garland around his neck would help. You got any more of them flowers?"

"Hunter."

I give her my most winning smile. "Did you find the package I left in your room?"

That shifts her mood like magic. She pats my arm. "I already sent Mabel over to the tailor's place with it. You didn't have to bring me anything, you silly goose. That green satin is divine, and you know how I like black lace."

"I thought it might be a pretty color on you."

"You spoil me. Try to stay out of trouble, I'll find you later," she shakes her finger at me and heads for the entryway where her first guests are arriving. "Mr. and Mrs. Kent! How lovely to see you both this evening."

I watch while she does what she does best. I'm not much good at talking to folks about the pins in their hair and the state of the weather. Anyone can see that snowflakes are falling outside. Happens every year, and every year people act like they're surprised to see it coming. Never been much for gossip either. I figure keeping my nose in my own business is enough. No need to go around collecting everyone else's. But Addy manages to balance the Charm of a gracious hostess alongside comments about this lady's dress and the latest goods that arrived at this gentleman's store. It's like she knows a little something about every person that ever lived.

The mayor and his wife arrive and wait their turn to be greeted. His suit coat stretches a little over an ample waistline, and he doffs his shiny top hat with a gloved hand. His wife glitters on his arm in her peach-colored organza. I fidget with the hem of the black waistcoat again and remember why I always avoid soirees like this one. At least I managed to pull my hair into a bun at the back of my head. I touch my plain silver necklace and fiddle with the little cross at the end. I imagine that Reverend Ambrose would be at ease here too, like Addy.

Johnny and I stay toward the back of the room where Addy's bartender is shining glasses and swiping dust that doesn't exist off the already gleaming counter. He gives me a jaunty wink and nods his head toward the growing crowd of fancy folk in the hotel's lobby.

"If you think you're safe here, you're wrong," he says. "In less than an hour this bar will be the busiest spot in the building."

I grumble a little bit under my breath. "You sure know how to make a girl feel comfortable, Andrew Hayes. Why don't you shine that counter up some more? You missed a spot."

He chuckles and offers me a glass. "Might as well start now. Get a bit of courage in you for the rest of the evening. I've been saving a special Gallington bourbon for just such an occasion."

A slim glass bottle appears almost out of thin air from under the counter, and he pulls the stopper, pouring the dark honey-colored liquid into the glass. I sip a little bit of fire down my throat and let the smooth aftertaste linger before giving my opinion.

"That's a good one."

He beams and pours a little bit more into a second glass, pushing it toward Johnny. "Drink up, little man. Put some hair on your chest."

Johnny takes too big of a sip and sputters. Hayes' big laugh fills the room, and he offers Johnny some water to chase away the burn. I set my glass back on the counter as an invitation.

"The usual?" he asks. I nod, and I guess I'm not surprised he remembers. I did drink a good deal when I stayed with Addy a few years back. He'd only worked for her three months when I came shuffling into town with Rip on my heels, and he'd never said a word about the Animated. None of Addy's people had, except Mabel. But then, Mabel always has a lot to say about everything.

Andrew pulls a bottle of Blue Island rum from the impressive line against the bar's back mirror. Farenese limes are a precious commodity this far inland, but I know that Addy stocks them whenever she can, and it looks like I'm lucky today. The pinch of sugar he adds to the mix is just enough to soften the tang of the lime.

That first sip chases the last of the bourbon aftertaste away. I haven't had a real good drink like this since the last time he made it for me. I lift the glass in his direction.

"You're a wizard, my friend."

He waves me away with a broad grin as he heads toward the other end of the bar to see to the portly man that just took a stool. Johnny tries another smaller sip of his bourbon and manages with just a grimace this time. Over on the far wall, I see the mayor and his wife pause near Rip.

"I say, what a grotesque spectacle to have on display at such a gathering," says the mayor, drawing a handkerchief out of his pocket and dabbing at his sweaty nose. His wife holds her own lacy hanky against her face as if the Animated smells like something that's actually dead. Addy is only a step behind them, and she smiles brightly.

"Oh he's harmless. Pay him no mind, he's just a little extra security for tonight's party. Much cheaper than a hired gun, and certainly more imposing, wouldn't you say?"

The mayor's wife looks at Addy with an expression that reminds me of a puckered fish. But the mayor manages to collect himself enough to continue the conversation. "I suppose it is, at that. But I hope he isn't meant to be a permanent fixture in your lovely establishment, Miss Sterling."

Addy pulls them along back into the crowd, throwing a glance over her shoulder at me. She mouths *watch the door* as she mingles in with her guests again. I'm not sure why until about two minutes later, when the big front doors open and a group of scrubbed-up cowhands tromp in, knocking a dust of snow off their boots. Most of them look common enough except for the tallest one. I mark him as a dandy from the minute I lock eyes on him. He wears a wide-brim black hat and duster that haven't seen a day's hard work, or I'll eat my own. He's a handsome enough fellow as far as they go, with a trimmed beard and mustache underneath green eyes. And with those good looks comes the easy arrogance that sort of oozes off his shoulders like slime. Shiny silver spurs hug the heels of his oiled boots. As they enter the hotel, he pulls a gold watch out of the pocket of his waistcoat and makes a show of checking the time.

I'd bet my shadesilver knives that's the new cattle baron. He has all the look of young money, ready to swing his weight around and flash his stack of banknotes at a party. They're a copper a dozen down south. He seems to like the way the heads turn to look at him when he comes through the door. The way the hubbub dims a little.

Even though I scrubbed up for Addy's soiree, the minute Martin Price looks across the room and those green eyes settle on me I feel like marching up those stairs and settling back into the tub. He doesn't linger on me long, he's too busy looking for someone else. And as much as I don't like him looking at me, I like him looking at Addy even less. My friend steps to the front of the crowd in her blue satin and offers the man an all too generous smile.

"Welcome to the hotel, Mr. Price. I'm glad you could join us this evening." She glances down at the gun belt strapped around his hips. "You can leave your iron with Mabel at the front desk and retrieve it when you're ready to go."

He tips his hat to Addy with a little smirk. "Thank you kindly for the welcome, Miss Sterling. I've heard your Charm is legendary in these parts. I'm pleased to see those rumors hold true. As for my guns, you can rest assured that they will remain firmly holstered throughout the evening."

Addy's smile tightens. "Mr. Price, I do not allow any

strapped guns in my hotel-"

"Don't you worry about a thing, darlin'," he says, reaching for her hand and bending over it. "It's my pleasure to provide a little extra security for this gathering at no cost to you."

I figure if I'm going to earn my keep as Addy's muscle around here, I might as well take my cue. I meander my way over to the entryway, my thumbs resting in the pockets of my trousers. My gun belt is upstairs with my shadesilver knives, and I don't like how naked I feel without them. I take hold of the tether to Rip, ready to pull.

"Mister, I believe the lady asked you kindly to remove your gun belt."

His green eyes lose a little of their glitter when he turns to me. "I don't think I've had the pleasure of making your acquaintance. Is it your habit to barge in on other folks' conversations?"

I shift my weight back on my right boot heel. I can smell the whiskey on his breath now that I'm closer to him.

"My name is Hunter. And as to your question, I only barge in on conversations where I'm needed."

Martin turns back to Addy again, the charming smile fading from his lips as he reaches to unbuckle the holsters. "I wouldn't want to cause a scene in your fine establishment. Though I do hope you'll consider an upgrade to your security. It's hard to keep the peace when you leave your guns at home."

I pull on the tether and hear a few shrieks and surprised shouts behind me as Rip leaves his place beside the piano and shuffles across the room. I can feel the looming darkness of him behind me and watch as Martin Price looks at the corpse with his jaw slack.

"From my experience, Mr. Price, a gun isn't always the most effective way of keeping the peace."

CHAPTER TWENTY FOUR

AN INTERRUPTED SOIREE

Martin pulls his gun belt free from his waist. His revolvers have silver inlay on the butts, and nothing on the holster or the gun is worn. There's a thinly veiled suspicion and anger in the way he eyes Rip after he gets over his shock at the sight of the dead giant looming over my shoulder. At a jerk of Price's head, the cowhands behind him pull their belts and head toward the front desk.

"I look forward to getting to know you better, Miss Sterling. My apologies for the unwanted suggestions," he says. There's no real apology in his tone. Addy graciously accepts it, though, and invites Mr. Price to step into the room and find some refreshments. He heads for the bar, and Johnny hurries to step out of his way.

Addy glides forward to my right and puts a hand on my arm. "Thank you for stepping in. Ever since he moved to Grand Junction, he walks around like he owns the place. His family is from St. Albane, and they have big money. I wouldn't be surprised if they gave him a stack of cash and sent him up north to be rid of him."

"I know his type," I say. "Waves a wad of bank notes at the

sheriff and gets away with whatever he wants. He's harmless as soon as you play a bigger card."

Rip's interruption seems to have now been relegated to the murmured conversations around the room. A few glances are still tossed our way, but at least folks are keeping to themselves. The piano player begins a lively rag, her fingers bouncing over the ivory keys while the feathers tucked into her hair quiver. Addy is quickly swept into the gathering again, and I make my way back over to the bar, pulling Rip along with me this time.

Johnny follows me like a baby duckling and waits until I have another drink in my hand before giving me his thoughts. "I don't like him. You think Miss Addy will be alright?"

I chuckle. "She didn't need me to put Price in his place. Just figured I'd give her the night off. Men like that are easy as long as you're facing them in a crowded room. When you turn your back in the alleyway, that's when they're dangerous."

The parlor has transformed into a dance floor, with brightly colored dresses spinning and bouncing through the room alongside the darker coats and vests of their partners. The mayor and his wife whirl past us in a flurry of peach organza, red-faced. There's not much call for dancing in Paradise, so I never did learn. Addy tried to teach me once, but I'm more graceful on a horse than tapping my heels across polished floors.

A small group of young men have congregated near Addy. To the eye of anyone else in the room, she's pleased with their awkward attentions. She laughs and smiles, and I can almost hear the heartbreak when she steps away from the pack. After gracefully disentangling herself, she heads my way in a flounce of blue satin. Her face is flushed and she grips my hand tightly.

"Talk to me. Save me from the insufferable attention."

I make a show of finishing my whiskey while she fidgets

impatiently next to me. "Seems you have quite a few admirers in town," I say with a grin. That earns me a glare. Addy pulls her fan from a loop at her waist and flutters it in front of her face, blowing back the black curls framing her cheeks.

She eyes her admirers with distaste. "Vultures, the lot of them. I'm an unmarried and rich woman who must certainly be in need of a husband to manage my affairs. They'd marry the hotel whether I came with it or not."

I raise my eyebrows. Addy has always been stubbornly dismissive of her looks, even though nearly everyone she meets does a fair bit of ogling.

"You never know, one of them might sweep you right off your feet."

Addy huffs. "Trip me, you mean. Look at them all preening their feathers." Then her lips curve in a wicked little smile and she tucks her hand in the crook of my arm. "It would ruffle them horribly if I dance with you instead of them."

"Sprawling on your oak floorboards might not be the best way to make an impression," I answer grimly. "You know I can't dance."

But Addy has set her mind to dancing, so dancing we go. She takes my hand and we enter the steps of a square dance right alongside the mayor and his wife. My enthusiasm is severely lacking in comparison to Addy as she stomps around that wooden floor like she is determined to put one of her heeled boots right through the boards. Miss Kay had once said that there was a fire in Miss Adelaide that put the fear of the Almighty into a person. I had to allow she was right.

I do my best to keep up with her while nursing the ache in my ribs and leg. Mostly she dances and I sort of take up space so nobody else can step in. I think Addy would have kept me out there all night, but soon enough I'm pressing a hand to my side and excusing myself to the back of the room where Johnny watches the dancing couples and fiddles with his suspender straps.

I sit down on one of the stools and clap Johnny on the back. "I've danced my last round, and if someone doesn't take my place, those good for nothing suitors will take their chance. Why don't you go dust your heels a little?"

Johnny's cheeks flush hot, and he looks like he'd rather animate a corpse than step out into the swiftly moving current of skirts. He tries to protest but I plant a palm firmly in the small of his back and push him out toward Addy, who graces Johnny with a curtsey as he shuffles toward her. She takes his hands and places one firmly at the curve of her waist. If his face gets any redder, Miss Kay can add him to one of her famous tomato soups. To his credit, he tries to follow her quiet instructions as they move in an awkward square, and a few minutes later, he's looking a lot more graceful than I did.

Addy's Charm works its magic, and it isn't long before Johnny's face goes back to its usual color and he's even smiling and laughing a little while they make some small talk. The piano player has slowed from jigs to a waltz, and the movement around the dance floor takes a different shape. Addy's group of would-be suitors hover at the edge of the gathering, looking like an irritated gaggle of geese as their object of desire stays happily on the dance floor with a green kid for almost an hour.

Suddenly, a loud voice to my left pulls my attention away from the dance toward a less pleasant sight. Martin Price and several of his cowhands are leaning against the bar while Andrew Hayes politely refuses to pour another whiskey for Price. He's already had several. The cattle baron is agitated and offering a string of obscenities in the bartender's direction. Price reaches for the bottle in Hayes' hand and nearly falls face first onto the counter as it is neatly whisked away from his reach.

I know Hayes can handle himself. And there's always the double barrel shotgun shelved under the counter in case he can't. Apparently Price comes to this same conclusion too, because he straightens out his waistcoat and sets his whiskey glass on the counter with a bang. Hayes pays him no mind and simply sets the bottle next to its fellows on the back shelf. But when Price leaves his seat at the counter and heads back into the gathering, I watch him. He disappears into the dining hall. I'm willing to bet he's not looking for refreshments, and I don't see Johnny and Addy on the dance floor.

I brush past a young woman in a dark red frock with way too much lace along the bustline. She turns and barely covers her gasp as Rip shoulders his way through after me. The dining room tables are still full of little cakes. I'm pretty sure Miss Kay made every flavor known to mankind, all bunched together in tiny square pyramids on scalloped platters.

Johnny and Addy are in the middle of scooping up a couple of the dainty desserts onto fancy plates when Price reaches them.

When he speaks, his voice is loud enough to wake the dead outside in the Grand Junction graveyard. "Miss Sterling, I wonder if you might consider a business proposition."

Addy still manages to look graceful even with a mouthful of cake. She dabs a small napkin at the corners of her mouth and makes no effort to smile. Instead, she fixes Price with a heated stare that could curdle fresh milk.

"I am not interested in a business proposition, Mr. Price. Especially not from a man so intent on harrying my bartender."

"Now hold on, there. You haven't heard my proposition yet," says Price, leaning forward over Addy. "I think you could use a partner in this hotel business. I'm prepared to offer you…" he pauses and lowers his voice. "Ten thousand for a half share. I'm a generous man."

At her full height, Addy barely reaches the man's shoulder. But she looks him dead in the eye. "Mr. Price, I would not sell you one room of this hotel if you offered me twenty thousand in pure shadesilver. You're a drunk, and I will not have you on my property."

Mr. Price chuckles a little and pulls away from the small angry woman in front of him. "As you like. But do consider my offer." He reaches into one pocket and pulls out a bit of cash, tucking it and his fingers into the front of Addy's corset. "Consider this a good will gift, madam."

Addy slaps him across the face so hard that he teeters sideways and crashes into one of the tables, spilling cakes and cutlery onto the floor. Before he knows what's happening, two massive gray hands close around his shirt collar and drag him off the ground, boots dangling a few inches from the floor. I ignore the gasps and shouts of surprise as the gathering slowly quiets to see what is happening.

I look at Addy first. "Are you alright?"

Her eyes flash like a forge fire. "Take his trash out with him," she says, handing me the wad of bills. I shove them into my pocket and march outside through the kitchen and down the back steps, tugging Rip along after me with Price slung over his shoulder. The man kicks against Rip's thighs, but he's helpless in the giant's vice grip.

There's a light carpet of snow on the ground and I crunch through it toward the nearest wooden fence. A soft snuffling sound comes from the little log lean-to in the corner as my footsteps wake the pigs. The fence isn't high, and when I push out through Rip's arms he sends the body of Martin Price flying into the snowy sludgy muck of the pigsty. Johnny comes up behind me with the bucket of slops that Miss Kay just set out for morning feeding time. The contents of that bucket fly across the pen to coat the man with another layer of slime. He scrambles around in the mud, slipping and sliding and trying to get his feet planted. All the while he's calling out curses and letting Johnny and I know that we've enraged a very dangerous man, a very rich man with grand connections. Johnny tosses the bucket aside, and before we return to the interrupted party inside, I pull the cash out of my pocket and let it fall from my fingers into the pigpen.

"You've made a fool of yourself! I am not a man you want as an enemy!" Price continues, stumbling toward one of the fence rails.

I tsk at him. "Mister, if I were you, I'd be thanking the Almighty that I tossed you out on your behind instead of Miss Sterling. If it had been her, you wouldn't have a behind to sit on."

And with that, Mr. Martin Price is uninvited from the soiree.

CHAPTER TWENTY FIVE

STRONG MAGIC

We don't hear a peep out of Martin Price or any of his men the next day. Most likely he's draped over a bowl in his bedroom throwing up his guts. He'll be needing more than one bath before he stops smelling like a pigsty. Addy oversees the cleaning of the hotel with a shorter fuse than she normally does. Her Charm fills the rooms with the warmth of a blanket in winter, but there are still sparks in her eyes. If Martin Price wants to keep his skin, I reckon he's going to want to abstain from any further business propositions.

The dark spot added to Mr. Price's own ungentlemanly actions comes when Addy and I pay a visit to the sheriff to inform him of the new baron's behavior. The sheriff talks a big talk about seeing to the protection of the citizens of Grand Junction but seems to think that a little drunkenness isn't anything to worry about. He says he'll let Price know to steer clear of the hotel, but Miss Addy shouldn't take these things so personal. Addy's redder than a boiled crab by the time we leave.

"That piece of tin he's wearing on his vest isn't worth a pan of dirty dishwater," she fumes. "Worthless, the lot of them. I spoke to the mayor about it last night before they left and he was perfectly sympathetic until I asked him to do something. Then he was all empty apologies and reassurances that it would not happen again. No doubt Price is slipping more than a few coins in that pocket as well."

I let her go on, doing my best to keep pace with her angry walking. Her silver-gray jacket comes up in a high collar around her jaw, looking more like a suit of armor than the top half of a dress. The fascinator pinned into her black curls sits at an angle, the white feathers tucked into its band jerking with every step as if they're just as angry as the woman they're attached to. At least she remembered to bring her furred muff. Despite the light dusting of snow still covering the boardwalk and street, it's a bit nippy for someone not used to bitter cold. By the time we get back to the hotel's front porch, Addy has run out of unflattering things to say about Mr. Price, the sheriff, and the mayor. At least for the time being.

She stops at the steps and faces me. "I do wish you'd stay on here, Hunter. I can handle myself, but I do feel better knowing that you and that infernal corpse are around. If you're going to keep him upright, I suppose he might as well be put to use."

"I don't think I'll be moving on till spring at least. Johnny seems to like it here, and like you said, somebody ought to teach him some things. Maybe Miss Kay can show him how to make those soft sugar cookies."

A smile reaches Addy's lips for the first time today. "I know you, Hunter. You've taken a shine to that boy, and don't think I can't see it. Maybe you can stop putting all your energy into the dead and start giving some attention to the living."

Once inside, Miss Kay manages to herd me into the kitchen for some late breakfast. Johnny is already at the table, and she's tutting over him as she fixes him a second plate.

"You just eat up as much as you want," she tells him with a

sparkle in her eye. "I won't have anyone going hungry out of my kitchen."

"Thank you, Miss Kay," Johnny says around a mouthful of pork sausage.

The sausages are crispy on the outside and taste of maple. I eat four of them before turning my attention to the stack of fluffy griddle cakes doused in syrup and melting butter. By the time I push my plate away, I feel rounder than the rainwater barrels outside.

"The stagecoach will be coming into town in a few hours," says Miss Kay as she takes my plate. "Miss Sterling is expecting some new tenants. You two might want to finish up whatever you're doing out there before they arrive."

Johnny and I manage to heave ourselves out of the kitchen chairs and make our way to the barn, still pulling at the waists of our trousers. If Miss Kay keeps feeding us like this, none of our clothes will fit by spring. The barn is colder today, and Johnny gathers his coat a little tighter around his shoulders. I pull Rip out of his stall and set him between us.

"Alright. Same as last time. I want you to reach out to Rip and then pull back. I'm not going to push you away this time."

Johnny splutters a little. "I don't think that's a good idea."

"Well, you aren't the teacher, so close your trap and try it."

He shuts his trap, and a few seconds later I can feel the necromancy tethers creeping out across the floor. They still feel nervous, unstable, but less so than the last time. He reaches Rip and the necromancy curls around the giant's feet. I don't push him away this time. The strength of his magic still surprises me, and I am more sure than ever that if Johnny wanted to, and knew what he was doing, he could pull the tether between Rip and I clean apart. I feel my magic stretching, giving way beneath the stronger pull.

"Now… pull it back," I say through gritted teeth. My forehead breaks out in a sweat from the effort of keeping the tethers steady. And then, without a fuss, the pull disappears and slithers back along the floor to Johnny.

I smile and nod, leaning forward with my hands planted firmly on my knees. "Well done, kid. We might make something of you yet."

Johnny's face glows like a firebug, and he looks down at his hands, surprised by what he's just managed to do. The freshly dead of Grand Junction aren't safe just yet, but it's a start. He looks up at me with some determination written into his face.

"Can I try again?"

For an hour we stay in that barn. Johnny reaches out to Rip and then pulls his necromancy tethers back toward himself. Every time, the pull against my magic gets less and less strong. Even so, I'm worn down to my bones with the effort by the time he finally stops for a rest. We both gulp down some cool water from the well and settle on some hay piles on the north end of the barn.

Johnny's worked up a sweat but still looks as bright-eyed as a new calf. He pulls a piece of hay from the stack and starts pulling strands off it.

"Miles Lightfellow… he's a necromancer too."

I side eye him, not sure why he's asking. "Yeah."

He points at Rip. "Does he have an Animated that he drags around everywhere too? Is he stronger than you, or weaker?"

I shake my head. "Dangerous game, asking questions about Miles Lightfellow. I don't think you and he would get on."

"If I do meet him someday, I'd like to know. And if I never meet him, what's the harm in asking?"

The kid has a point. I spit onto the dirt floor. "He's older and stronger than I am, and he'd love to hear me admit it. He's mostly a drunk and a lecher. When he's sober, he's a bounty hunter like me. Works in the south. Drunk or sober, he's one of the fastest gunslingers in the Territories, which makes him one of the most dangerous people to be around."

Johnny listens, still pulling at his piece of hay. "How'd you meet him?"

I don't know as I'm entirely comfortable sharing the story, but I tell him a little of it. "I met him six years ago, not long after I left the north with Rip for the first time. I wanted to get as far away from home as I could. Got into a fight in Gallington with a man on the street who threw rocks at me. Turns out that man was Miles' mark. Shot him dead as a possum in the middle of the street. The bullet went right past my ear. Then he took me to the nearest saloon and bought me a drink."

"You ran away from your home too."

I don't want to unpack that particular sentiment. "To answer your question, no, Miles doesn't keep an Animated with him. Down south, they call him The Puppeteer, or Miles Lightfingers."

"The Puppeteer?"

"He doesn't raise corpses unless he makes them first. As soon as he's done, he drops them where they stand."

CHAPTER TWENTY SIX

LAW AND ORDER

The stagecoach full of new boarders brings something else along with it that is even more welcome. Owen finds me in my room taking an afternoon nap and knocks on the door with an urgency only found in young children who believe they have something of grave importance to share. I swing my stockinged feet over the side of the bed stiffly and turn the doorknob to see his smudged little face staring up at me gleefully.

"A letter come for you, Miss Hunter!" he says, holding out an envelope that has been slightly crumpled by his small hand. "I brung it up right away when Miss Mabel found it in the post bag."

I ruffle his golden hair and flip him a copper, which he snatches out of the air and sets between his teeth before running back down the stairs with all the grace of a herd of elephants. The handwriting on the envelope is as familiar to me as my own, and I carefully slice open one end with the letter opener on my desk.

Dear Hunter,

I am relieved to hear you are with Adelaide this winter. It's going to be a bad season up north. Everyone is a bit worried about getting in enough supplies to outlast the snow, but the Almighty has seen me through fifty-nine winters thus far and I believe that He will continue to do so. I will be praying for you and the boy Johnny.

There was a man here not long after I received your last letter. He is from McBride's company and was asking around town to find out what holdings near the Cathedrals were unsettled, and if anyone was looking to sell. Gerdy told him about your cabin, said it had been vacant a long spell.

I don't want you to worry about it. I'll see to it that they don't sell out from under you. Gerdy talks big, but I believe she knows better.

I made sure your mama's gravestone was cleared before the snows came. Some brush had grown up beside it, and that's all taken care of.

Since your Mama and Pops aren't here to worry after you, I hope you'll forgive an old man's meddling. I hope you stay in Grand Junction and make a life for yourself there, if you can't come back to Paradise. I understand that it may be too hard for you here. But you deserve a measure of happiness, and I believe that it's being offered to you if you're willing to take it.

It's never too late to start a new life. You'll never run so far that you can't come back.

The forge is warm if you come by.
Your friend, Reverend Ambrose

I fold the letter, running my finger gently over each smooth crease and feeling the slight ripple from Owen's crumpling hands. A little piece of home. The sadness creeps up on me, and I can almost smell the cold air and the promise of heavy snow. I close my eyes and make a picture in my mind of the towering mountains crowned with their snowy caps, the rush of black water over icy rocks in the stream near the cabin. I feel the warmth of Reverend Ambrose's forge heating my cheeks and hands while he pumps the bellows and shapes some iron tool on the anvil with practiced hands formed by decades of metalwork. In another life, perhaps I could have stayed. In another life, perhaps I would not have been a necromancer at all.

I imagine myself as a schoolmarm at the end of a classroom full of boys and girls sounding out their letters and learning the distance between Ferensia and Gandrin. I imagine myself a cook, or a tailor, or more likely a horse dealer. Even in my head it feels like I'm stealing someone else's skin. In fairness, I can't imagine Addy as a schoolmarm either.

One day I will go back to Paradise. I'll ride right into that fickle town and order a whiskey at Gerdy's saloon, nice as you please. And if she tries to shoot me with that blasted gun of hers, I'll just use Rip's hand to bend the muzzle of it right up toward the plank ceiling. It's a nice thought.

I set the letter among my things in the top drawer of the bureau. Most of the letters from the reverend are locked in my safe back at Tabitha's. I'll send her some money this week and a letter to let her know I won't be back until spring. She'll probably fuss when she gets it, but I know she won't rent the room out. She likes me too much.

Addy catches me with a gloved hand just as I come out my door. "Hunter! I was just looking for you. One of the new boarders that came in on the stagecoach is a solicitor from the law school in Whitebridge. He's planning on setting up a practice here in Grand Junction. Perhaps we may have an ally against Mr. Price if we need one in the future."

Despite her wink and excitedly flushed cheeks, I figure I'll believe in an honest solicitor when I see one, especially when it concerns the likes of Mr. Martin Price. I don't say as much to Addy, though.

"Sounds fine. It's an improvement on the law and order of this place riding on the shoulders of one circuit judge, I expect."

Her nose wrinkles like the judge brings a sour smell to mind. "Judge Bower is a relic. He might as well pound his gavel on his own bald head for all the good he's done this community. He'd rather stay in his bed eating quail eggs than put on a robe and be forced to think. Anyway, come downstairs and have some tea."

The hotel is calm and homey with all the boarders gathered in the dining room and lounge sipping from their porcelain teacups. There are a couple men leaning against the bar counter with drinks, and Andrew gives me a wink and a nod when I follow Addy into the lobby. The dining room, like most of the rooms in the hotel, has Addy's signature lavish taste stamped all over it. The blue drapes over the windows, gold trimmed porcelain and silver cutlery, and lace tablecloths over the delicate wooden tables all manage to bring a bit of southern finery to the north.

Sitting alone at his table near the window, the solicitor manages to look right at home in the stylish finery. He peers down at a newspaper through the spectacles perched over a wide nose. His suit is neatly tailored, and there isn't so much as the shadow of a beard or mustache on his clean-shaven face. I place him at about thirty years old, if that. He reads the paper with stoic disinterest and sips his coffee. The cup clinks back onto its saucer as Addy sweeps up to his table.

"Mr. Pruitt! I hope you've been settling in comfortably. How was your coffee?"

He unfolds himself from his chair and respectfully offers to pull out the chair next to him for Addy. She settles into it. He looks me over and apparently decides I can pull out my own chair, which I do.

"You run a very adequate accommodation, Miss Sterling," he replies. "The coffee here is certainly not what I expected, but I believe I will become used to it."

If Addy dislikes the word 'adequate' in relation to her hotel, she doesn't seem to pay it any mind. "Wonderful. Mr. Pruitt, this is my associate and friend, Hunter. She's been helping me keep an eye on things around the hotel."

One of his thin eyebrows lifts over the spectacles. "Pleasure."

"What brings you to Grand Junction, Mr. Pruitt?" I ask. I'm not much good at small talk, but I know it's something most people expect to be asked in a situation like this one. I already have my own assumptions about what brought him up this way. Probably looking to get away from the big southern cities and make a name for himself apart from the crowd.

"Progress," he says, adjusting the cup in front of him so the handle is slightly closer to his fingers. "I believe that the stability of law and order must be brought to less civilized regions to unify the Territories."

"Seems a mighty big job for one man."

"Advancement begins with the individual pursuit to better one's own environment. I presume by your dialect that you are from a northern settlement?"

"Paradise."

"Ah." He settles back into his chair. "And who is responsible for the law and order in Paradise?"

Gerdy comes to mind with her fossil of a musket and her wild eyes. "The folks in the town manage their own law and order."

"Of course. And from what you've observed, would you say

that justice is served well?"

My jaw gets uncomfortably tight. "Justice is different in the north than what you're used to, Mr. Pruitt."

He smiles, a thin thing that makes a crooked line in the smoothness of his face. "In that we disagree. And that is exactly why I am here. I am a simple servant of law and order."

"Simple justice usually means the fastest bullet in these parts, Mr. Pruitt."

"So it would seem. I was surprised to learn of your proclivity for magic, Miss Hunter. I was under the impression that necromancy was not well thought of, especially in the northern half of the Territories. It must be difficult to find work beyond the likes of bounty hunting."

Addy clears her throat and shoots me a glare that makes me swallow whatever words were about to come out of my mouth. "Hunter has been an invaluable help to me here at the hotel, Mr. Pruitt. Perhaps the north could benefit from a better sense of justice in the future. I look forward to your contribution," she says. "You've drained that coffee right down, I'll make sure Miss Kay sends another cup out for you."

I don't want to cause more of a scene in Addy's hotel after the evening with Mr. Price, so I nod as respectful as I can manage to the man across the table, who seems to be not the least bothered by my irritation.

"Best of luck with your pursuit of law and order," I say. Mr. Pruitt reaches inside his suit coat and produces a small square of paper.

"And with yours. If you have any need of my services, I intend to settle here permanently."

As I head to the kitchen, I turn the business card over in my fingers. There are no embellishments, just a simple black type that reads:

Gilroy Fitzthomas Pruitt
Solicitor
University of Law, Whitebridge

Some people think that a long name and title makes you important. But it just makes me uneasy. The sort of person who wants to be judged by the title on a card doesn't want to be judged as the person they are when no one is watching.

Mr. Gilroy Fitzthomas Pruitt thinks he's bringing justice to the north. We'll see how long he lasts.

CHAPTER TWENTY SEVEN

A SQUARE PEG IN A ROUND HOLE

"Really, Hunter."

I shouldn't be surprised that Addy is pointing her disapproval in my direction. More than one person has told me I'm a bit blunt for polite company. That's why I generally avoid polite company. Rip drops an armful of hay into one of the barn stalls, and then I send him back for more. I retreated to the barn after my conversation with Mr. Pruitt, hoping to avoid both him and Addy. I was half successful.

"I don't understand why you try so hard to make people dislike you."

Rip steps around Addy to drop his next load of hay. "I'm not good at charming people, Addy. That's why you own a hotel, and I track folks down for money. I'm the square peg in a round hole in your world, and you know it, no matter how hard you try to force me to fit."

She huffs. "Don't you put this on me. You made up your mind on how you felt about him before we sat down at the table. If you gave people a chance, you might have more friends than just me, the reverend, and Miles Lightfellow."

I push Rip toward the hay pile again. Stalks of straw stick out from the holes in the sleeves of his tattered shirt. "You forgot Hayes and Owen. And Miss Kay. And Johnny."

"Hunter, he's a solicitor, and he might be able to help you with the folks up in Paradise."

Rip stops short with an armful of hay, and I look at Addy in disbelief. "Is that what this is about? Me going back to Paradise?"

She presses her lips into a tight line and leans against the barn wall. "I always thought that's what you'd want, eventually. I know it hasn't always treated you well, but maybe things could be different if you really wanted them to be."

I grit my teeth. "Adelaide Sterling, you do beat all. First you nag at me to stay in Grand Junction, now you want me to skedaddle back to Paradise?"

"Of course I want you to stay!" she snaps. "But every time you come down here it's like a piece of you is missing. And something tells me that you're going to have to go back up there to find it. You just get so drawn into yourself sometimes. And then you start to look through people like they aren't there. And I wish you wouldn't."

I gnaw on my lip a bit. I can see her eyes going red around the edges, and she looks away out the barn door. Addy's a worrier when it comes to those she cares about, and it's downright cruel that she ended up as my friend. I give in to the little voice in the back of my head for once and walk over to give her a hug.

She sags against my shoulder like she's been holding herself upright for too long. I pat her back a little, and she takes a shuddery breath.

"We're all alone against the world, Hunter. People like us have to take whatever we can get to stay above the water," she says, real quiet. "I wish there was a place where things weren't so hard for you. And I wish it could be here."

"If I didn't get into some trouble now and then, I think I'd just sit around and eat quail eggs and grow a few chin hairs."

She laughs and pushes away from me, wiping her hands beneath her eyes. Outside, there is a surprised yell. Seconds later, Owen runs giggling into the barn and makes it as far as one of the stall doors. He tries to climb over before Johnny comes in after him and grabs him by the back of his shirt. The older boy's hair and the shoulders of his blue shirt are soaked through. He wrestles Owen off the stall door and down to the hay.

"Come here you little feather-bellied sap," Johnny says in a real tough voice. "I'll get you for that."

The boys tussle on the barn floor for a few minutes, which ends up with both of them wearing enough hay in their hair and clothes to look like scarecrows. Owen half-heartedly calls for help amidst his fits of giggles. Finally, Johnny stumbles back in possession of a pair of small boots. He nods at me and Addy and pushes his black hair out of his face. I notice that he doesn't look as much like a ghost as he did when we first rode into town. His cheeks have some real color in them now.

"Evening, Miss Addy."

She crosses her arms and looks down at Owen. "I'll remind both of you gentlemen that I don't hold with this kind of violence on my property. This is a respectable business."

Johnny's eyes crinkle up with his wide grin. "Yes ma'am. It was self-defense."

"Well in that case I suppose I can let it slide this one time."

"Much obliged to you ma'am."

Addy reaches a hand down and pulls Owen to his bare feet. "How many times have I told you to put socks on your feet before your boots, young man? Get on up to the hotel and ask Miss Kay to give you a bucket of water and a brush. I don't want to see a speck of dirt on your feet when you come in for supper."

Owen tiptoes out of the barn with Addy shooing along behind him. Johnny sets the boots down on the barn floor and starts to shake off a bit of the straw clinging to his clothes. I reach over and pull a long stalk out of the back of his hair.

"Feather-bellied sap?" I say with a pointed look. He shrugs.

"I figured I'd pass it along." He snags his thumbs in his belt loops. "Miss Kay said you'd probably leave in the spring. She said you never stay long."

"Well, she's right on both counts. I'll bunk here for the winter to help around the place and then move on when things thaw out. I never want to outstay my welcome. Besides, bounty hunting requires a bit of moving around."

He nods and puts on his thinking face. "I guess that makes sense. Where will we go next?"

My chest gets a twist in it. I push Rip toward the next stall with his hay. "Johnny, I think it would be-"

"I read a pamphlet about Merenessa once. They say it's a holy city. I'd like to see that." He walks over to the haystack and gathers his own armful.

"Maybe someday you will," I say. "They don't accept magic folks into their Order, if that's what you're hoping. But it seems like you've been doing well enough here in Grand Junction. I figured on you staying here."

He drops the hay over the roan mare's stall door, and she lips at his hair. He dusts off his hands and turns to face me. I see the way he tries to look like a man with his mind made up, and that twist in my chest gets a little tighter.

"I want to go with you."

"You're safe here with Addy. She'll see you get the rest of your education and learn a trade, if you want it."

He studies me. I don't like the way he seems to look right through me the way Reverend Ambrose does. "Miss Addy is a kind lady. But like you said, I'm a necromancer, and nothing is going to change that. So I think it would be best if I stay with you."

I know he can't stay with me. I know that if he does, he'll end up restless and angry and then Addy will have to worry over both of us riding off and getting a bullet through our brains. I remember the last time I left Grand Junction. Addy refused to see me off, and the last thing she said to me was, "Hunter, someday you're going to ride away down that road and that'll be the last time I ever see you alive."

I'm too far gone to leave my road now, but I'll be damned if I let Johnny ride it in my shadow. I start shaking my head, but Johnny beats me to it.

"Grand Junction is too close to Lamarnais, anyway. If my… if he comes looking for me, I think I better be farther south. Or north. I'd like to see the Cathedrals too, the way you talk about them."

"No."

He looks at me with a bit of surprise. My voice sounds dark, the way it does when I've found my mark at the end of a long trail. I hold onto that darkness like a crutch.

"I'm not taking you with me." I step toward him, lean in so he can see my eyes up close. "I brought you here so you'd be safe. You think riding with me is a dandy trip to see the world, but it's a whole lot of blood and dying and getting shot at and spit at and having to watch your back every waking minute so you don't get a knife stuck in it. I can't afford to have a soft kid like you underfoot. We'd both be dead. Sometimes you got to know what you can't do."

He pulls away from me and pulls his hands into tight fists to stop the shakes. "I think you're more scared than me," he says. "I think you're scared because you don't know what's going to happen either."

Turning hard on his boot heel, he strides out of the barn with his shoulders stiffer than a corpse. Pushing back the rage, I slam my knuckles into the closest wood. The roan mare spooks a little and stares at me out of one wild eye with the white rolled back. A dark shadow looms behind me, and I push hard against the magic until I hear Rip's body thud against the opposite wall.

My fingers itch to draw my knives and cut him into a thousand pieces. I should've done it years ago. Addy's right, the reverend is right, and I know Johnny will be right too, in time. They all see through me, and I feel naked inside all the walls I've built. I'd rather drown in the blood of a thousand bounties than face their pity and the fears that they bring up in me.

I huff out a deep breath and watch it gather in a little gray cloud when it meets the chilly air. If I have to, I'll leave before spring. Tipping my head back, I breathe. It's time to start letting them go. It's easier that way.

CHAPTER TWENTY EIGHT

HELLFIRE

It makes me uneasy, the way Martin Price seems to vanish after the soiree. Snakes have this unfriendly habit of hiding away under a bush or a rock, only striking if they're sure of success. Some people do the same. Addy and I don't even smell a whiff of him in town. A couple of his cowhands are regulars at the card tables in the saloon across the street, but they pay us no mind. Addy figures we've given him a reason to behave himself, but I keep an eye on the bushes and rocks. I bruised him a bit, and that surely wounded his pride.Could be that he's biding his time until I ride off in the spring. That thought keeps me awake for more than one night.

Winter closes in on Grand Junction, finally making its way down from the north and spreading some snow over the town. Owen tells Johnny that they're going to make a big snow fort when the drifts pile up. The stagecoaches bring in fewer and fewer travelers to Grand Junction as the weather starts to turn cold. Everyone in town starts wearing their heavy coats and furred muffs, scarves wrapped around their necks and faces. It still makes me smile after all these years. I'll be fine in my regular duster for most of the winter. Addy will force me to wear a scarf and gloves eventually. But while everyone else seems to shrivel up in the cold, it makes me feel more alive.

By the time December rolls around, there's enough snow on the ground that the boys start work on their fort out behind the barn, except now it's not a fort because Owen wants to make a mining operation instead, complete with shadesilver ore veins. Miss Kay starts baking more cookies and pies and thick fruitbreads with the dried stock from earlier in the year. She pushes hot teas and ciders into the boys' hands when they come inside to warm their fingers and noses.

I spend most of my time fixing the fences around the place and repairing things that Addy had left on a list for 'when somebody has a minute to see to it'. I oil door hinges, add a shim to a table leg that is too short, and chop enough firewood to keep the fireplaces burning most of the way through the winter. One of the lumber mill workers, Dan Griffiths, even finds some time to come over and help me with some fresh planks. I settle into a rhythm of sorts, the kind that keeps your body working and your mind quiet. I make Johnny help me with the fences. He's awkward with the tools at first but he's eager to learn.

Then one night after a light snowstorm, hell shows up at the hotel's back door. I polish off one or two of Miss Kay's sugar cookies and cozy myself up in one of the lounge chairs to read a little of the newspaper after most of the hotel has turned in for the night. I start nodding off after reading a particularly thrilling column about the price of beef cattle hitting an all-time low.

I don't know how long my eyes are shut, but I wake with a start amidst a horrible ruckus and yelling. Owen is shaking me by the lapels of my shirt, his wild eyes full of terror. It only takes me a second or two to realize that he's yelling about a fire in the barn and then I'm on my feet and hurtling downstairs and toward the back door.

It's a cold night, blacker than pitch outside with only a sliver of moonlight. Heat hits my face almost as soon as I leap off the back steps. Big angry flames lick out of the back corner of the barn where the hay pile is, snapping through the wooden beams and up into the air with a crackling roar. Owen starts frantically working the pump, getting a trickle of water going into one of the slop buckets.

There are six horses in the barn, and I hear their terrified screams as the fire spreads. The doors have been flung wide and smoke billows out through the opening. Pulling my shirt over my nose, I plunge into the haze. I can hardly see a thing, but I feel my way along the stall doors until the fire overtakes the smoke and I can see the back half of the barn is completely alight.

The roan mare is halfway out of her stall, eyes rolled wide and pulling back against the halter rope. Johnny is there, putting all his weight against the line and begging her above the sound of the flames to follow him out. The heat sears my skin, but I pull my neckerchief out of my pocket and reach up to wrap it around the mare's face. Blind now, she drops her head and I slap a hand against her haunches. She leaps forward, dragging Johnny down the aisle and out the doors.

There isn't enough time. I throw General's door open and wrap an empty feed sack around his eyes. Someone's voice screams at me through the roar of the fire, but I can't stop or the horses will die. A shower of sparks rains down around me and the chestnut gelding. I throw my arm up to protect my own face and pull the trembling horse out of his stall. He follows me, his steady nature saving both our lives as boards crash into the empty space behind us.

I shove the gelding's lead rope into someone's hands and

push back into the smoke. Johnny must have come back in for another horse, and someone else is with us now. I narrowly miss being run over by a terrified carriage horse and head for another stall. A burning beam has fallen in front of the door and the flames are reaching the barrier too fast, too greedy. I reach out to the tether and pull.

Out of the whirling fire and clouds of smoke, Rip appears like a demon of the Dark After, wreathed in flames that try to grip the nothingness of his skin. Black mist pours off his body, and his eyes flicker as red firelight illuminates the dead veins spidering across his face.

He wraps his arms around the beam and lifts, throwing it back into the inferno behind him. My will flows through his hands as he grabs hold of the door's top edge and rips it free of its hinges. The terrified animal inside is succumbing to the heavy smoke, the eyes glassy as its legs begin to buckle. I throw the lead rope around its neck and duck as something drops over my head. Needles of hot pain trickle down my neck and back. The horse stumbles out after me, Rip's body pushing it from behind. The heat is unbearable, and my vision blurs.

There are hands on my shoulders and elbows pulling me out into the winter air and patting down the back of my clothes. The lead rope disappears, and I'm surprised to see the red welts on my palms. Someone says my name.

"Hunter! Oh Almighty save us. Hunter!"

Addy's black hair is a wild mane around her pale face. She's crying and holding my cheeks between her palms. I try to answer her, but my voice comes out as a raspy croak. We're being pulled further away from the barn amidst shouts and the roar of the fire. Beams crack, and the walls collapse in a bloom of flame and sparks. I can see a small crowd of people, some dressed and some in their nightclothes, all carrying buckets.

There's a line of them, passing water from the pump to the dwindling remains of the barn. It does no good, but they stubbornly toss the bucketfuls into the blaze.

I look around for Johnny. He's sitting a few feet away from me, black with soot and smoke and coughing. Miss Kay is sitting with her arms around him, wrapped in a thick knitted shawl that she's using to try and wipe his face. Owen is still madly working the pump as if he can stop the fire with his own small hands.

Addy leaves me and grabs her own bucket, throwing the contents at the giant bonfire devouring the pile of beams and planks. Most of the hotel boarders come out to help, and Gilroy Pruitt leads the efforts of the firefighting line, handing buckets to Hayes, who is closest to the flames. The barn is gone. They just need to keep it from spreading to the hotel.

The cold air feels sharp against my reddened skin. I grimace at the rope burns on my palms and fall into a fit of coughing that strains my freshly healed ribs. Rip stands silent nearby. There's not a mark on him from the fire. It occurs to me that without Rip both the horse and I would surely be lying beneath a pile of burning rubble. I cough again, and bile rises in my throat. I feel like a rag doll, limbs loose and numb.

"Hunter?"

Miss Kay holds out a glass of water. Her spectacles are askew, and she must have gathered her hair in a rush. The loose bun has slid down lopsided on her head. My eyes are stinging and watering so much it's hard to see her.

Between the cold and the rope burns, my hands don't want to close around the cup. She holds the rim to my lips and gives me a drink, fussing over me. "Oh sure, you're a right mess. Let me get some herbs and wraps for those."

She hurries into the hotel. My voice comes back enough that I can manage a few gravelly words in Johnny's direction.

"You alright, kid?"

He coughs and spits phlegm onto the ground before hunching over himself and laying down in the snow. "I'll live," he rasps. Scratches cover his arms, and I'm willing to bet he'll have a few nasty burns to deal with. "Hunter, someone must have set the barn on fire. I took the lantern in with me."

Even though he's seen some of the worst in people through his life, Johnny still says it with the kind of simple surprise that comes to folks who can't believe someone else capable of evil. I cough and nod slowly, watching the line of determined firefighters holding the ground between the barn and the hotel with their little buckets of water.

It seems the snake has slithered out of its hiding place.

CHAPTER TWENTY NINE

SNAKES AND THREATS

"Now, Miss Sterling, I understand you are upset about the loss of your property. The townsfolk will do everything they can to help you out until you can get another barn built come spring. I've told you that I will investigate this and find out if anyone was behind the fire. Trust the law to do its job. You've been through a terrible night. You ought to take the day to rest."

It wouldn't surprise me if Addy clubbed the sheriff over the head with his own revolver butt. She lifts her chin and stares at him with disgust written in every line of her face. She stubbornly insisted on coming to talk to him this morning.

"Trust the law?" she bites at the words. "Sheriff Molby, I want you to investigate Martin Price and his men. I want you to find out where they were last night."

The sheriff has the audacity to look annoyed. "Ma'am, there is no more reason for you to suspect Mr. Price than anyone else in Grand Junction."

My smoke-damaged lungs rattle as I drag in an angry breath. "That's where you're wrong, Sheriff. After the altercation during Addy's gathering a couple months ago, he made threats against both of us."

Sheriff Molby isn't a stupid man, but he has what Pops would call the 'turtle sickness'. Once he's got his mind made up about how a thing should be, he'll pop the veins in his neck pulling his head back into that thick shell. When he looks at me, I see just how much he'd rather I was somewhere else.

"A drunken exchange without weapons or violence is hardly a concerning threat. And from what I was told, Mr. Price has a better complaint against you. I will investigate the fire with Deputy Skinner, like I told you before, Miss Sterling. But I will have to ask you to stay out of the way and let me do my job."

Addy jams her hands back into her muff. "If you did your job, Sheriff, I wouldn't be in your way. Perhaps someone ought to speak to the mayor about the way you seem to ignore the concerns of Grand Junction's citizens."

She's pushed him too far, and I can see that we aren't going to get anywhere else with the man as soon as his eyes narrow. He points toward the door of his office.

"I'm going to have to ask you to be on your way, Miss Sterling. If you come up with actual evidence, come back and see me. And until then, be careful the company you keep," he says. "You've a good reputation with the people here."

I don't know if Addy is going to burst into a rage or into tears as we leave the worn building and tromp back toward the hotel. A bit of both, as it turns out. She swipes one gloved hand beneath her eyes.

"Insufferable man," she says. "All this talk of law and order and Molby wouldn't know true justice if it hung him from the gallows."

The idea of justice has always confused me a bit. Men like Molby and Pruitt and Hector McBride sit behind their desks and promise to uphold it, but in the end, it's only their vision of justice that wins out. Seems an awful dangerous thing, to put justice in the hands of folks who take the word of one person or another because of prejudice or money. I settle my sore palms on the butts of the revolvers at my hips. Even if I had caught Martin Price or his men red-handed in the act of setting fire to Addy's barn, they'd expect to see justice done their way. The law-and-order way. That doesn't sit right in my gut.

Addy would just say I'm too savage for civilization, and maybe she's right. Like I told Mr. Pruitt, law and order is different where I'm from. Gerdy points her gun at me, and I point mine at her, and then we decide maybe we don't want to die today.

"You're thinking awful hard. Don't hurt yourself," says Addy with a small smile.

"Thinking maybe I ought to saddle up and go for a ride."

She slows down and side-eyes me. "Don't put yourself in any danger on my account, Hunter. If Martin was behind the fire, we don't know how he would react if he saw you on his property."

"I'll take Rip along."

"Bullets may not kill him but they'll certainly kill you. Luck won't save you forever."

We turn at the front steps of the hotel and find Mr. Pruitt waiting for us in the lobby. He is examining the oil painting on the left wall, a blue and white checkered tablecloth under a white bowl of peaches. The fruit looks good enough to eat, and I wish I'd taken Miss Kay up on her offer of breakfast.

"Miss Sterling," Mr. Pruitt greets us, removing his bowler hat. He looks a bit less stuffy today. I certainly can't fault him for cowardice after seeing him jump in to help with the fire.

Addy smiles and bobs in an unnecessary curtsey. "Mr. Pruitt, thank you so much for your help last evening. I don't know what we would have done if you all hadn't been there."

Mr. Pruitt shakes his head. "It was my pleasure to be of assistance after your hospitality these past weeks. Besides, my role was minimal compared with the bravery of others." He reaches out a hand toward me. "Hunter, I believe we may have stepped off on the wrong foot when I first arrived. Consider this an olive branch."

I take his hand and am surprised when he shakes it gently to avoid troubling my burns. "I'll accept that, Mr. Pruitt."

He turns back to Addy. "I believe I am going to purchase the old barbershop building that Mr. Conway is selling a few doors down. I'll need to do some repairs, but I believe I should be able to set up my practice within a few weeks. If some nefarious conduct comes to light in the investigation of the barn fire, I would be pleased to assist you."

"That's so kind of you, Mr. Pruitt. I may take you up on that."

He places the hat back on top of his head and tips it, leaving us alone in the lobby. Addy pulls her scarf away from her neck, her cheeks still rosy from the cold outside.

"I don't think you should go."

I'm already a few steps toward the kitchen. "I'll take that into consideration," I reply with a wink. I'm rewarded with the sound of her muttered complaints following me as I enter the warmth of the kitchen. Miss Kay is there with a hot cup of tea for me.

"There now, you need to be drinking plenty of water and tea, love. All that smoke in your lungs was a bad thing," she says sternly. "It's nothing to be taking lightly, and that's for sure."

The tea does perk me up a bit, but before long I'm heading out to the pens where the horses are being kept. The roan mare doesn't like me catching her. She's more jumpy than usual, and

I guess I can allow her that after nearly burning to death. My saddle is a charred heap somewhere in the rubble, so I climb up on her back with nothing but the halter and lead line tied around for reins. Rip has a little dusting of snow sitting on his head and shoulders, but it trickles off as I pull him out of the pen after me. Little bits of cold sneak up through the sleeves of my duster and sting the raw red skin still healing from the fire.

My guns ride comfortably around my waist beneath my knife belt. The mare doesn't like me sitting on her without a saddle, so every few steps she hitches her back legs up a little and pins her ears flat. I ignore her and she settles as we ride through the main street of town and out the south side toward the big cattle ranch a couple miles away. I keep Rip closer than usual, and the mare doesn't much appreciate it. But I don't trust Price and his men farther than I can throw them, which admittedly isn't as far as I'd like.

The cowhands have brought the herds closer to the buildings for the winter, and the pens are full to bursting with fat, lowing Lorray beef cattle from the big ranches around Hannesburg. The hides make a pool of brown-black against the surrounding white. A two-story house sends a steady stream of smoke wafting into the sky from the brick chimney. One cowhand notices me and rides over to the fence.

"Howdy, stranger," he says. He curiously looks at the roan mare and the lack of saddle. Then he stares a long while at Rip. "Bit cold for a ride, ain't it?"

"I'm looking for your boss," I say quietly. "Up at the house?"

He nods. "Should be."

I ride on without saying another word. This house isn't as grand as the one Hector McBride built in Silver City. It looks like someone sort of fancied up the original farmhouse after the outfit got bigger than a simple homestead. It's good land around these parts. Decent grazing for big herds around the hills with the occasional stream, plenty of space for the pens nearer the barns and house for winter. Whoever settled here first knew what they were after.

I tie the roan mare to a small tree in the front yard, and walk up the porch steps to the door. The old floorboards creak under my boots. One knock on the door, and it opens, as if he's been expecting me. Martin Price appears, that self-satisfied smirk fixed on his face like he's nailed it there, hoping I won't notice the look of fear that passes through his eyes. The presence of the giant corpse behind me makes him go a little green in the face.

"Morning, Mr. Price."

"You're either brave or stupid to show up on my land," he says, still trying to convince me or himself that he's not knocking his knees together a little.

"Thought I'd come by and see this cattle ranch I've heard so much about. The way the folks in town talk about it, I figured it was a little piece of the Holy After and came to see for myself."

He narrows his eyes. "Well, now you've seen it. I don't need you over here spooking my cattle with your filthy corpse."

I lean back against one of the porch railings. "He's not a corpse the way you think he is. He's got no smell of death on him. And things that would drop a man like you deader than a fencepost go right through him. Bullets…" I pause. "Fire."

"I heard about Miss Sterling's barn. Real shame," he says. He licks his lips and crosses his arms over his chest.

"Lucky we saved all the horses. But that barn was a fine building. And the funny thing is, we can't for the life of us figure out how it got started." I wave one hand out toward the buildings near the cow pens. "You'd best be watching your own barns, Mr. Price. It would be a shame to lose part of your fine establishment here."

Price glowers at me like a spent ember trying to pluck up enough heat for a flame. "Oh, I assure you I will be vigilant."

"That's good." I shift my weight back into the heel of my right foot. "If you hear anything about someone who might know a thing about how that fire started, I trust you'll be the good neighbor and tell us what you find out."

He sneers. "It was probably one of those half-grown street rats you keep around as pets."

Patient, I push back the side of my duster and rest my palm gently on the hilt of one of my shadesilver knives. "What I do know, Mr. Price, is that I'd hate to be the man responsible. Miss Sterling has a kind heart. You'll find me less forgiving."

"You can't threaten me. You're not the law."

A broad smile pulls at the corners of my mouth. "I think you're banking on that very fact, Mr. Price. But I'm a bounty hunter. I'm the one they send when the law doesn't want to get its hands dirty."

With a tip of my hat, I leave the porch and pull myself up behind the roan mare's withers. She tosses her head and pulls at my hard hold on the makeshift reins. Rip shuffles after me, and I turn my back on Martin Price. No gunshots ring out after me, but I know that in his mind he's pulling a trigger.

CHAPTER THIRTY

THE EASIEST THING IN THE WORLD

A few days after the fire, puffs of black smoke still curl above the pile of charred beams and walls. Mrs. Gentry from the boardinghouse down the street offers to take our six horses into her barn. It's not as spacious as Addy's was, but it'll put a roof over their heads and straw under their feet. Sheriff Molby does his rounds asking questions about the fire. He meets with everyone who was in the hotel that night. In fact, he spends all his time in the hotel and poking around the smoking ruins. Nobody is surprised when his half-hearted efforts produce a whole heap of nothing.

He talks to Owen and Johnny at length, asking them over and over again if they had tried smoking or had taken a lamp back out to the barn. Of course they hadn't, but he doesn't seem to believe them and keeps asking until Addy finally tells him to talk to somebody else. The atmosphere in the hotel gets more and more sour. Even Addy's Charm can't fix the frustration building like a simmering soup pot. Miss Kay bakes so many cakes, pies, cookies, and scones that she could feed the whole town. Hayes polishes the bar counter until it can see its own face in the gleam. Johnny and Owen start a new snow fort since their last one melted away next to the barn. But this time, they dig and scoop to have something to do. The fun's all gone out of it.

Mr. Pruitt moves into his new office, fixing the place with a brightly painted new sign with his name in fancy letters and 'solicitor' underneath it in big bold print. There's a small apartment above the shop space, so he moves his things out of his room at the hotel. I think Addy is sorry to see him go.

Even when Martin Price rides into town and starts playing cards at the saloon, still Sheriff Molby doesn't seem to take any interest in him. It's nothing new. I tell Addy about the way Hector McBride has Sheriff Brady tucked in his back pocket with a few coins. Money and iron do the talking. Sheriff Molby and Deputy Skinner can't take on the whole Price outfit by themselves. And even if they could, they didn't pin on their tin stars to face any real trouble. Not the kind that could get them run out of town or killed.

A stagecoach brings in a few boarders, and Addy brightens a little with some new folks to fuss over. I'm happy for her, but the restlessness in my bones starts to become an unbearable itch. Grand Junction isn't the type of town where I'll find much bounty hunting work, but I consider going out onto the blinding-white prairie to see if I can chase down one of the poorly drawn faces on Molby's wanted posters.

I find myself hoping that Price tries something else and gives me a reason to go after him. But he does nothing except play poker and drink at the saloon. Addy hires a couple of the men in town to help Hayes and I lay a foundation for the new barn. Pops always did allow that I worked hard when I set my mind to it, so I throw myself into the work, only stopping to eat because Miss Kay threatens to use salt instead of sugar in the next cookies she gives me if I don't take better care of myself. I think she's just mad that I stay lean as a fence rail despite my excessive consumption of her food. Rip proves to be as useful lifting newly cut beams as he is lifting ones that are on fire. The men are skittish around him, but they just give him a wide berth.

Somewhere in between the work and falling exhausted into my bed, I manage to get another letter written to the reverend. I tell him how Miss Kay has fattened Johnny right up, and he's working like a man now. I tell him about the fire and Martin Price, and Gilroy Fitzthomas Pruitt. I tell him how Gilroy invited Addy to see his new office as soon as he got everything fixed up nice. It feels good to get it all off my chest.

The winter takes a nasty turn just as we're putting up the roof beams of the barn. A snowstorm rolls in, howling and hurling itself against the windows and doors and shrieking along the outside walls. On the second night, Addy knocks on my door. She's wearing long underwear under the white nightdress and holding a candlestick. She sits on the end of my bed, and I put a small strip of leather in my book to mark the page.

"You're reading?" she says, surprised.

I shrug and set the green clothbound book to one side. "It's one of those adventure stories you gave to Johnny a few weeks back. I figured I'd see what all the fuss is about."

Her black braid sits over her shoulder like a thick horse tail, tied with a white ribbon. "Mrs. Gentry finished that new dress with the green satin you brought for me. It turned out real pretty. I thought I might wear it for the next party at the mayor's house. Or maybe come spring for another soiree here at the hotel."

"What are you going to do about Price?"

She sets the candlestick on the trunk next to my bed. "I don't know. The only thing any of us found out was about those two cowhands being at the saloon that night. Hayes said they were rip-roaring drunk. Gilroy says he will have a court case drawn up faster than a blink if Price tries anything. I'm just tired of it all, Hunter. I'm tired of feeling like there are always people in the world that want to see me fail."

I smile and fold my hands over my belly. "It's Gilroy now, is it?"

Her eyes flash with that famous Adelaide Sterling spark. "Oh you hush. Don't even start with me, Hunter. He's been kind and thoughtful."

It's too good to pass up, especially when I catch a glimpse of her cheeks going a little rosy. "A kind and thoughtful eligible bachelor who wants to save the uncivilized and lawless of the world. Adelaide, I do believe you're out of your league."

She grabs a small pillow and throws it at me. "You're worse than an old gossip, you know that? We're friendly, and that's all."

"I don't recollect Gilroy Fitzthomas Pruitt inviting any other women around to see the new office and his freshly painted sign. In fact, I don't recollect as he asked a single other soul."

Addy rolls her eyes in a huff. "Hunter, you know I'm not interested in being paraded around on a buggy and stepping out with someone like a fresh-faced doll. I'm a businesswoman, and Gilroy is a businessman. I think we've just found an appreciation for each other."

"I asked Pops once why he married my mama," I say. "He said that when you find the right person, everything just sort of falls into place, like a nicely oiled gate latch."

Addy bursts out laughing, and I glare at her. I don't know what's so funny about that. It always seemed to make a whole lot of sense to me.

"Fine then, like something else," I grumble.

"I'm glad you're here, Hunter," she says, wiping her eyes.

"Nobody makes me laugh like you do. Goodness knows I need it. Ever since the fire it feels like I'm just waiting for something bad to happen. I've never been so nervous in my life."

I reach out and pat her hand on top of the knitted blanket. "If it was Price, he won't get away with it again. If he so much as pokes his nose in the front door, I'll be there with some cold silver and iron."

Addy crosses her arms and looks around the room with a sort of motherly affection. "I'd protect this place with my life if I had to. It's everything I have, and I built it even when everyone told me I couldn't. It's a bit extravagant, but I wouldn't have it any other way."

"You're a bit on the extravagant side too," I say.

"Hunter, you're still walking around wearing the same duster you had on when I met you eight years ago. Of course you think I'm extravagant. I change my clothes every day."

I curl my lip a little at that, but I know she's just looking to get a rise out of me. I do, in fact, change my clothes every day when I'm in civilized company. Most of my clothes just look the same because I don't see the point in having duds in every color of the rainbow. A plain shirt and vest with some well-made trousers suit me just fine.

"Johnny seems kind of quiet lately," Addy says, interrupting my thoughts on the color of my shirts. I start to say something about how Johnny is always quiet, but she's right. He's been almost ghostly quiet the past week or two. He goes out with Owen sometimes or helps Miss Kay in the kitchen. Once I even saw Hayes teaching him how to make the special lime and rum drink at the bar counter. But whenever I ask him to go out and practice his necromancy with me, he always seems to have some excuse.

"I think he's sore at me."

"At you? Why?"

It's a guess, but I think it's a pretty good one. "I told him that I didn't plan on taking him along with me in the spring."

Addy raises one eyebrow. "Don't tell me you're surprised he'd be mad at you for that?"

"I'm not, but I don't like the way that everyone seems to think I'm cruel for refusing to take a green kid along with me to get shot at when I go back to bounty hunting. He has no idea what that life is like. If I'm trying to keep him alive, we'll both be deader than a doornail before we get paid for our first mark."

"You know that bounty hunting isn't the only thing you're good at, Hunter."

"I don't much fancy sewing dresses."

She's not interested in my cheek. "You know I'm right."

"Not a lot of folks wanting to hire a necromancer, Addy," I say. "Especially not one dragging around a big corpse like Rip."

I know the look of pained frustration that crosses her face then, because I've seen it many times since I first showed up on her doorstep with Rip in tow. She'll never understand why I won't let him go. She doesn't understand it because she doesn't carry the burden. It's the easiest thing in the world for a person to let go of something that wasn't done to them. They'll tell you what would be best, and how you can live for more. But it's not their wound that's bleeding out.

CHAPTER THIRTY ONE

THE DARK AFTER
CATCHES UP

Pops always used to say that the Dark After has a habit of chasing after people until they finally gasp their final breath and drop into the grave. Some people drag it along after themselves, and others just can't seem to avoid it no matter how hard they try.

I sit in my room reading the last pages of the adventure story when the next stagecoach arrives at the depot. I have a good line of sight to the platform from the window above my desk, so I glance up when the lathered team of horses pull in. An older man steps down from the carriage and then three more men appear behind him. They all wear traveling coats and holsters on their hips. Something about them keeps my eye as they walk up to the depot window to talk to the ticket seller. The man inside says something to them and points down the street. Their hats cover most of their faces, but one strikes me as familiar.

The book can wait. Something has the hair on the back of my neck standing straight up, and I buckle my gun belt around my waist before heading down the hallway to the main staircase. Down in the lobby, everything is quiet this early in the morning. A few boarders are eating a hearty breakfast of sausage hash in the dining room. Mabel gives me a sour look from behind the desk. I think that's just how her face is.

The sound of boots on the boardwalk precedes the arrival of the three men through the front doors of the hotel. As soon as they tip their hats, I know why my hair stood on end. The first two men I've never seen before, but their faces seem eerily familiar. The third man is none other than Paulie Torrence. As soon as he sees me, he gives me a wide grin and slaps his thigh.

"Hunter, in the flesh! Well, I'll be bloody fluxed to the After."

If only that were true. I can't imagine what has Paulie Torrence swaggering into Grand Junction, but I doubt I'm going to like the answer. His two companions are also eyeing me now, their similarities possibly marking them as father and son.

"You running tours of the Territories now, Torrence?" I ask. "Seems a bit too tame for you."

He shrugs, tapping the fingers of his right hand against the butt of his gun. "Just thought I'd get out and see the world. You understand. Can't bring myself to stay in one place."

"This the bounty hunter?" the older of the two companions asks, still eyeing me with a bit too much ice in his gaze. I keep my hands calm and relaxed at my sides and meet his eyes. An uncomfortable truth is settling in my stomach as I look at the eyes and the tilt of his cheekbones. His cleanly trimmed beard and mustache, the clean and fresh shirt. I've seen this man's face before, but a kinder and younger version. He steps forward.

"I was told that you took my son."

I want to trade the ugly truth for a pleasant lie, but there it is. "I'll need a name first, mister," I say evenly. Even Mabel seems to realize that there's a chill in the air, because she gets up from behind the desk and hurries upstairs.

"Jediah Holt," says the man. "From Lemarnais."

"Lemarnais." I roll the name of the city off the end of my

tongue lazily. "I haven't been there for a few years."

He scowls, and I already know enough about him to distrust his patience. There's not a chance in the Dark After that I'm going to let him near Johnny. Far as I'm concerned, any man who raises a hand against their child isn't enough of a father to have any claim.

I gesture toward the young man behind him. "This your son?"

"I have two sons, and you took one of them with you out of Silver City a few months back. His name is John, and I'm here to take him along back home."

"Seems to me if he's run off maybe he doesn't want to go along back home," I say. Neither Jediah or his son seem like the gunslinging type, but I'm not fool enough to think Paulie Torrence wouldn't hesitate to shoot a couple holes in Addy's hotel. Or me. I reach through the tethers and feel Rip's presence at the other end. I won't bring him in unless I need to.

Jediah Holt is done pretending to be polite. "Listen, I know what you are and what you want with my son. You'll turn him over or I'll come back with the sheriff and a warrant."

"Don't make things hard for yourself, Hunter," says Paulie Torrence. "Mr. McBride sent me along to be sure the boy is returned to his family." The placating tone he uses makes my trigger finger twitch. If McBride is tied up in all this, there's a reason. A reason I can guess all too easily.

The sound of Addy's heels tap across the wooden floor and then thud onto the carpet. Mabel follows her like a stern shadow. Instantly the room feels softer, and the tension fades out from under my skin. I shoot her a surprised glance, but she doesn't return it. Her Charm fills the room like an invisible blanket, suggesting more than demanding an urgent calm. I've never felt her use it so intensely before.

Her smile seems a little less warm than usual. "Gentlemen,

welcome. My name is Adelaide Sterling, and I am the proprietor here. What seems to be the problem?"

Paulie Torrence pulls his stiff new wide brim off his head and slicks his hair back with a quick bob of his head toward Addy. "Ma'am, it's our pleasure. We've just come to return a runaway to his family and were informed that he has been staying here at your fine hotel. We will collect the boy and be on our way directly."

Addy tilts her head slightly in Mr. Holt's direction, a bit of steel in her eyes. "Forgive me, but if there is indeed a boy here from your family, I will need to discuss it with him to confirm that you are his family and he will be safe in your care."

"I've had enough of this," mutters Jediah Holt gruffly as he steps forward to push past Addy. "Where are you keeping the boy?"

Two strides and I'm in front of him, blocking his path toward the back of the hotel. We're nearly the same height, and he flinches away from the palm I hold up to stop him, eyeing my hand as if it might burn.

"You have to be dead for my power to work on you, Mr. Holt," I say quietly.

"Don't touch me, Soulless. I have a contract." He pulls a folded piece of paper from the inside pocket of his duster and waves it up in the air for all of us to see. "I will not leave this town until I have the boy."

I don't want to know, but I ask anyway. "What contract?"

"He's been contracted to work with Mr. McBride and learn an honest trade." He lowers his voice and leans as close to me as he dares. "And I will not have any son of mine in the company of a corpse defiler. Your kind belong in the Ice Wastes with the Shades."

A half-smile curves across my mouth, but there's no amusement in it. "He's a son of yours now? I imagine the contract is only valid if you admit he's your flesh and blood."

"Hunter."

I step back when I feel Addy's touch on my arm. She holds out her hand. "May I see the contract?"

Holt thrusts the paper at her, annoyed. Addy skims over the words written on it and then folds it carefully. "Thank you, Mr. Holt. There is a solicitor here in town with expertise in such matters. If it is agreeable to you, I'd like to have him take a look at this before any further decisions are made. It is important to make sure everything is as it should be."

My stomach drops when I hear familiar soft footsteps from the back hallway approaching us. There's nothing I can do. Johnny appears from the doorway to the kitchen carrying a pitcher of water, and his eyes widen in surprise as he looks between us all. Finally he sees his father. His face loses half its color and leaves him with that same ghostly pallor that he wore when I first met him in the woods. Ice clinks in the pitcher, and I expect the glass to shatter on the floor.

"…Pa."

Holt sneers at us, ignoring the boy staring fearfully in his direction. "So he is here. You can take that contract to any solicitor you please, Miss Sterling. I'll be back for my boy directly. And if this Soulless creature attempts to stop me, I'll have the sheriff along."

He whirls toward the door, followed by his son, who throws a glare back toward Johnny as they leave. Paulie sweeps his hat to the side and gives Addy a smile darkened by yellow teeth.

"Pleasure meeting you, ma'am. Hunter-"

"Don't say anything you don't mean, Paulie Torrence."

He pats his hat back down onto his head. "Between you and me, I'd like to see what those guns of yours are worth when they're not pointed at a man's back."

CHAPTER THIRTY TWO

CONTRACTS

"I'm sorry to be the bearer of unfortunate tidings, Adelaide, but this contract is binding. Mr. Holt is the boy's legal guardian, for better or worse. He is only sixteen, and this contract would hold him legally until he turns eighteen. We could possibly send for a circuit judge to review the terms to buy some time, but I don't see any other loopholes."

Gilroy sets the paper on his desk and pulls the spectacles from his nose with a sigh. Addy sits rigid in one of the chairs across from him. Johnny slumps next to her in the other. It's only been an hour since his father walked out of the hotel, and already all the light has gone out of him. I stalk back and forth in the back of the small office, half tempted to get Johnny in the saddle and ride south. Rip hovers behind me, motionless. I've kept him close since the moment Holt left the hotel. Addy looks more tired than I've ever seen her.

"Thank you for looking at this, Mr. Pruitt. I have little hope for the Sheriff to be of any help to us, but perhaps I can persuade the mayor to give Johnny some asylum until we can find another way to protect him."

"The boy's right here, Addy," I say shortly. "Let him speak for himself."

She grips her gloves so hard that her knuckles turn white. "I'm not the enemy, Hunter. We all want a way out of this."

I've chewed my lower lip to ribbons. The coppery taste of my own blood fills my mouth as I suck at the latest wound. I could take Paulie Torrence. I could get the drop on him, if I can just get him running his mouth. He's a fast draw, but Miles Lightfellow was a good teacher. I shake my head. My first instinct to fight has gotten me into trouble more than once, and I know that if Torrence were to drop me in the street, no one else would be able to stand up to him. Pops would say that folks who think with their trigger finger are the first ones buried.

No, better that Johnny and I ride for the south as soon as night falls. With some providence on our side, we'd have a couple hours head start if they mean to follow us. Paulie Torrence may be a fast gunman, but he's no tracker and I know how to disappear.

"We'll leave when it gets dark," I say. I look up at Rip, and his dead eyes stare straight back at me. For once, I don't feel the cold shiver up my spine.

Addy turns to me with a pinched expression. "Hunter, the first place Mr. Holt went after he left the hotel was straight to the sheriff. If you take Johnny with you now, you'll be on a wanted poster by tomorrow. Let me talk to the mayor."

"The longer we wait, the less chance we have to make a clean break. Holt is one thing, but he's got McBride on that contract. If he gets his hands on you, kid, he won't give you a choice. He wants a necromancer, and if he can't have me, he'll make do with you."

Johnny picks at his thumbnails. "He can't be worse than going home."

I stop my pacing to put a hand on his shoulder. "You said you never wanted to bring anything back. Remember your sister? McBride thinks it's as simple as weighing out a few pinches of shadesilver. He sees the numbers of things, the business gains. You won't be a person to him."

"I wasn't much of a person to my father either."

He's giving up, and it burns me. My comforting hand turns into a firm grip on his jacket, and I pull him up out of the chair. "You're not a coward. Don't act like one."

There's no hope in his honest gaze. "Then what do I do?"

"Addy, if you're going to talk to the mayor, you best do it now. If he won't step in, I'll have Johnny out of Grand Junction as soon as it's dark enough to hide us. They'll expect us to run, but if I can get a head start they won't find us."

Gilroy shakes his head. "I can't condone that, Hunter. Better that we try to handle this the way of the law. I'll send for the circuit judge."

"No offense meant, Gilroy Pruitt, but it doesn't matter if you condone it or not. If Holt is Johnny's legal guardian, then he can take him anywhere while we sit and wait for the judge to mosey on over here. He'll be locked in McBride's vault by then."

Addy isn't convinced either. "If they're expecting you to run, they'll be watching us. You won't get out of town before they catch you."

"We move the horses."

"What?"

"The barn is nearly finished. If we move the horses back, they'll expect us to ride out from the hotel. We'll take two mounts from the boardinghouse stables. I'll leave money for them."

"If you take him, you're on the wrong side of the law," Gilroy tells me. "They could claim that Johnny is the victim of a kidnapping."

I shrug. "Pruitt, I'm a necromancer. I've been on the wrong side of everything since I was born. My own neighbors wanted me dead when I was still shorter than a fencepost. If the law is behind men like Jediah Holt and Hector McBride, maybe I don't mind being on the wrong side."

He doesn't have anything to say to that. I know he's got his heart set on the law being helpful to folks, but he's not me. Our best chance is to get clear of Grand Junction and lose Holt in the miles between here and one of the big cities. But I can't expect Johnny to act like a man if I don't treat him like one. So I let him have the last word.

"I can get you out of here, Johnny. We'll go south, I know folks in every town from here to St. Albane. It's your choice."

He looks up at me. "You really think you can do it?"

I'm not about to add my doubts to his. "Sure."

"What about Rip?"

"He'll come along with us."

Johnny casts a skeptical glance over the massive corpse behind me. "He'll slow us down."

"I'll tie him to a packhorse if I have to."

The boy sighs. "Alright. Let's do it."

"I can have Miss Kay pack some food for you," says Addy. She blinks a few times to chase away tears. I reach out for her hand, and she tucks her smooth palm against my calloused one.

"We won't take anything from the hotel, Addy. I don't want them to say you helped us."

Addy rolls her eyes. "Someday you come back and stay with me for good, y'hear?" she scolds me half-heartedly. "Once you've finally gotten into enough scrapes to satisfy yourself."

I nod. Gilroy hands the contract back to me, and I tuck it into my duster pocket, ignoring the urge to rip it into thousands of tiny pieces right there on his waxed floor. I'm already hours ahead in my mind, following every possible track we might go. There are a few things I need back at the hotel, but I'll have to throw off the urgency riding my shoulders.

The street is clear and quiet. Gilroy's front door swings open silently, not even a squeak. It's snowing again, lazy flakes drifting down to freshen up the dirty white blanket on the ground. I'm irritated to see the Sheriff standing on the front porch of the hotel with the Holts lurking behind him. I don't have time for this. A sigh sends a big puff of smoky air out in front of my face.

"Already seen the contract, Sheriff. Mr. Pruitt is looking it over."

The Sheriff pulls his duster aside and produces his own piece of paper, holding it up between his fingers. "Hunter, this is a warrant from Sheriff Brady in Silver City. You're under arrest for the murder of Ulysses Hadley."

CHAPTER THIRTY THREE

A DEAL WITH THE DEVIL

Murder. It's pure stupidity, and I believe it the minute the words come out of Sheriff Molby's mouth. It's simple math that Hector McBride would have this farce in his back pocket to keep me from messing up his contract. I should've seen it coming a mile away. He let me run once already. And I should know better than anybody that McBride doesn't let anyone run.

My hand slips toward my gun belt before I know what I'm doing. Rip crouches behind me, ready to spring forward. Sheriff Molby goes for his gun, and for one breath I see myself drawing iron and squeezing the trigger. But I've heard the soft step behind me, the click of a gun hammer being pulled back. And it's not pointed at me.

Over my shoulder, I have a perfect view of Paulie Torrence with his arm locked around Johnny's neck. Without the gun barrel pressed into Johnny's ribs, it almost seems a familiar gesture, like they are brothers about to have a tussle. Rip slowly turns away from the Sheriff and faces Paulie Torrence.

"Keep your corpse where it is now," says Torrence in that chipper tone I wish I could rip out of his throat. "One more step and Johnny Boy might lose an ear. Maybe a finger."

I squint over at the Sheriff. "That warrant also say that Hadley drew first?"

"You can say your piece in front of the judge. But I've got a warrant to serve and I intend to bring you in." A pair of handcuffs dangle from his hand, but he's still hesitant to come closer to me. There's no sense in me trying to argue that the warrant he's holding is a lie. He probably thinks Brady's done him a favor, cleaning up the streets of Grand Junction.

Torrence is still grinning at me. He was a witness to Hadley's death, but he'll side with McBride. Probably gets a new silver trimmed saddle out of the deal. I talk to him over my shoulder, still watching the sheriff with my hand loose and ready by my hip.

"You hurt that boy, Paulie, and you'll be missing more than a finger."

Sheriff Molby looks jumpy, like he might just go and shoot me for breathing. He'd be dead before his iron cleared the holster, but Torrence won't hesitate to make good on his promise. I start calculating in my head. The circuit judge won't be here for a week or two, and by then Johnny will be locked up with McBride. If I'm being arrested for Hadley's murder, chances are McBride intends to see me swing for it too. The only other person who could stand as a witness is Jo Farstep, and she could be anywhere in the Territories by now.

"I'm not going to ask you again," says the sheriff. He lets out a sharp whistle, and a group of horses and cowboys appear from the side streets, riding in to circle around Rip and I, each one armed with a pistol.

"Curse you with the bloody flux, Martin Price," I mutter under my breath. The coward himself is sitting on his horse right in my line of vision, his gun barrel trained on my chest with a satisfied smirk under his trimmed mustache.

"Come along quietly now," he says.

I grit my teeth so hard I feel it in my temples. I can't look at Johnny, and the hot flush of anger that creeps into my face makes the winter air feel like summer. My hands go skyward as I mutter a few choice words under my breath.

Sheriff Molby shuffles down from the boardwalk with his handcuffs, round face red as he puffs big clouds of air out from between his lips. Four cowboys ride forward and toss their lassos around Rip, pulling the rope taut. I feel the magic shiver. Addy cries out from behind me.

"This is the devil's work, Sheriff Molby, and you ought to be ashamed of yourself. You let her go or I'll see you run out of this town!"

Johnny's voice cuts through the air. "Don't! Let her go!"

Gilroy says something but I'm not listening anymore. My teeth saw into my lower lip as Molby pulls my hands behind my back and the cold steel clinks shut around my wrists. Breathing becomes harder as my chest tightens around old memories. I focus on the tether to Rip, feeling that faint pulse of soul echoing back toward me.

Molby unbuckles my gun belt and my knives and hands them to the deputy. "Now, you got two choices. Either you let go of that corpse magic, or the boys are going to have to ride him out a ways and take care of it."

"Sure seems like there should be a trial before you treat me like I'm guilty, Sheriff."

"Suit yourself," he says. "Price, see to it."

Martin Price spurs his snorting bay forward, nearly running the horse's shoulder into me as he wheels over to lead his men out of town. Rip has six lassos around him now, all pulled tight. They'll have to drag him. He tips forward, crashing to the ground and spooking several of the horses. They're heading north out of town. I'll remember that. None of them know how far they will have to drag him before the tether grows too thin for me to hold onto. Chances are they don't even know if they can. They can't cut him apart, and they can't sever the link between us without killing me first or dragging him clear to the next town.

Satisfied with that small victory, I relax a little. Sheriff Molby pushes me toward the office at the edge of town. Jediah Holt stomps down the hotel steps and heads toward Johnny, fire in his eyes and the promise of Hector McBride's money burning a hole in his pocket.

"Holt," I call out. He pauses, turns to glare at me.

"You're the mark."

Molby pushes me along toward the jail and tells me to be quiet. I don't look back. Addy and Gilroy are trying to argue on Johnny's behalf. But they can't win. McBride holds the trump card for now. Pops always said that patience brings you a better hand. I'm already adjusting, my mind racing ahead to the next steps.

I know that behind me, Johnny is being handed over to his father, that Paulie Torrence will likely have them mounted and riding out within the hour. Waiting only offers us more chance to stop them. Addy will go to the mayor, but I won't hold my breath on that one.

Molby's office is bare bones, nothing but a desk, a couple of chairs, and a small stove churning out heat to mix with the smell of sweat. He pushes me roughly into the single cell and pats down my pockets. Then he pulls the wide brim off my head. I wait for him to unlock the cuffs, but instead the door clicks shut behind me with the scrape of a key in the lock. I shuffle over to sit down on the only piece of furniture, a rickety wooden cot. Molby plants his bulk in the chair at his desk and pulls out a sheet of paper, no doubt ready to write a simpering letter back to Silver City.

The tether to Rip shudders, and I feel the ghosts of heavy blows. There's no real pain, but even the echoes of whatever violence Price is enjoying seems to drive some of the air from my lungs. My lip curls in disgust. Coward. Blows turn into the short, sharp blasts of bullets. Breath hisses from my mouth as ghost bullets dully thud into my chest, head, and back. They're shooting him from all sides.

I'm up against the jail bars in an instant. "This your idea of justice, Molby? Letting Price throw a tantrum while you sit and pat yourself on the back for what an excellent job you've done protecting Grand Junction from a necromancer and a sixteen-year-old boy? What did McBride promise you? A new set of balls since you seem to be missing a pair?"

When he stands, red-faced and mean, and opens the door to the cell, I don't move away. I see the punch coming and let my shoulders carry me backwards with the momentum when Molby's thick knuckles meet my jaw.

"Keep sassing, girl," he grumbles as I spit a wad of blood and saliva on his floor. "I'm the only thing standing between you and Price's mob. You can take your chances with the judge, or you can swing from a tree over the cow pens."

My next wad of spit lands on the toe of his boot, mixing with the snowy slush melting off the leather. He raises his fist to me again but shakes his head and returns to the chair. Deputy Skinner stomps in, kicking snow off his boots. He hangs my gun and knife belts on a wall hook and crosses to his chair without giving me so much as a glance.

The cot isn't comfortable. I sink down to the unforgiving wood and kick my own boots up onto the thin blanket. Breathe.

Think. My throat constricts, and I struggle to swallow. I wrap myself up in anger like a shield. With every other mark, I've always imagined the final moments of the chase, the pull of a trigger or the swing of a fist. I've always been drawn to that rush, wondering if I'll live or die. So I chase it now, and Holt dies in all manner of unspeakable ways in my head. I push other older memories into the space he inhabits within my mind and let them all jumble together like a stampeding herd, wild and dangerous until there's nothing left but cold certainty.

No one comes. Sometime in the evening, Molby unlocks the cell and brings me a plate of beef and bread. He switches my cuffs to the front while Skinner keeps his gun pointed in my direction. It's fresh bread, and I'll know the smell of Miss Kay's baking until I'm dead and gone. It warms the very edges of the coldness I've wrapped around myself.

The food settles like a bucket of rocks in my stomach. Molby comes in and puts my hands behind my back again. Now I can only wait.

CHAPTER THIRTY FOUR

THE PROTECTION OF THE LAW

I doze off but it only feels like minutes before the mob comes. They're a loud bunch of drunkards, and I can hear the whiskey in their words through the walls of the Sheriff's office. Molby is standing by the door and whispering to Deputy Skinner. They both flinch as something crashes against the outside wall with an encore of breaking glass. *I'm all that stands between you and Price's mob,* that's what Molby said, but I guess there was some part of me that thought he was being arrogant. From the sounds of things, there's a bunch of drunk men outside who don't think much of his standing in their way.

Molby steps outside and tries to play nice. His voice is muffled through the cracked-open door. "Now then, gentlemen, this isn't the kind of behavior we hold to here in Grand Junction. No mobs. We've sent for Judge Bower, and he'll be along directly to see that justice is duly served."

He's trying to reason with a hornet's nest, and it sounds like he's kicked it by the way they shout back at him. Rip didn't sate their need for violence. I guess it's only fun to beat up somebody who can feel fear. I swallow carefully and rise from the cot. I don't like the way my throat feels like somebody's hands are around it.

"Skinner."

He's got the pinched expression of a man who doesn't like his situation but isn't brave enough to do something about it. I make it a little easier for him.

"Make sure Addy gets my guns and knives. They're too valuable for the likes of Price."

He seems surprised, but I wait patiently by the cell door for Molby. When he comes back into the office, he's lifting his keys out of his pocket. Price and two of his men appear through the office's front door. They're wearing bandanas over the lower half of their faces, and despite the deadly chill spreading through my limbs, I manage a mirthless smirk at the absurdity of it.

"So it'll be the tree over the cow pens then, Sheriff?"

Molby unlocks the door and grips my arm with a grimace. "You'll swing for murder one way or another. They'll shoot the place up if I keep you in here."

"Better my neck than a good citizen like yourself."

He doesn't answer. I pull on the tether to Rip, but the resistance feels like I'm pulling against a mountain. Whatever they did to him, he's not moving. The moment I'm through the door, hands close around my arms and shoulders and drag me out onto the porch. Price leans in and his breath flutters the bandana over his mouth.

"Seems you can't hide behind good people forever, Soulless. Give me those keys, Sheriff."

Price pulls a rough feed bag over my head, and I'm shoved into the midst of the mob like a rag doll. Pressed against the side of a skittish horse, it takes me three tries to get my foot in the stirrup, even with the pushing and shoving from the men behind me. Without the use of my hands, I nearly fall right off the other side of the saddle. The horse bucks a little, and I tip forward. The saddle horn punches into my stomach and makes me cough.

I've gone numb. The saddle doesn't fit me right and by the way it pitches on the horse's withers, it doesn't fit him either. Blind in the canvas bag and hidden from the shouting crowd around me, I'm surprised when my breath shudders. Fear creeps in.

"So much for your prophecies, old man," I murmur. "I guess the darkness swallowed me up after all."

The horse jolts underneath me and then we're trotting, my bones jarring against the hard seat of the saddle. Gritting my teeth, I try to figure out how many of them are around me. Scattered voices hollering back and forth seem to come from every direction.

"…taking her to the big tree with the corpse?"

"Careful she doesn't pull some old bones out from the graveyard."

"Drake, you got that bottle of whiskey on you?"

"Give me a swig when you're done."

"You think she really murdered that fella over in Silver City?"

"Course she did. She's a necromancer. They all turn bad."

"She's touched with the Dark After, that's for sure."

"I figured there was something going on between her and that pretty hotel broad."

"Price will get that sorted out."

The horse lurches into a canter. The edges of the handcuffs are cutting off the circulation in my hands, and my fingers feel thick and dead. I wonder if I should pray. I wonder if it would help. I've always left the prayers to Reverend Ambrose since I know he means them. But I can only manage a single word.

Please.

Fear takes me then, and I know without a shadow of a doubt that I do not want to die. That wherever Price and his men are taking me, and whatever they plan to do, I want to live. The numbness tries to protect me, but it's not enough.

Johnny.

I promised him I'd help him get away from McBride and Holt. And I surely can't do that if I'm hanging from a tree somewhere. The fear and the anger fight against each other like cats and dogs as I try to come up with a plan.

We slow to a walk, and the horse below me snorts and sidesteps. More hands close in, pull me from the saddle. Someone's fist lands against the side of my head, and my knees buckle. Please.

The only goodness in the world is hidden away like little lights across a dark sky, tiny glimmers of hope in a wasteland of hatred and greed. I think of those lights. Addy, Reverend Ambrose, Hayes and Miss Kay. Owen. Johnny. I'm desperate to see them one last time. Desperate enough to pray and hope I'm heard.

With a jerk, the bag comes away from my face, and Price grabs hold of my hair. Horses are milling around me and the flicker of torch fire glares in the dark. My vision is blurred, and he gives me a slap across the face to clear my head. "Wake up, Soulless!"

I manage a bleary smile. "Didn't think you'd be willing to look me in the face. Doesn't seem like your style, Price."

"I promise you I'll be looking at your face while you swing," he says. "Look, we've got your corpse waiting for you."

He grips my chin and forces my face up and to the left. There's a big old tree behind us, branches thick and skeletal reaching up into the sky, leafless. Hanging from the lowest and biggest branch, suspended in midair by ropes around his arms and neck, Rip's gray skin is broken by black veins everywhere I can see. He stares down at us, his face frozen in the same expressionless mask he's had since I shot him in the mine shaft all those years ago. My throat still faintly burns with the pressure of the noose around his neck.

One of the cowhands is throwing another rope over the branch and knotting a loop in the end. My hands sweat while my breath freezes in the air.

"I've never been one for necklaces," I manage. Then I look at the man in front of me, and I don't want to make light of it anymore. "Don't do this, Price. You don't want my blood on your hands."

"It's not murder to kill a murderer," he says. "That's the trick, isn't it? You can violate any corpse you want, but you can't bring yourself back. Bet you're sweating under that duster."

My boot heels leave furrows in the snow down to the dirt as two men drag me under the branch. Price goes back to his horse and pulls himself into the saddle. "String her up nice and tight, boys. We don't want her slipping the noose and causing any trouble."

The rope snags in my hair, and then I feel the Dark After closing around my neck. Price rides his gelding close and draws his revolver, waving it in the air. The sharp report of a gun cracks through the cold night, and I expect to feel some kind of pain or coldness until I realize that the sound came from somewhere out in the dark, and one of the men behind me is on the ground. Price whirls his horse just in time for another bullet to knock him clean out of his tooled saddle. That's no revolver. It's the deeper crack of rifle shot.

Milling about in confusion, horses stamping and blowing, the cowboys draw their iron and fire into the night. But there's no way to tell where the bullets are coming from. Another shot fires, and the man to my left drops like a rock, writhing in pain as he clutches at his collarbone with a broken scream.

The rifle fires three more times before the last cowboys set spurs to their mounts and gallop away into the dark like Shades are on their tail. A few feet away from me, Price's bay jerks his reins out of the hands of the downed cattle baron and takes off after his fellows with his tail held in the air like a flag. One lone horse remains tied to a scrub tree, whinnying so loudly that it shakes his whole barrel. Price groans and rolls onto his side.

I imagine all sorts of saviors riding out from the dark line of trees, but never the one that appears. At first, everything is quiet and still, and I wonder if the Almighty himself fired that rifle. Then something moves in the nothingness, and a horse comes trotting toward me, its rider holding the long barrel of a gun against their shoulder. Moonlight glints off the metal.

Nothing on the good green earth can prepare me for seeing Jo Farstep's face. But sure as death itself, there she is. She shoves the rifle into its case alongside her saddle and slides off her flea-bitten gray mare to fix me with a squint.

"Got yourself in a real speck of trouble, I see."

I blink at her a couple times, and then all the nearly dying I just did comes up the back of my throat and I vomit into the snow.

CHAPTER THIRTY FIVE

JO FARSTEP

Jo finds the keys to the cuffs in Martin Price's duster pocket while I heave everything I've eaten for the past day out of my guts. A minute later, the scrape of metal against metal clicks and my hands are free.

I wipe my arm across my face, hoping to take the tears away with the last traces of sick. It takes me a minute to get the shakes under control. Jo doesn't say a word about it and gives me some time while she goes over and puts a boot on Price's shoulder to roll him onto his back. He's still groaning, barely alive after the shot that took him through the chest.

Jo kneels next to him and manages to stuff a wad of handkerchief against the wound. "I suppose we'll need to cut down your corpse," she says. "Best we get on our way before they come back."

She whistles for her mare, and the horse trots over. Jo leads her under the branch and beckons to me. "You'll have to cut him down, if you can. My leg won't handle standing on saddles anymore."

My mouth won't move. It feels like it's full of cotton. Jo pulls a long hunting knife from her belt and comes over to press it into my palm. "Hunter. Either cut him down, or we're leaving without him."

The cold hilt of the knife brings me back a little. "They took Johnny."

She nods. "So I hear. But we can't do a damned thing about it with you standing here and staring at me like I'm a ghost. Get yourself on that horse and cut down your corpse."

I climb up in the saddle and start sawing through the ropes. Black smoke wreathes his neck as the undead skin tears and heals from the noose over and over again. I can barely get the knife through to cut the rope. Below me, Jo watches the surrounding landscape with her hawk's eyes. One or two torches still burn stubbornly in little patches of melted snow.

Finally, I break through the last loop of rope, and Rip drops like a sack of rocks to the snow. Jo retrieves the bay gelding that was left behind and hands me the reins when I climb down from her mare. For the first time, I look at the bodies of the two men who were about to hang me in the tree. Neither one of them moves, and their eyes have the glassy stare of death. But Price isn't dead.

Jo offers me her revolver without a word. I crouch down beside him and place the muzzle of the gun against his forehead. He stares at me, half delirious.

"You're not worth the bullet it would take to put you out of your misery, Price. But there's a blood debt between us now, and if you live another day, you best pray to the Almighty you and I never cross paths again. Jo, help me get him up on this horse."

Together, we manage to lift Price behind the saddle and tie him there with a bit of rope. I turn to Rip and reach out for the tether, pulling him to his feet. The black veins on his arms and chest have disappeared, leaving only the spidery webs around his empty eyes and no trace of the violence Price and his men tried to inflict.

I clamber up onto the bay's saddle and check Price's pulse. He's unconscious but still breathing. Somewhere out in the night, someone shouts.

"HUNTER!"

A haphazard group of nine or ten rides into our line of sight, led by a familiar black-haired woman riding my roan mare. Behind her are Hayes and Gilroy Pruitt, along with a few other faces I recognize from around Grand Junction. Even Owen bounces along on General, a revolver strapped around his tiny waist.

I manage to dismount just as Addy throws herself down to the snow and grabs me in the hardest bear hug I've ever received. "Oh thank the Almighty, I thought we would be too late!" she sobs in relief, her hands frantically searching my face and arms for any wounds. "Are you alright?"

"I'm breathing."

"We were coming up with a plan to save you," Addy says breathlessly. "When Jo came into the hotel, I thought for sure the Almighty had sent us an angel."

It occurs to me just then how odd Jo's appearance was, and how lucky I am to be alive. "How did you know?"

"Just got back from Barnesville and heard around Silver City that a man named Holt had come looking for his boy," says Jo. "I got wind of him signing a contract with McBride and saw them ride out of town. Didn't sit right, so I figured I was about due to move on out of Silver City anyway and followed them. Got to town today just in time to hear about the warrant." Jo leans over her horse and spits. "Load of codswallop."

Addy squeezes my hand. "She came into the hotel and said she was a friend of yours. I couldn't believe it."

I manage a wobbly grin. "I am capable of making friends besides you, Addy Sterling."

"I would never have forgiven myself…" she trails off. "When Deputy Skinner came around with your things, why, I nearly dropped him dead on my lobby floor."

"We wasn't gonna let them hang you, Miss Hunter," says Owen sternly from atop General's broad chestnut back. He patted the butt of the revolver on his hip. "Mr. Hayes said I could shoot one."

"Come here you rascal." Hayes reaches over and pulls the boy onto the back of his own horse. "I expect you'll be needing to take Johnny's horse with you."

I take General's reins and look down at Addy. She's got dark fire burning in her, same as I do. She unbuckles the holster belts around her waist, and hands them to me along with my wide brim hat. The feel of my guns and the hilts of my shadesilver knives pull me the rest of the way out of the Dark After's doorway. Dan Griffiths appears from the ring of horses and ponies the roan mare to me.

"Glad to see you're alright, miss. It's not right, a mob like that."

I take the reins and give him a nod of thanks. The roan lips at my boot as I get my foot in the stirrup and dances sideways. I don't even scold her.

"Miss Kay filled your saddlebags with food to last you a few days," Addy says. "Hunter…"

I wait for her to tell me to be careful, to come back safe, or not get myself in a scrape that I can't get out of. But instead, she surprises me.

"Don't come back until you've got Johnny away from that man. Take him somewhere safe." Tears pool in her brown eyes. "Take both of you somewhere safe."

"I promise."

She lets go of me then. "I'll see that Price is left with the Sheriff. He should take care of his own."

"You're bringing your corpse along?" asks Jo.

"He gets along fast enough to set a steady pace."

I don't need to ask Jo if she plans on going along with me. She sets there like an old mountain cat, patiently waiting to set out for the kill. I take one last look at the people that came to rescue me and then set my heels against the roan's sides.

Jediah Holt and Paulie Torrence are marked men, and I aim to see this through.

CHAPTER THIRTY SIX

MARKED

We ride through the night. Paulie Torrence will set a hard pace back to Silver City, but he'll have two men with him that aren't used to that kind of riding, so they'll have to stop and rest. The snow and cold is also on our side. Jo and I ride like shadows through the dark, coats and scarves pulled around our ears. Addy even remembered to pack thick leather gloves in our saddlebags. Of course she did.

Both of our mares charge through the snow-covered prairie at a slow lope, eating up the ground with each stride. General is ponied behind my roan, the long rope tied around my saddle horn. Rip jogs along behind us in that strange, broken marionette way of his. Every so often we stop for a few minutes to let him catch up, but we set a good pace just like I promised. The tracks we follow lead north along the river: four horses moving at a decent clip.

Finally, dawn breaks and floods the ground with soft colors. And with it comes a sign that improves my dark mood a bit. I pull the roan mare back to a walk. She's puffing and blowing and stretches her neck out when I slide down from the saddle to inspect a melted circle of charred wood. Horse dung litters the tramped earth near a close copse of trees.

I kneel and pull one glove off to hold my fingers over the charred remains of the fire. The warmth has all but gone, but there's a small and stubborn flicker of heat in the heart of the coals. I slide my glove back on.

"Late last night, I'd guess." I gesture toward the piles of dung. "They rested for a while."

Something near the copse of trees makes me pause. I hand Jo the roan mare's reins and step over to a thick young river birch. The river side of the tree has bark rubbed away, and there's a depression in the snow of someone sitting with the scuffs of boot heels around the edges. Several small reddish-brown stains color the snow near the depression, frozen into tiny gems. I nearly grind my teeth into powder.

"They tied Johnny to the tree. He's hurt too, by the look of things."

Jo crosses her hands and rests them on the horn of her saddle. "You shooting to kill?"

I roll one of the frozen red jewels around between my thumb and forefinger, squinting north after the tracks. It thaws against the warmth of my skin, and for the first time in a long time, I feel my stomach turn at the sight of blood. I pick up a handful of snow and wipe my hands clean, then pull the gloves back on before the cold starts to eat at my fingers.

"I'll shoot to stay alive."

We let the horses set a steady pace. Both mares are wiry and have the endurance of the desert breeds that make up their ancestry. General plods along with a bit less enthusiasm but manages to keep up with the mares. To our left, the middle of the river burbles along like a black snake through flanks of ice. As we ride, Jo matches my stoic focus on the path ahead. She's an impeccable horsewoman and sits her saddle as if she were relaxing on a porch swing. The steel in her spine gives me a little bit more strength in mine.

"Is it worth drawing iron on McBride just to save my hide?" I finally ask her after a few miles of silence.

"No laws against defending oneself," says Jo. "McBride is one of a thousand folks who think they're better than everyone else, and that gives him the right to change the law as he sees fit. And he might slip betwixt the cracks of laws written on paper. But that's different than a law written inside your chest. The one that tells you it's wrong to leave a boy like Johnny to fend for himself. Plenty of us fight over paper laws, but the wars that really matter are when you draw iron to protect the laws that go deeper than that."

I know I'm pushing on old wounds, but I ask anyway. "Why'd you fight in the war?"

"Same reason a lot of us did when we were too green to wear our britches properly. Somebody told us there was a bit of glory killing other people in the name of a great cause. Didn't really matter what the cause was. We were going to be soldiers, and soldiers were important."

She paused then, thinking. I tossed her the water canteen and she took a swig. "I was in the sharpshooters corp, back a ways from the killing. But walking through all those bodies after the first battle… some of 'em crying and begging like children, old ones and young ones. It burns something out of you every time until you don't see much difference between a breathing body and a dead one.

"One time we opened fire on a caravan of civilians, thinking they were taking supplies to the Secessionists. I stopped counting my kills after that day."

"So why'd you become a bounty hunter after all that?"

She doesn't take her eyes off the horizon. "Same reason you

did, I expect. Pain always looks for a way out."

We're a day out from Silver City when we catch up to them. The last horse dung we passed was only just starting to freeze. Jo pulls her rifle out of the long holster and settles it comfortably across her lap. We'll need the element of surprise that Jo offers, because Paulie Torrence knows me as a loner. He might not be shocked to see me slip out of the Dark After's fingers, but he doesn't know Jo is with me. She takes General from me and turns her gray mare down toward the river. There's a thicker layer of ice all the way across the water here, and the horses take quick, careful steps to the other side. I'm not the only bounty hunter who knows how to disappear when she wants to. Once she's gone into the trees and brush, it's just me, the roan mare, and Rip.

The cold prairie is quiet, other than the occasional shifting of the river ice. I bring the air into my nose with deep breaths, letting the chill wake up my senses. I'd rather hunt in the north but this will have to do.

Tensing underneath me, the roan mare picks up on the change. She skitters to the side. I push her at a canter, pulling Rip along behind us. It's not long until I see the dark figures of horses ahead against the snow. Six rounds in each revolver chamber should give me more courage than it does.

They catch sight of me, and Paulie Torrence wastes no time circling his little band into a tight group. A glint catches the sunlight as he pulls his guns clear of their holsters. I lean over the mare's neck, keeping my head and shoulders behind her. When I'm inside fifty yards, I pull the reins tight again, and the roan tosses her head as she slows to an angry stop. Rip lumbers up behind us, and I push him in front of the mare like a shield.

I'm off her back and aiming my revolver at Paulie Torrence, and that's when he finally figures that I'm not in a talking mood. My first shot flies past his face as he falls to the side and tumbles off the back of his horse. Jediah Holt shouts and fumbles for his guns. The roan mare squeals and kicks, barely missing my head as she jerks the reins out of my hand and pulls away. I let her go.

"Go, go, get him out of here!" Paulie yells at Holt, waving his hand toward Silver City as he scrambles to his feet.

I stick tight to Rip's back and feel the first bullet snick into his chest. The older Holt boy fires on me from the side, but the shot goes at least a foot behind me into the packed snow. Ducking to the side and gripping Rip's shoulder with one hand, I steady my left revolver on my right forearm and sight down the barrel at the pair of horses that just whirled away from the fight. Letting out a breath, I squeeze the trigger. The rope between Jediah Holt and his son splits, and Johnny kicks his feet free of the stirrups. The horse beneath him keeps on running as Johnny falls into a bank of snow.

The spiral of a bullet zipping past my ear sends me back behind Rip, sucking in quick breaths. I push Rip forward into a closer firing range and hear a shouted curse from Torrence, who is using his nervous palomino to hide his body. I steady my hands.

"Give it up, Torrence! I ain't gonna quit!"

"You oughta be strung up in a tree about now!" he yells back.

The Holt boy can't get his horse under control, and saws on the reins as the animal turns in a circle, eyes rolling white. He's not a threat, so I focus my whole attention on Paulie. Wherever Jo is across the river, she hasn't gotten a clear shot yet.

"Hunter!"

Hands still trussed up, Johnny bolts from the safety of his snowbank. Jediah Holt is right behind him, gun finally out of his holster. My stomach drops into my boots. He's never going to make it against four guns. I shove Rip forward at a desperate sprint.

Paulie spins his palomino out of the way, but it's Jediah Holt who aims his revolver at Johnny's unprotected back. The sound I let out is more wild animal than human. My thumbs glide over gun hammers and swing up to fire around Rip. The tether frays, and then something pulses through the magic and knocks the breath out of my lungs.

An inhuman burst of speed carries the corpse ahead of me, pulling him away from my grip as he reaches for Johnny. A revolver shot snaps just as Rip wraps his huge arms around the fleeing boy and curls around him toward the ground. Two more revolver shots in quick succession, and then the sharp crack of a distant rifle.

CHAPTER THIRTY SEVEN

DEEP ROOTS

Jediah Holt topples from his horse and lands with eyes staring up at the sky. Blood oozes from a bullet wound straight through his temple. Confused, Paulie holds his revolvers steady on me now as he stumbles back into the cover of the brush. He fires again and misses me by inches.

Another rifle report shatters the sudden quiet, and Paulie screams as he falls into the tangled arms of a barbed cageweed. My cheek feels wet and ice cold. I reach up to touch my face, and nod at the blood that comes away on my fingertips from the small groove that Paulie's first bullet tore through my skin. The wind suddenly sinks its chill beneath my scarf and duster, and I don't like the way my hands shake.

"Hunter!"

Rip slowly rises from the ground, releasing the boy beneath him. Johnny runs to me, finally getting his hands free of the ropes. He grabs hold of my arms just as I lose control of my knees. We sink to the snow, and I see drops of blood beneath my right leg. Figures that Torrence would finally find his aim.

"You murdering Soulless!" screams the Holt boy, lifting his gun in our direction.

Johnny pulls one of my guns free from my hand and stands over me, the barrel pointed at his older brother. I feel the tendrils of desperate necromancy shoot out in all directions, reaching for the corpse still cooling in the snow. Wild, untamed magic surges through the ground like tree roots.

Necromancy floods my senses, and out in the snow, black veins begin to break out around Jediah's staring eyes. I reach up to take hold of Johnny's arm. He looks down at me, his own eyes red and dry. Pushing back against his magic with my own, I shake my head.

"Pull it back. Control it."

He draws in a ragged excuse for breath and chokes on a sob. "I can't bring him back."

"No, you can't. Let him go, kid."

The heavy thrum of necromancy lets up a little, and the black veins on Jediah's face fade back into the natural color of his skin. Johnny points the gun back toward his brother.

"Jack, you get on out of here!" he yells. "I'll shoot, I swear it! I'll shoot!"

But the older boy is off his horse and kneeling over the body of Jediah Holt, screaming at his pa and paying no attention to Johnny's threats. His revolver drops from his hand, forgotten. Johnny walks over to his father, each step planted firmly on the ground as his magic retreats back to his Core.

The fire from the bullet wound in my side finally reaches my head, and I press my hands against the bleeding entry hole. Based on the sharp pain in my back, I'm willing to bet it went all the way through. Rip comes back to me, and the magic between us wobbles a bit, then steadies. I glare up at him.

"Worthless corpse," I mutter. "Him over me, huh?"

The soft hum of the soul fragment inside his chest calms me, and I have a strange clarity that only comes with pain. I smile.

"Yeah, I wanted you to save him too."

Jo's fleabitten mare gallops up the east side of the riverbank and tears over to us like the Shades are on her tail, the chestnut gelding huffing along behind her. As soon as the horses slide to a stop, Jo is over at my side with her rifle in hand. She grabs the side of my duster, and I try to wave her off.

"Don't fuss about it. The Dark After can't have me just yet."

"You let me be the judge of that," she says as she prods around the wound. "Went clean through, but we'd better sew you up before you ride. That was a lucky shot."

"Torrence?" I ask.

"Breathin'. Hold this on it now."

I look over at the pair of boys hovering above Jediah Holt and try to staunch the blood with Jo's neckerchief while she heads back to her saddlebags. "Thought you weren't shooting to kill, Farstep."

"He wasn't going to miss. Neither was I."

I've seen men die before, but this one hits me different. Jediah Holt isn't the kind of man to change his ways, but any hope Johnny has of hearing a good word from his father dies with him. It'll eat at him for a long time, but at least I stopped him from making a bigger mistake.

"I don't know where that fool roan is." I scan the snowy hills around us, but there's no sign of her. "Just as well, I suppose."

"We'll find your horse, Hunter. Lay back and hold still."

She sews me up like a soldier, strong enough to hold and ugly enough to make a surgeon cry. The bullet went through, so she doesn't have to fish it out of my guts. After poking and prodding around a bit more, she seems satisfied that the thing didn't nick any of my organs. Small mercies.

"You good enough to get up on a horse?" she asks me.

I nod. I don't have a choice. We're far too close to Silver City to stay long. Jo leaves me and grabs hold of Jack Holt's coat lapels, dragging him to his feet.

"Time to grow up a bit, son," she tells him. "Your pa tried to kill somebody and got himself killed for his trouble. You're going to help me get his body up over the back of your horse and then you're going to ride back to Silver City. Follow the river, you'll make it in less than a day if you keep moving." She points at Paulie Torrence, groaning softly in the brush. "We're going to strap Torrence on his horse and tie it to yours. It's up to you if he lives or dies now. You hearing me?"

The boy looks like he's about to raise his fist in Jo's face, but he doesn't have it in him. He wilts like a snapped flower stem and nods, snot and tears freezing on his face. Within a few minutes, Jediah Holt is thrown over the back of one of the horses. Paulie Torrence is harder to move. He's only partially conscious, and he flops around a bit before they can get him tied up proper. Jo tosses his fancy gunbelt and iron under the cageweed.

Johnny grabs hold of his brother's stirrup before they ride out. "Jack… I'm sorry. Tell Mama I'm sorry."

And then they're gone, riding away toward Silver City and the judgment of Hector McBride. Jack Holt he won't bother with, but I'd hate to be Paulie Torrence when he comes to. Jo swings back up onto her horse and canters off in the direction my roan mare disappeared. With any luck, she'll have stepped on her own reins somewhere over the next rise.

I make it to my feet, still a little unsteady. Johnny hasn't moved, staring off after the disappearing forms of his brother and father. He's crying, but I don't say a word. Better out than in, I figure. When he's done his bit of crying, he wipes his arms across his eyes and turns around, squaring his thin shoulders.

"I'm proud of you, Johnny."

His eyes snap to me, surprised. I nod and squint out over the prairie. "You're going to turn out to be a decent enough man, I expect."

That seems to bolster him up a bit. "You okay?" he asks.

"I'll live. Might be a bit uncomfortable in the saddle for a bit."

"My father would've killed me."

It sounds sudden, but I know that his brain is starting to put together the pieces now that the adrenaline is relaxing its grip.

"Yes."

"I didn't think he would do it."

"Folks will always surprise you by what they're willing to do."

He looks over at the corpse next to me. "Like him?"

"Like him."

I shuffle over to the cageweed and crouch, picking up the discarded gun belt from where it lies in the prickly stems. The pair of guns are fine quality, bought with Torrence's blood money. I hold them out to Johnny.

"If you're going to ride with a pair of outlawed bounty hunters, you'd best carry some iron."

The belt is a little big for him, but we can add another hole to the leather. He seems uncomfortable with the weapons so close to him. We all were, once. Someday he'll feel naked without them. I hope that day doesn't come too soon.

Over the snowy rise comes a sharp whistle, and then Jo appears, my roan mare trailing along after her gray.

"Found her holed up by a little gulley," says Jo. "She was standing on her reins."

"Here," Johnny pushes past me to kneel by the roan mare's side on one knee, cupping his hands over his leg. I'd seen him do it for Owen once or twice when the younger boy was trying to ride a horse that was too big for him.

The climb up to the saddle is less than comfortable, and I know when I wake up in the morning my body will feel like a beaten hotel carpet. Jo eyes my bandaged side like a mother hen. But we've got more important things to do than fuss over it.

"Less than two days' ride to Ellestown, and then south. We can't waste any time getting out of these parts," I say.

Jo holds General's reins as Johnny mounts up. "How far south are we going?"

"To one of the coast cities. McBride will be spitting mad when that Holt boy gets back. Wouldn't put it past him to send a few men after us if he thinks it's worth his time. We'll need some extra iron."

Jo frowns. "Who'd you have in mind?"

If there was any better option, I'd have done it. But I know whose guns we need if McBride comes after us. I gather up my reins. "There's a man we need to find. Last I saw him, he was dead drunk at a bar down in one of the south cities. I expect he's still thereabouts."

Jo doesn't look pleased with the idea of moseying all the way down south just to find some deadbeat drunk, but she doesn't have a better idea. McBride's a bloodhound. It may take him some time, but he won't let go of the scent now that he's got it.

Tired and dreading the ride ahead, I grin at Johnny. "Ever been to Gallington, kid?"

"No."

"Well, it's your lucky day."

EPILOGUE

THE LAST MARK

The Tart's Barrel leans against the other buildings in Red Blossom Row. Naming a street after a flower doesn't much improve the smell or the sight, I find. The nicer folks in Gallington like to pretend that Red Blossom Row doesn't exist. The cobblestones disappeared under a thick sludge of Almighty knows what decades ago, and our boots squelch into the mud as we pick our way through the beggars and sour addicts toward the broken-down façade of the Tart's Barrel. Johnny presses close behind me as a few beggars hover as close as they dare. We avoid the usual groping and pawing by keeping Rip close behind us.

Somewhere nearby, a gunshot goes off. The only one in the whole street that flinches at the sound is Johnny. One sour addict stumbles a little closer to us and grabs at my duster. Her blue eyes are vacant, the skin around her mouth chapped and covered in sores from the harsh powder.

"Just a copper pithing, just one and I'll give you a grope," she murmurs. I push her back into the crowd of her fellows, careful not to bruise her already mottled skin. I hate these streets. I hate the sour powder that spreads like a plague of the bloody flux through the crowds, made by greedy folks and filtered down through to the broken streets like Red Blossom and others. Not for the first time, I wonder if I should turn around and leave this mark to his death at the bottom of a dark glass bottle. But I need work, and Johnny and I can't show our faces farther north for a while. Johnny looks from one side of the street to the other, his face as green as the sludge at our feet.

The sign for the Tart's Barrel hangs on rusted hinges and the carved woman who had once been visible on the square bit of wood is nearly worn faceless by years of weather and foul air. I pull my neckerchief over my nose and try to imagine the clear cold air of the Cathedrals. The door opens with a horrendous squealing of hinges. It's nearly impossible to see in the dim lighting after the daylight outside, but I can see the counter in the back and the huge man that leans over it, balding head ringed with bits of brown, bushy hair. He squints at us over meaty cheeks as I step around the drunk and stoned customers perched on stools at rickety tables. A few barely dressed women give Johnny and I a quick onceover before deciding we're not worth their time.

A small man in a bowler hat is playing an out of tune piano is being played in the corner; though calling the merciless pounding of playing might be a bit generous. I know well enough to step up to the counter and order myself a drink before looking for my mark. I've already spotted him at the table in the western corner of the building, draped over the wood like a dead man.

"Whiskey."

The barkeep scowls but doesn't even seem to notice Rip behind me. After a minute, he hands me a glass that might have been washed at one point in its life and pours me a drink. The whiskey is nearly black and has an unpleasant burnt flavor that lingers around my molars and the roof of my mouth. I finish the glass. Insulting a man like this on a street like Red Blossom would not be good for my health.

"Thank you kindly. I'm looking for a friend of mine. Tall, bad-tempered gunslinger with a black beard. Drinks like he's already dead."

I'm not sure if the barkeep smiles or grimaces at me. But he nods toward the table I've already seen in the corner. I narrow my eyes at the man passed out in a mess of bottles, and my fingers twitch toward the holsters at my hips. There are smart ways to do this, and drawing iron isn't one of them. So I leave the weapons alone and wander to the edge of the table with Johnny so close on my heels I'm surprised he hasn't faceplanted into the back of my duster.

I reach out and thump my fist on the table hard enough to rattle the bottles. One of them rolls off the edge and clatters onto the floor, saved from breaking by a small pile of dirty rags. There's no response from the man. His hat is lying next to his hand and his black hair spills around his face, obscuring everything but the two gold rings pierced through his left ear and a bit of his chin.

"Wake up, drunk," I say loudly, leaning over the table closer to the exposed ear. There isn't so much as a twitch in response. The past few years drain away, and I feel hot anger bubbling in my belly as I stare down at the man drowning in his drink. Nothing has changed.

I ease one hand around the butt of my right revolver and slide it free of the holster. Clenching my jaw, I shift my weight into the heel of my right boot and thumb back the hammer with a soft click. The man lunges upward, nearly upsetting the table. Before the bottles start rattling, his guns are out of their black leather holsters and twin steel barrels are aiming at my forehead. His eyes glare out at me from behind the screen of hair, lips curved down somewhere in the overgrown brush of his mustache and beard. Then he blinks twice and looks up at the massive Animated hovering over my shoulder.

"… Hunter?"

I cock the hammer of my gun down and nestle it back into the holster. "Morning, sunshine." Reaching behind me, I pull Johnny forward by the sleeve of his duster.

"Johnny, meet Miles Lightfellow."

To be continued…

THANK YOU & PLEASE READ

I am so grateful to everyone who takes time to pick up one of my books and step into the worlds I've made. Each story takes months or even years of love, blood, sweat and tears, and there is nothing more rewarding than seeing it in the hands of a reader. It is the readers like you that make it possible for authors like me to write, create, and eventually publish the stories that mean so much to us.

If you enjoyed *Cold Silver for Souls*, please consider rating and reviewing it on Amazon and other platforms. Every review makes a huge difference and can help share your favorite stories with other people looking for their next book amongst the thousands of options out there. Leaving a review is one of the most meaningful things you can do to support authors and help them stand out in the crowd.

As an author who deeply loves the craft of storytelling, I will always bring you my best. I will always challenge myself to create bigger, better, and bolder. I look forward to walking into new worlds together.

Love always,

Tori

ACKNOWLEDGEMENTS

Writing this page is one of my favorite pre-publishing moments, because it offers me a chance to reflect on the journey and the people who walked it with me. Writing a story is a labor of love, and it takes a lot from its author. It's a price we're all too willing to pay to see our stories come to life. But the cost is made easier by the people who support us along the way. It is my honor to include them here.

To my fearless alpha team, who dug into the story when it was new and rough and finding its way, thank you. Kayla, you were the first person to read this roughly drafted story when I needed someone to talk to about the first half, and your gentle support and encouragement helped me find my way back. Andrew Meredith, friend and mentor, who always tells me to challenge myself and has helped me become a better and bolder writer because of it. And thank you for making sure my tech-challenged self wasn't formatting this book alone. To Brian Bell, who jumped in to the alpha team and gave me valuable feedback on short notice.

To my beta readers: Pete, Nuclear Katie, and Andrew Wizard. Thank you for helping me tweak and hone and for always answering the call when I ask for your feedback. To Matt, who saved the day when my website malfunctioned a day before the cover reveal and preorder launch. I am lucky to have friends like you. And to J.L. Odom and her husband, who gave me a wealth of information about guns from the 1800s and their range and accuracy. Accurate gunfights matter.

To Casey, who answered the call for a boss-level editor to help me smooth out all the rough edges of this story. And for generally being one of the most awesome people I've ever met. Here's to many more years of analyzing K-drama characters together.

To the incredible artists who helped bring this story to visual life: Helena, Jack, and Dewey. I'm beyond honored to have your talent represented on the cover and interior of this book.

To my Mom and Dad, who have a nerdy daughter and love her for it. Thank you for always being there.

To my cherished children. With every book I write, I am reminded that you are the most important story I will ever be part of. I love you, I love you, I love you. Being your mom is the greatest gift.

To my soulmate and the best man I know, my husband Ben. This year you supported and loved me through everything, and every day I am more and more grateful that I get to live my whole life, every day, with you. Thank you for loving me so deeply, and always being the first person to fall in love with my stories.

And finally, to the God who is Faithful, and knows every part of my story.

OTHER BOOKS by TORI TECKEN:

The Blood Stones
Legends of the Bruhai #1
Dark Epic Fantasy

His name is not worthy.

A traitor is executed, his name ripped away from history. Now the kingdom stands on the brink of a succession war that could bring the country to its knees. Forces stalk the darkness, moving pawns into place in a deadly game.

Gehrin and his brothers were not meant to witness the execution, but now they find themselves trapped in the center of a political quagmire. When Gehrin faces the loss of everything he knows, will he also lose himself?

To the south, tribal warlords clash in an endless cycle of violence. Syndri, the daughter of a chieftain, kills for the honor of her people. An alliance with a foreign queen offers the power to unite the tribes, but at what cost?

Someday, history will remember them as legends.

Phased
Phased Duology #1
Dark Paranormal/Urban Fantasy

According to the Department of Domestication and Assimilation, Val and Lyla Blackwood are the most dangerous kind of werewolves. Raised in the wild, their trueblood heritage has made them little more than experiments for years. Now, their freedom depends on their ability to become as human as possible, thrown into an assimilation school with humans and werewolves who have never known what it means to be wild. Trapped in a world where they don't belong and fighting to stay one step ahead of the horrific past that chases them, any wrong move could send them back to those stark white cells, losing their last chance of freedom.

You can find more information and links to purchase all of my books at
toritecken.com

Hey friends! I'm Tori. When I was a little sprout, my epic fantasy storytelling involved small pirate and animal figurines invading rival lego villages. I was obsessed with characters I couldn't get out of my head and the possibility of worlds undiscovered.

After writing a few books, becoming a self-published author at age 14, and teaching at Young Writers' Conferences for a few years, I went to college. I married the weirdest boy I'd ever met. We now have three small humans of our own who are just as weird as we are, but much more wonderful.

Today, I'm a wife and a stay-at-home mom, and I'm still a storyteller. I write beneath the supervision of two feline overlords in a chair that is older than I am. And I wouldn't have it any other way. Pull up a chair and join the chaos. I hope you find a world here that you can't wait to go back to.

https://toritecken.com/
@ToriTalks2